AND THEN YOU WERE GONE

AND THEN YOU WERE GONE

A Novel

R. J. Jacobs

CROOKED
LANE

NEW YORK

Published in the United States by Crooked Lane Books, an imprint of The Quick Brown Fox & Company LLC.

Crooked Lane Books and its logo are trademarks of The Quick Brown Fox & Company LLC.

Library of Congress Catalog-in-Publication data available upon request.

ISBN (hardcover): 978-1-68331-959-7
ISBN (ePub): 978-1-68331-960-3
ISBN (ePDF): 978-1-68331-961-0

Cover design by Melanie Sun

Printed in the United States.

www.crookedlanebooks.com

Crooked Lane Books
34 West 27th St., 10th Floor
New York, NY 10001

First Edition: March 2019

10 9 8 7 6 5 4 3 2 1

To Bob and Linda

ONE

Paolo's black hair was everywhere in the wind, whipping against the Wayfarer sunglasses he always wore. He'd confessed once that he thought they made him look famous, or—unable to find the word in English—"Hollywood." Later, when I'd teased him about being "Mr. Hollywood," he'd frowned and acted sullen, so I'd dropped it. But the memory still made me grin. He drove with one hand on the wheel of his Jeep and the other on my leg all the way to the lake. It was the first weekend of October but warm enough to still be summer.

"I'm suspicious of you," he said.

"Me?"

I couldn't see his eyes behind the dark gray lenses.

"You're . . . what do you call it? *Fidgety*. You're hiding something," he teased, his voice barely audible over the wind rushing in. "What are you smiling about over there?"

I shook my head, turned up the radio just as the Allman Brothers came on.

"Wait, this is 'Ramblin' Man,' right?" He sounded pleased to have remembered. "That last song was about Bob Seger's erection." He had been in the country for less than two years but picked things up quickly.

The engine growled.

"Emily, you're going to love this marina. Perfect boats. Crisp white sails. Tight. Everything. Tight," he said, his thumb and forefinger pinched, lips pursed.

I laughed out loud and rolled my eyes, and he caught me doing it.

"I thought you were past trying to impress me," I said. "A long time ago." Early on, I'd scrubbed the honey out of my voice, trying to act tough. A year into the relationship, I'd let that go.

He shook his head, smiled. "Oh, okay, Dr. Firestone." He was nearly finished with a doctorate himself but liked to tease me about being a psychologist. As if evaluating him was my intent. He raised his palms mock-defensively. "So, I like nice things. It's not my worst quality."

"It might be, actually."

He considered the notion a second longer than I expected.

"What's mine?" I asked, playfully.

"You're stubborn," he said. "And you think you can do anything."

"That's two."

"Then it's that you think you can do anything. That's your worst," he concluded. "That opens the door for all the others."

It stung, but I wasn't about to let the day be anything but fun. He seemed relaxed in a way I hadn't seen in weeks. If he was going to drag me out on the open water, we were not going to be in a fight.

With him, love was like speeding in the Jeep with the doors off. The rest of the world rushed by as a blur, but he remained in focus even as I imagined tumbling onto the pavement. When I hit the ground, all I could break was my heart, right?

I picked up my phone. No cell service. I tried the Internet, reloading the page a few times. Nothing. No messages.

"How much farther?" I asked.

"What are you looking at there?" he replied instead of answering. "The helpless children of Tennessee will survive without you for one night, I promise."

"Hold on. How is the biggest workaholic I know picking on me for wanting to check email?" I squeezed his shoulder.

Paolo winked in response.

"It's . . . going well in the lab?" I asked after a beat, my hand moving from his shoulder to the small curls above his ear. "You haven't even talked about work this week."

"Going great," he said. "I left work behind for the weekend."

Grinning, I made my eyes look startled. "You're not going to check at all? No one last thing to send to Dr. Silver? No questions that can't wait till morning?"

He glanced at me, smiling. He shifted gears, sending the Jeep's engine to a lower octave.

"All weekend? Even if, what's his name? The guy who glares at you?"

"Matt."

"Even if Matt sets the lab on fire?"

"Even then, no."

Really, I was only half feigning surprise. Paolo's principle investigator, Jay Silver, was known for his devotion to research. He seemed to know no boundaries between work hours and personal time, sometimes ringing Paolo's phone with questions or ideas before the sun had risen—a habit Paolo defended, urging me to understand the pressures of grant funding, publishing, NIH grants. I'd questioned Silver's calling at such odd hours until realizing that Paolo didn't seem to mind. And who was I, really, to lecture anyone about moderation and balance?

When Paolo quieted, I assumed he was troubled by the pressures of his work. Then again, if I let myself think about what Paolo had taught me about epidemics, I'd lie awake at night, too. He'd said that it wasn't a matter of *if* a pandemic would strike, but *when*, and that because of globalization an outbreak *anywhere* could mean an outbreak *everywhere*. Half the country's hospitals would run out of beds within three weeks in the event of a serious outbreak.

On average, an H1-N24 outbreak occurred every two years—a time frame that seemed to fuel their pursuit of creating a vaccine.

Paolo had said soberly that everyone in the lab had a plan for where to go if an outbreak started. All I could do was bug out my eyes in terror. I could never tell if he fully sensed my discomfort when he talked about epidemiology—if he noticed me flinching or my toes curling, or a dampness in my eyes when he described the potential spread of the virus that had killed my father, who was famous among certain researchers for being the first American known to have contracted H1-N24 and died from it. The CDC in Atlanta had held on to his body for two full weeks when he was brought back to the States.

I pushed his silhouette from my mind and focused on the road we were rushing over, and on the round, purple flowers passing by, blurred by our speed.

When Paolo worked late, I thought about how his research would save lives—save kids from the gaping absence of losing a parent. It was what I focused on when Paolo hadn't texted me back for hours. "Well, here's to freedom," I said, toasting with an invisible champagne flute.

He flashed a quick thumbs-up. "We're almost there."

It looked like we were almost nowhere. Every so often, a mailbox marked a clay driveway spilling from opaque brush.

The Jeep jolted and I folded my hands on my stomach to cap the nausea rising inside me, leaning back in the seat. I inhaled slowly through my nose, holding the breath for two beats until my lungs became uncomfortably full—the same relaxation strategy I taught my patients. It must have been love, I thought, that had made me agree to spend the night on a sailboat on the largest lake in Tennessee.

I reached between us for his ever-present stainless-steel water bottle. Paolo put his hand over mine, then touched his throat. "Don't drink after me. Throat's sore."

"Oh, please."

"Really," he said. "As your personal microbiologist, I insist."

I put my hand over my heart. "My own? Really? *My own personal*? I like that."

We passed the remains of a house. Crumbling brick painted white. The roof had collapsed as if stepped on from above. Black rings of ash or paint, I couldn't tell which, circled the windows.

"We're really almost there?" I raised my phone toward the sky. Still nothing.

"You really think I don't know the way," he said with a grin. He covered his uncorrected teeth, making him seem all the more mischievous.

I guess everyone is insecure about something.

From the corner of my eye, I could see the metal case that contained his camera equipment.

"You've shot here before, right?"

He put his eyes back on the road, downshifting as we took a serpentine curve. "Last fall." A sudden dip in the road took me by surprise. When it straightened, he said, "Colors all reflected on the lake, like a mirror. One side real, the other like a painting of it, like tiny brushstrokes."

He never sounded more excited than when he talked about photography. I pictured him with his camera around his neck the previous year, his first autumn in the States. Red and gold in every direction around him, infinitely. The innocence in his eyes, the childlike wonder.

The road narrowed further, the Jeep's tires crunching gravel on the right side. We passed the sign for the marina. In the parking lot, he slowed to a stop, and my stomach had the feeling of having ridden roller coasters all day, like a part of me was still flying.

But he was already out of the Jeep. "Coming?"

"Just got a little carsick," I said. "Give me two minutes."

"I'll get the boat, okay? I'll be right back."

A trail led through the woods to the marina. Paolo literally skipped. I went around to the front of the Jeep and threw up, then dug through my purse for gum. My hand passed over the prescription bottle I'd brought, just in case.

Not yet, I thought. At least get to the boat first.

In the lazy buzz of late-afternoon insects, I collected myself.

Paolo seemed almost giddy when he came back. "Better?" he asked.

I shook my head.

He found a tube of sunscreen. "Turn around," he said. He slid the straps of my tank top down my arms. The sun was hot on my skin, and the cool sunscreen made me shiver. His hands were soft as he rubbed them up and down my shoulders; the sensation took me out of my head. My stomach eased.

"You're beautiful," he told me.

I turned my head. "I've already agreed to go. You know that, right?"

He laughed playfully as his fingertips brushed my shoulders.

He picked up the cooler, and I took the backpack with our other things. Limestone poked against the bottoms of my sandals along the rocky path. His shoulders bowed under the weight of the sloshing cooler as he said something that sounded like "All of this was once under water."

All of this.

Suddenly I wanted him to tell me one of his stories about him and his brothers to distract me and normalize what we were doing. I pictured their smiles and tan shoulders as they waded with reedy fishing poles in Argentina. A part of me looked forward to Paolo having a chance to show off, to let me further into his life, even if at the year mark I was still the only one talking about *partnering* and *life*.

When I'm focused on something, I'm bad at knowing the difference between what I want and what should be. Falling in love gave me a sense of letting go, of relenting. The danger in that loss of control only deepened the passion. The notion that loving him was a terrible idea dimmed as time wore on, but giving myself to him seemed truly foolish. How could I not notice he seemed preoccupied, even in our most intimate moments? Sometimes after we had finished making love, he would check his phone and then disappear into another room, leaving me alone. I never saw his eyes follow another woman out the door, but something sinister like jealousy nagged at me, knowing deep down that his heart wasn't entirely mine.

Sweat ran onto my lips. I could taste sunscreen. When my

sandals touched the wood of a deck, the sun reflected off the water like ten thousand tea lights. Paolo pointed at the sailboat he'd rented, and I nodded. He took my hand and tugged, turning back when he felt my resistance.

"What's wrong?" he asked, voice gentle now, aware. "You're still carsick?"

His fingers wove through mine, his eyes the color of Easter chocolate.

"I'm okay. It's just going to take me a second."

"Just a little ways out. Really."

"We can come back in if I don't feel right?"

He laughed. "Please. Why would you not feel right? You won't get carsick on a boat."

I shrugged.

He sounded so light and sure. I was not about to act like a child.

"We'll fish tonight, snap a few photos, enjoy the sunset, wake up together. Romantic." He put his hands together, as if it had been decided just in that moment. He started down the dock again. "We're not going to Cuba, I promise. This perfect place—I want to share it."

I wanted it, too. He gestured toward the sapphire horizon, extended his hand to help me onto the dock. I thought I might throw up again but drew in a deep breath and squared my shoulders.

Across the wobbly line of boats, bearded fishing guides blew smoke as they shared a joke about my body language. I could hear the chatter of birds as sun-brittle boards creaked beneath my feet. We loaded our things onto the boat. Around the lake, the pines looked the way they do on vintage postcards—stately, wise—though the shore was too far away to clearly make out. The sailboat itself was more spacious than I'd expected, with a sturdy fiberglass deck and navy-colored cushions. In the center was an opening through which I could see the shadowy corner of a bed sheet.

"See, it's beautiful," Paolo said encouragingly.

I hated my vulnerability even as I longed for him to accept the irrational part of me. "I like looking at it as much as anyone else. It's getting near it that I don't like," I said. I shut my eyes over the wave of unease.

"Hey," his voice light as air, "it's *okay*. Tomorrow we'll go back to Nashville. Go hiking, whatever you want." He put a hand over his heart. "Promise."

He turned my shoulder, pointing me to the place where I imagined the sun would rise.

I glanced at the guides, the blue haze of smoke around them. I twisted my ring finger.

"If you hate it, we'll come right back. I won't take us anywhere near where the sharks are."

That made me laugh. "Really," I said. "I was sort of hoping for a shark encounter."

"Well, you'll just have to keep waiting, in that case. I'm going to sign out. Be right back," he called, striding to the rental counter. "No sharks on this trip." His teeth flashed in the late-afternoon sun.

When he was out of sight, I stepped onto the white deck top and spit over the side. I told myself that sailing is smooth, that a little alcohol would ease the gnawing in my stomach, distract me from my sense of helplessness. I grabbed two life jackets off the rack and dipped into the cabin, which looked comfortable but smelled like a rustic campground. Sticky wood paneling lined the walls. The mattress felt like a tile floor. Through the porthole, I glimpsed Paolo waving to the guides. I imagined us setting off, then anchored together at sunset. My heart felt like a flag whipped by the wind.

Up top, I checked my phone. Still no service. My mind started to wander, but I centered it. Fear of being on the open water, and more specifically of the helpless feeling I associated with it, wouldn't limit me.

I helped people beat their fears; I could surely help myself. Structure the time, focus on other things, stay busy. Sip wine. I flipped open the cooler and ran my hand through the ice around our chardonnay. I glanced at the time. Technically, drinking wouldn't approach legitimacy for another thirty minutes, but this being a Saturday, I started digging around for plastic cups. My fingertips found the glass cylinder, pulled it out, gripped the top and twisted. The tiny fireworks of a seal breaking.

I washed down an Ativan with a quick, cool sip, then poured some for Paolo, too.

When he came back, my feet were propped on the rail as I swirled what remained of the wine I'd poured for myself, the inside of my mouth both stinging and numb. I wore a skipper's hat that I'd found hanging in the cabin, and a life vest. He clicked his tongue, shook his head, and smiled, like he could tell I'd taken the pill. Maybe it was obvious.

His face was smooth as he leaned over to kiss me. "Feeling better?"

"I'm working on it."

At the far end of the dock, a kingfisher sat stoic atop a pylon. Along the seawall, a handful of wrens peered impatiently at the ripples. They seemed to sense the contents of the yellow bait bucket as Paolo lowered it into the boat.

I sipped the cold chardonnay and looked down at the panicked cloud of silvery fish, fighting an urge to pour them overboard. I tried handing Paolo a life jacket, but he made a puzzled face and waved it away.

"Are you planning on falling in?" he asked.

"Safety first," I told him.

He laughed. "That's not something you say." He knelt and began clearing a space in the cabin for his camera gear.

He'd taught me a few basics with the camera the year before, mainly so I could take shots of his softball team, but I'd spent most of the game snapping photos of his friend Cal's daughter, Olivia, who usually sat beside me on the bleachers while Paolo and her dad played ball.

"When I win the Powerball," Paolo called over now, "I'll be a famous wildlife photographer."

He said this every Saturday.

Then he turned the boat key, and the tiny engine began to cough. "Just to get away from the dock," he said. "Then it's all wind." He revved the throttle on the way out of the marina.

Moving felt better. Anticipation is the worst part of fear.

When we cleared the other boats, he cut the trolling motor and raised the mainsail. "My brothers would have teased me for using that engine at all."

He took a sip of wine from what I'd poured him, tilted his head back to the sun, and swallowed, throat bobbing like a bird consuming fish. "You're good, now? Right, Emily?" *Em-ih-lee.* "If anything happens—which it won't—we'll swim back in. You can see the shore—look. Worst-case scenario, I lose these sunglasses. Not you."

"I don't really swim." My voice sounded whiny as I said it. It was as close to an admission as I was going to come—even with him, showing certain vulnerabilities felt impossible. Without the life jacket, I would sink like a stone in the water.

He made an incredulous face. "You mean, at *all*?"

"At all. It's not something I'm proud of. I worked summers, then started playing soccer. Everything was soccer."

"Nothing at, like, a friend's pool?"

I shook my head. My friends didn't have pools, aside from public ones at apartment complexes.

"Or at the country club?" He covered his mouth and smiled.

"I'll never understand your fascination with country clubs. Waiting tables in a clubhouse was the closest I ever got to the pool."

He pushed again. "I thought they made everyone learn swimming in America." He touched his fingertips, reciting a list. "Golf, tennis, swimming . . ."

"I had one or two swim lessons when I was really little but hated every second. Though I did date a lifeguard in eleventh grade," I announced, only because he was asking for it. I folded my arms and added impishly, "But he wasn't that interested in giving me swim lessons."

Paolo clenched his jaw, the slow burn of a wound beginning, and returned his attention to the horizon.

I'd made peace with knowing that Paolo hadn't just appeared the night I'd met him. I wanted to hear his exes' names and their stories, despite the raw rub of listening. I was the kind of person who liked walking through the grass with bare feet, even if it meant getting scratched or stung occasionally. Paolo, on the other hand, found the mention of my exes intolerable.

Waves pushed against the side of the boat. My toes gripped my sandals as I stood. I uncrossed my arms and put a hand on his shoulder as a way of apologizing. He rubbed his cheek against my hand to say that we were okay, but his eyes stayed focused ahead. I sank into a warm plastic cushion and adjusted my new hat. When I glanced back, I noticed how quickly the pier had shrunk away.

Being on the lake smelled something like I imagined a cloud might smell—the opposite of dusty. The air told my body to fill my lungs, and my body did.

The boat rose and fell, rose and fell. I took off my tank top and let my skin absorb the sun. My eyes closed, but nausea found me instantly, and they sprung open again. As we slowed, I felt my toes uncurl. The breath I'd been holding finally escaped.

When I looked back to shore, I could barely make out the dock. The umbrellas at the campground looked like blue beetle shells dug into the stony sand.

Paolo took his camera case from the cabin and opened it, revealing a cushioned tray of black instruments. "I want to get these trees," he said, nodding at the shoreline.

I looked over my shoulder. The shoreline was a jagged, sandy line, and the boat was rocking. "The trees? Won't the boat moving kind of—"

"The light's just perfect right now." He knelt to steady himself and adjusted the lens. The camera clicked in his hands; there was no sound in the world like it.

"I was thinking," he said after a moment, "does being bipolar have anything to do with it? You not swimming?" He always lowered his voice when he said bipolar, like it was a secret.

"Being bipolar just means I get a lot done," I told him.

"Seriously," he said. He squinted and scanned the shoreline with the camera once more.

I finished the wine in my cup, then reached to pour myself more. "I'll tell you a story. The way you say that word *bipolar* makes me picture my grandmother on my dad's side, who tried to kill herself just about every summer, usually by throwing herself in the Cumberland River. When I was maybe ten, my grandfather answered a phone call and said, 'Yes, yes, okay, okay.' Then he set the receiver down hard and told me Grandma Jane needed our help. He grabbed some frayed rope from his shed and a couple of pastel pool noodles, and we sped in his Buick down to where I could see her wading, waist deep through the current."

Paolo clicked and adjusted, eyes still on the shoreline. He paused. "I'm still listening," he assured me.

"He tied a knot around the bumper, then put the rope through his belt loops. He tucked a noodle under each arm and told me that, if they both went under, to shift the car into reverse and step on the gas."

Paolo shook his head. "You were ten?"

"If that. I could barely see over the dash. Then he strode down the boat ramp into the water, calling her name. When he put his arms around her, she tried to wiggle away. I was positive they would both drown. She beat on his chest and kicked at the air as he carried her to the car, but when she saw me, she stopped like a switch had flipped. My grandmother smiled and kind of shrugged as she wrung out her hair and asked me if I could believe what an ever-loving mess she'd made. Then my grandfather put aside the pool noodles and the rope and told me to not worry about the seat getting wet. Ten minutes later, ice cream was dripping down our hands at Bobby's Dairy Dip. So, when you ask me about having bipolar disorder, I don't mean to brush it off, but I'm nothing like she was. I'm just busy. Focused."

Paolo looked like he was trying to keep his eyes on me, but they kept getting pulled back to the images on his camera. The story was a little more intimate than I guessed he'd expected, and his posture was rigid and upright. "You think that's why you don't like the water? Because you couldn't go in after your grandmother?"

"Yes and no." If only it were that simple. "Her wading in the river didn't help, but my fear wasn't made in one place. I mean, my one swim instructor held my head under water until I started to panic. But I think I was afraid even before then." My hand dropped onto my chest as I searched for a way to describe the feeling. "When I'm in water, I'm powerless. I feel pulled down."

Engulfed, I'd almost said. Or immersed, like I'm surrounded by feelings I can't control.

I realized my pulse was racing. "Let's talk about something else. You get so serious about stuff like that. I'm fine, and she was fine. She lived to a happy, kooky old age."

But I'd intentionally left my own terror out of the story—springing off the soft carpet of my grandparents' house when the call came, seeing the water's surface as a mirror that reflected a second grandma. The apron tied behind her back carried in the current while her peroxide hair blew around her head like a blonde tornado. When my grandfather extended his hand, she'd cried out in a voice that sounded nothing like her. In the stillness after her shrieking subsided, I'd heard the car engine and the wind rustling the oak branches, maybe a barge horn from somewhere. On the drive home, my grandma sang along with the crackly radio as the sky dimmed to a color for which there was no name.

I touched my chest, my hand cold from holding the cup. "And my bipolar isn't even that bad," I assured Paolo.

But it was, really. Even if, most of the time, I'd learned to function well enough. *I* was that bad—or much worse—in ways I never wanted him to know.

TWO

Paolo looked downward, his expression pensive for a second. Then he stretched his arms over his head and reached for his cup. After a sip, flirtation returned to his eyes. "Want to see how to find the fish?"

He reached inside the camera case and passed me a round piece of plastic the size of a soy sauce dish. "That's a filter."

I squeezed it between my thumb and forefinger. "What does it filter out?"

"It makes colors brighter, cuts out haze, things like that. That one's a polarizer, maybe the most important type. Some stuff you can make look better on the computer, but this one changes what the camera can catch—things you can't really add or take away."

I liked it when he sounded like a scientist. "Like the opposite of a flash."

"Yeah, in a way. It basically eliminates reflected light, which, for your camera, makes blue skies bluer, clouds pop. Look at the water without it and you just see a sheen on the surface, a reflection. But with the filter . . ." He snapped the filter in place, then pointed to the water and handed the camera to me, watching my expression.

The display was a wide rectangle, big enough for us both. Through it, the water was transparent, like looking into an aquarium.

"Not bad, right? It's why fishermen wear those polarized sunglasses."

After a year together, he was still teaching me things. My legs wobbled, but I had to hand it to him, spotting the fish was more exciting than I'd expected. I sat again and pushed up my sunglasses, which kept slipping down my nose.

"That top doesn't have to stay on." He raised an eyebrow, no doubt knowing I was one more glass of wine away from really taking it off.

I might have, too, if it hadn't been for the sound of another boat approaching. The throaty mumble of an old motor, hints of kids' voices—word fragments and exclamations, the rest of their sentences lost in the breeze. Paolo leered at me comically, then squinted at the oncoming boat, which slowed nearby. I sat up a little.

On the boat was a family—two Midwest-pale parents and three grade-school-aged kids streaked with sunblock, stepping over each other, gently arguing as they came to some decision. The father waved to us. Paolo's eye roll toward me was almost imperceptible; he was never rude. He leaned toward them.

"Do you like one place better than another for fishing?" the father called.

"Not at this time of day," Paolo said. "Better around the edges in the morning, but now there's no difference."

"First trip to the lake," the father said, shutting off the engine.

I spoke to the oldest boy, who'd propped up his foot and stood proudly beside his father. "How about you? Enjoying your summer?"

He nodded shyly as his two younger siblings tangled behind him, a sudden squall.

Then the mother shrieked, and kid voices rose in blame.

"You!" one said.

"I didn't!" the other insisted.

They crowded onto the bow and studied the surface of the water.

"Did something go over?" Paolo called.

"The keys!" the mother hollered, in almost a pantomime of worry, hugging herself. For a second I thought she meant the physical place off the coast of Florida, but she meant the ones that started their boat, of course. The youngest of the kids began laughing.

I glanced at the orange float hooked to our set.

"This'll be fun." Paolo slipped off his white polo shirt and dropped it on the seat beside me. He flicked open the console and pulled out a dive mask.

"What'll be fun?" My voice sounded shrill, even more worried than the mother on the other boat. "What do you mean? What's going to be fun?"

He spit lightly into the mask and rubbed flecks of his saliva over the plastic surface. He moved eagerly, ready for the challenge. Like me, he could find a thrill. I realized I was gripping the handrail, and that the part of me that had adjusted to being on the water had retreated. I felt helpless again. I couldn't imagine doing what he was about to. "That's going to be freezing," I said.

The mother looked grateful as Paolo slipped his legs over the edge. He shook his head at me. "Don't worry," he said, pulling the mask over his eyes, "I can swim better than your lifeguard."

Then, all at once, he dropped, vanishing beneath the surface.

I reminded myself that I'd probably, hopefully, laugh about this later. I grabbed his camera and stood, pointing the lens at the sphere of his dark hair. The depth seemed unfathomable, like there was no bottom, the rolling waves flexing like muscles.

I tried not to think of the impossibility of what he was doing—looking for a set of keys in a lake so big and deep. But I loved him for trying. Through the camera lens, it was like watching a movie, and I thought back to the stripes of sunlight on the curtains that morning and the warmth of our bodies against each other. On the other boat, the family stared at the water's surface while the shadow of a cloud passed over. My pulse throbbed in my neck.

A minute passed that felt like ten. Then the kids started shouting, and the father clapped his hands over his head as Paolo's face appeared beside their bulky engine. When Paolo propped the mask on his forehead and tossed the keys into their boat, my stomach began to unclench. I drained the rest of the wine from my cup.

"Thank you, thank you," they called, voices overlapping.

He waved to them, then looked at me for some recognition, as if to say, *What did I tell you?*

Once he was back on our boat, I raised his camera, pressing my elbows into my ribs to steady my hands. He wiped at the water running down his face and at the jagged strands of hair on his forehead.

"I'm going to take your picture," I told him. "So look triumphant."

He raised his hands and bowed, like he was accepting the adoration of a crowd, then took a long drink from his stainless water bottle, eyes closed with self-satisfaction in the fading sun.

I closed one eye and captured his image with a click.

An hour later, the sun had nearly set. A pair of birds glided high overhead, black boomerangs across the tincture of yellow.

I poured more wine.

Later, he took a fishing pole and tested the hook against the soft center of his thumb until I thought he might draw blood. He pulled a bait fish from the bucket and pushed the metal through.

I couldn't not look at the fish's blank eyes as he did this, and I needed to laugh at the kind of basic horror of it all. "So, the concept here is that we stab hooks through these little fish, and hope that the bigger fish down there will eat them?"

Paolo's laugh was like music. "Well, when you put it that way, it doesn't sound so good, especially for the little fish." He cast his line and turned his back to the darkening sky. "Actually, for any of the parties involved. The little fish, the bigger fish. or us. But yeah, that's basically the idea. Those big fish are going to eat something for dinner, and if we didn't have our cooler with us, we would need to have something for dinner, too. Besides, it's more fun than you're making it sound."

It was the logic my uncles used around the wooden table at my family's cabin when talking about fishing or hunting. I flipped the switch in my mind that lets me observe what I'm doing from a distance, where my actions are just a machine doing things. That switch let me play half the season my junior year with a torn rotator cuff. "All right," I agreed. "Let's do it."

Paolo's eyebrows rose playfully. He grinned at my bravado as he took hold of one of the poles. "Okay then, Miss Fisherman, I'm assuming you want me to bait this for you."

"Nope," I told him, the word coming out impulsively. "I want to do it."

Paolo put up his palms and stepped back.

I tried to think of the last time I'd voluntarily done something so disgusting. I couldn't. I'm a piece of work, I know, and was glad, in that moment, that Paolo seemed to be able to put up with it all.

"Just push it right through the middle. In one side and out the other."

My shadow darkened the surface of the water in the bucket, and even though I knew it was a little crazy, I was aware that I was about to end a life. The baitfish were silver streaks in different directions, but when I reached my hand in, they scattered as a school.

"Need some help?"

I shook my head, closed my hand around one, but it slipped away. Then I closed my hand around another and pulled it from the water, where it wiggled against my skin, terrified.

Paolo seemed to sense what I was thinking. "Doesn't hurt," he assured me. "No nerves."

He placed the hook between my thumb and forefinger, the fishing line catching the sun like a spider web at dawn. The fish's tiny mouth opened and closed, urgent and spastic, maybe trying to bite onto my thumb, or anything it could. Then Paolo put his hand on my shoulder and started to say something, and like I was in a dream, I tossed it into the lake. It hit a small wave with the broadside of its body, making a little splash before it disappeared with a grateful wiggle of its silver tail.

"You changed your mind?" Paolo asked. He was squinting, amused.

The capture and killing had suddenly seemed monstrous, but I was reluctant to say so, to make too much of the feeling.

Paolo squeezed my shoulder before withdrawing his hand, laughing gently. "Luckiest day of his life."

———

That night the water turned still. For dinner, we ate soft French bread with a sharp cheese I'd bought that morning, finished the rest of the wine, and opened another bottle. I'd hoped for a full moon, but clouds made the sky dim, distant. The cabin light caught the water a few feet from the boat but lit nothing further. I leaned my back between Paolo's legs and he put his arms around me, whispering in my ear.

I remember thinking that, when I laughed, the sound vanished the way the cabin light did. Nothing to reflect it back, no echo. The sound just disappeared.

Memory is an interesting thing. It's woefully inaccurate. People think they capture moments perfectly, but they don't. Images fade and change over time. When a person remembers something, they remember the last time they remembered it, a copy of a copy. Then the next time is a copy of that. Each time, a little less of the original.

I don't remember anything more from that night. Everyone asked me later, of course, in one way or another. My mom tried to jog my memory with specific questions, mining for irretrievable details. As if I hadn't thought of everything possible. As if I hadn't asked the same questions myself.

As if a small prompt would make me remember.

There was nothing to find.

THREE

Right away I knew I would throw up.

My head rolled into the wooden paneling as the boat rocked. It was hot already, my chest and back dewy. My tank top, which I'd slept in, clung to my back.

I called out to Paolo.

No answer.

The cabin door clapped closed and absently swung open again. The sheets were tangled between my feet.

I sat up.

That did not go well.

I dropped back to my elbows, but the horizon spun there, too, so I fell onto my back.

"I think I'm hung over," I announced toward the tiny door. My head rolled to the side, searching for the bottle that we'd been drinking from. After we finished the chardonnay, he'd opened something red, big, and bright, one he knew to buy. From Argentina, I remembered. I was happy he'd picked it up, actually. Because left to me, we'd have been drinking like college kids: rum and cokes, bottles of beer, tequila shots. I remembered thinking that Paolo being in charge of alcohol was a good thing, that we'd stick to wine. And I'd looked forward to waking up feeling relatively nontoxic. Except I didn't. My body felt beaten.

I pinched the bridge of my nose, closed my eyes. I had to find something immediately to throw up in, which ended up being a dusty wastebasket. I filled it halfway, a line of spit trailing from my lips to the plastic liner. It's not as though I didn't drink. More often than I would have liked to admit, I turned the veritable corner from buzzed to staggering. But it had been years since I'd woken up *sick*.

The rocking boat wasn't helping.

I'm not drinking any more of that wine, I thought. Not tonight, not ever. "Honey? Are you okay up there?"

I wondered if it had hit him, too.

The door slammed, then opened lazily. I imagined Paolo with his camera around his neck, his eyes on the pastel fish darting about. I pictured his steady hand, his left eye squinted closed. "Honey, come back down." I wanted his cool hands on my back, his lips on my neck. Then I'd feel better.

The boat rose on the crest of a wave, then dipped in its trough. I reached for the wine bottle on the bedside table and examined the remainder—it was the second we'd opened and was still a third full. My other hand stayed on my stomach, as if anchoring it.

"If you don't come down here right now, I'm going to kiss you without brushing my teeth. I swear I will." I forced myself to stand and turned on the cabin's tiny faucet. Warm water flowed into my cupped hands. I rinsed out my mouth and splashed water over my face and neck, then dried off with the bottom of my shirt, as if I were on the soccer field again and had nothing else. When I turned off the faucet there was only silence. I steadied myself on the wet countertop.

The door was aimless in the waves. I caught and latched it as I went up the stairs, covering my eyes, knowing I'd find him, smiling, shaking his head, telling me he thought I knew how to drink.

"What are you *doing*?" My voice broke on the last word as I climbed up onto the deck. I was alone.

My heart began to pound. I took a deep breath, fighting the edge of panic rising inside my throat, just beneath the nausea.

The horizon was nothing but sun. Looking around, I realized that we were no longer where he'd lowered the anchor—sometime during the night we'd come unmoored and drifted. The marina looked like I was peering backward through binoculars.

"Paolo!" I screamed. Not even an echo returned.

I looked at the water, then jerked my gaze away, recoiling. Was it possible he'd gone for a swim? Tried to swim to shore? And if so, why on earth would he do that?

Had he *fallen* in? The water looked unmanageable, opaque—pressing, pressing. The lapping waves sounded like cruel laughter. I shoved aside my fear as best I could and dropped onto the deck, my chest pressing between the faint gray footprints of his deck shoes. A single leaf, streaked with autumn orange, clung to the hull. When the boat rocked down, the coldness of the water shocked my outstretched fingers.

I stood and paced the tiny space, two steps, swiveling, repeating, until I made myself stop. My hands shook and I clasped them together. Inside me, panic pushed aside my nausea, spreading outward from my heart. It was the fear of being lost as a child, realizing the enormity of what it meant to go missing—never finding the person you love again, or a way home. Existing among strangers.

I imagined the horror of no breath, Paolo reaching for help in the dark—how long before?

A sob erupted from my throat.

"No, please no," I prayed desperately, telling myself it would be okay, that he knew how to swim—I'd seen him do it the day before. But knowing that he could swim was not the same as an explanation for where he was. It didn't mean he was safe.

I dropped to my knees and threw up again, this time over the side. I watched the pieces of my dinner spread and dissolve, and I could taste the stickiness of the wine. Tears streaked my cheeks. Were we the only ones who had spent the night on the water? Where had the family gone—the one with the missing keys? I pulled back my hair and let the sun warm my face, then screamed his name into a wind that swallowed my voice.

I dug into my purse for my phone though knew I'd have no signal before I tried it. I threw it down. Then I beat the cabin door like a kid throwing a tantrum.

There was no one to ask what to do. The feeling was like the uncertainty of a midday power outage, but much stronger—when lights, computers, appliances just blink out—half of me accepting the suddenness of a new plan—like it or not—but at the same time sensing pure terror.

Terror too powerful to look at directly.

Back in the cabin, I went through his things, looking for something—I didn't know what—pulling through the pockets of his clean shorts, then tossing them onto the half-wet floor like dirty laundry. There was nothing. Of course there was nothing. I emptied out his bag, picked everything off the floor and looked though it again.

Beneath the silver steering wheel was a radio, which seemed comical to try to use, like I was in a high school play. I flicked it on, turned a dial, and spoke into the handset.

Nothing, then a screech, then nothing.

I told myself to calm down, that I would figure it out. I'd call somewhere—shore, someone at a desk, and they would send a boat out to help me. They would take me back in, tow the boat, and I would reconnect with Paolo later. I told myself that.

Then I would lovingly wring his neck for doing this to me.

The radio crackled when I turned the dial. For a second, I heard a voice, clicked a few buttons, and spoke at the same time, like a kid with a CB. Then music played—'70s gold, something like ABBA. "Dancing Queen." I pressed it again, turning a dial, yelling. Once, I heard a man's voice, but he wasn't speaking to me. I was overhearing his conversation with someone else. He muttered something. I yelled, but he spoke in a low, calm voice about his weekend, his catch. It was like searching for extraterrestrial life among the stars.

The horizon shifted through the porthole. The impossibility of one shade of blue touching another. Back up top, I tried to gauge the distance to shore. Part of me felt that to leave was to abandon him. Another part knew I needed help.

Sunlight glinted off the water, which was coming from a midmorning angle but seemed to arrive from every direction. I squinted. The brightness alone made me sick; it made me want to throw up again. I ran my fingers down the mainsail, slick from morning dew. I looked at the levers, the shiny rivets, touched the taut, rough ropes. Figuring that out would take forever.

I turned to the ignition. Right—that. The orange float-thing. I stuck the key into the ignition, turned it. The little trolling motor chugged to life. I thanked God.

This I could do.

I yanked up the anchor, set it beside me, and a puddle the gray-green color of silt spread over the white surface.

I called Paolo's name a hundred more times as I splashed through the chop, little waves biting at the side of the boat like piranhas. Finally, I turned away from the emptiness, toward the marina, steering the boat like a car.

A trail of froth bubbled up in my meager wake as I wiped tears and asked myself if he'd abandoned me, or I'd abandoned him. *This is my gasp for breath above the surface of this lake.*

Eventually I ran straight into the dock we'd left the afternoon before. All the birds were gone. The boat hit the dock solidly, and when the sound of the fiberglass hull scraping along wood reached the office, a teenager in deck shoes came running, waving his arms. He hopped down, looking over his shoulder toward the office window. "Hey, uh . . . That's not the way to . . ."

The boat might have drifted if he hadn't dropped to his stomach to grasp the bowline. Gritting his teeth, he rolled and planted his feet, streaks of limestone gravel up the front of his blue T-shirt. He started to say something about the right way to tie off when I cut him off.

"I need to find my boyfriend. He wasn't with me when I woke up."

I leaned onto the dock, stomach scraping on the wood as I pushed myself to my feet.

The boy's neck was ropy, straining as he wound the rope around his forearm. "I have to get this boat secure. You can't just—"

I was scanning the marina, the path through the pines. Even then, part of me thought that Paolo might still appear—with two cups of coffee and a mischievous smile; that I would spend half the day furious with him and then return to having a wonderful weekend. That this might actually be funny someday.

The boy went on as he frantically secured the boat, muttering to himself more than talking to me, "There could be some serious damage to a boat if it doesn't. That siding is . . ."

A voice came out of me that belonged to someone else. "I don't give a fuck about the boat."

He stopped, looked up, held still.

"It's an emergency. I went out with my boyfriend yesterday, and he wasn't on board this morning I don't know where he could be. I don't know where he is."

The boy held up a palm and wrapped the bowline around a cleat. Light from the rippling water reflected in his gray eyes. "Can he swim?"

"Yeah."

"So, maybe he swam in."

Like I hadn't thought of that.

"Maybe. I *hope*." I was pacing. "Have you seen him? Black hair. About this tall?" I raised my hand six inches over my head.

His eyes followed me, the summery ease in them fading by the second. He shook his head.

"Do people just . . . ? I mean, has this happened before?"

"Lady, my boss just ran out. He'll be back in about twenty minutes."

No way was I going to hang out for twenty minutes. "Do you get cell service out here?" I asked.

"Uh. Depends on the carrier."

"*Do you?*"

"Sometimes," he said.

I glanced at the corner of his phone peeking out from his pocket, and before he could back away or refuse, I plucked it out and called 911.

I handed the boy his phone and stepped back onto the boat for a last look around, as if being docked might illuminate something

I'd missed before. The sound of the boy's fast footsteps echoed off the dry dock as I opened the cabinet where Paolo had stored his camera case. My heartbeat whooshing in my ears, I slipped the camera case into my overnight bag between my still-folded clothes and set the bag on the dock as I climbed off. Paolo loved that camera, I knew, and I wanted part of him with me. Besides that, I knew I wouldn't be able to bear watching it be potentially mishandled or, worse, dropped accidentally in the water.

Ten minutes later, the tires of a police car crunched to a stop in the limestone gravel. The officer was an enormous man, with a pale, moonish face that made it impossible to tell his age. His hair was ballplayer short, and the polo shirt he wore made him look oddly informal—almost like an actor who'd been hired to stand in at the last minute while the real police took care of more pressing concerns. I expected him to flip open a pad, the way police do in old movies, but his fingers hovered over a tiny laptop.

The more rushed a person feels, the slower everyone else seems to move. He was no exception. He introduced himself, but my mind couldn't store the words. I was a hundred feet ahead. I tried explaining but I couldn't. The tall cop typed at a glacial pace. He looked at me like I was insane.

I looked for the teenager who'd tied off the boat. I wanted some kind of support—as if he might validate the truth of my story, having witnessed the sincerity of my panic. But he'd retreated back behind the rental counter, slouching with the intention of invisibility.

I gave Paolo's physical description, down to the details of the clothes he was wearing—medium T-shirt, gray deck shoes.

"So tell me, from the start, what happened yesterday," the cop said. His shadow was the exact length of mine across the sun-bleached boards.

I tried to sound calm. I told him how we arrived, got on the boat.

"You were getting along?" he asked. "Any arguments yesterday?"

"No."

"Just a regular start to a vacation," he confirmed.

"Yes."

I desperately wanted to see what he was typing.

"Then we took the sailboat out. Late afternoon. Paolo knows the water, knows boats. He did everything, I didn't pay much attention. He wanted to spend the night on the boat."

"Rented from this marina?" He pointed.

"Yeah, right here, this one," I explained. I told him about fishing, about the other family.

He perked up like a retriever. "Did you catch their names?"

"No." I thought, trying to form their images in my mind.

"Maybe they were staying near here? Maybe he went back in with them?"

"No, we don't know them." I shook my head. "They were gone before sunset."

"Okay."

He snapped the laptop shut and walked up to the marina office.

When I looked at the water, I wasn't sure if what I was seeing was real anymore. It looked set-like, like something that had been specifically designed to be horrific.

I checked my phone again for service. I needed a familiar voice—my mother, or Marty, my first supervisor, who now served in the role of my dad. But to tell them what? I had no idea.

Soon, people arrived. Handshakes and low voices.

From doing evaluations during my postdoc, I knew enough about police work to understand the basics of what was happening, but no more. I understood who was who, what questions they would probably have. What they were looking for. Not that I had any intention of outsmarting anyone. I wanted to help but I could hardly hold myself together.

Another minute and two more officers appeared. One in uniform, one not. They wanted to look around the boat. I nodded, watching it rock when one, then another, stepped aboard. A minute later, they were holding up Paolo's clothes with a wooden dowel.

Then the tall cop was back. "We're going to try to track down the family you mentioned. Maybe they saw something."

Then my ear caught the word *drowned*.

"He couldn't have drowned," I insisted.

The police looked up, then one looked away. "Okay," one said.

"I'm serious. He grew up fishing. He can swim, *well*. I watched him, diving for a set of keys."

I was raving. I didn't care.

Ripples reflected off the sunglasses of the cop who couldn't look at me. His neck had the slow, mechanized swivel of an animatron.

There was a limit to what I could do, answering these questions. One too many, and I'd break. The tall cop seemed to sense that point was nearing, pursed his lips and squinted, working the puzzle behind his eyes. He twirled a red stick in his Styrofoam cup and furrowed his brow. The others stood up against the rail, talking quietly. One of them raised a set of binoculars that reflected what remained of the sunrise. Then he dropped the binoculars, and they swayed back and forth against his round belly. I looked, but the horizon was mist. No visibility.

On the boat, someone raised my prescription bottle.

"Does Mr. Fererra take any prescription medication?"

"No. That's mine."

"It's—"

"For anxiety. I can't swim." The admission choked me. I made a determined face, but I sounded defeated.

He nodded like I'd said some magic words. "Did he take any of that?"

"No way."

Hardly pausing, the tall cop approached the same basic question with slightly different wording. "Mr. Fererra takes no life-sustaining medication?"

Surely, he would have said something. "I wish you'd stop

calling him *Mr. Fererra*, and yes, I'm positive. I took one when we left. He had a few glasses of wine, that's all. It's not like that."

"Do you remember how many were in the bottle yesterday?"

"Um, ten, fifteen? I don't take them much."

"That bottle looks empty to me." I knew he didn't mean to antagonize, but it felt as though he'd slapped me.

We both watched as the cop on the boat shook it, then shook his head.

"Did you two argue at all?"

"No!" I yelled. It slipped out like a tiny bird escaping from my lungs. I gathered myself, rubbing my palms up and down the outsides of my arms as if trying to stay warm. "Look, I know you're just doing your job. But no, we had a great night. We had dinner, then we went to sleep."

If there was sympathy in the officer's eyes, it was obscured by the sunglasses he was wearing. "Has he ever done anything like this before?"

"No," I replied, flatly.

"Would you mind if we had a look through the vehicle?" he asked.

The request made me furious, but I agreed. I watched other boats heading out. People going about their usual routines. Other people spreading blankets, preparing to enjoy the lake. I watched them. From the corners of their eyes, they watched me, too.

I ached for a simple explanation.

Then there was a female cop with hair-sprayed bangs who wore a dolphin necklace that she tucked inside the collar of her polo shirt when she caught me looking at it. She seemed to think I should be crying. Should I have been? Would that have helped? Would people move faster if I screamed?

Her presence made me want to call Allie, if only just to translate somehow. My old friend, working as the public affairs officer for Nashville Metro. On my college soccer team, Allie had been a scholarship player who seemed not to need the scholarship—which

might normally have engendered bitterness among the other play-
ers, but she was so consistently gracious and supportive, resentment
toward her was impossible. The words *Allie* and *ally* twisted in my
mind. She was normally the person I called when I had any contact
with the police.

The female cop wanted to know if there had been any inappro-
priate contact between Paolo and me the night before.

I couldn't begin to answer that.

I described him again. I went through the details of the trip,
when we'd arrived, what we'd planned. The way they talked about
him made him seem less than real. Someone I'd dreamed up, my
imaginary boyfriend. My description of him sounded distorted to
me when she read it back. I hated her without knowing why.

An air conditioner began to hum. I searched the landscape for it,
aware of my longing to be back indoors, to be clean and safe again.
It seemed like a week had passed since Paolo and I had left my
apartment—departing our own private, curtained world. What happened should not have, I told myself. We should never have left that
protected, warm space.

Eventually, the female officer sat beside me on a bench outside
the front office. I smelled coconut oil. The morning haze had
cleared and the pine branches shifted lazily, perfectly. I was grateful
at least to be away from the water. Her dolphin necklace had reap-
peared, and she tucked her pale hair behind her ears.

"So what happens now?" I asked.

"We've established command," she said. It sounded both like a
line from a movie and something that I wanted to hear—a good
sign. "The marine unit's been called and will run searches of the
coastline. We've got aviation support that'll be flying over shortly.
The captain is looking into a K-9 search by this afternoon."

"Good," I said. I tested my latest cup of coffee again, but it was
still too hot.

"Right now the best thing for you to do is go home and get
some rest."

"Go?" I thought. No part of me wanted to leave. "I'm fine to stay here," I said.

Again she spoke with the patience of an elementary school administrator, somehow calming and infuriating at the same time. "It's best to let the search team work independently." She assured me they would be in touch *immediately* and that she had her phone with her "at all times."

"So, I'll drive his Jeep home?" I wondered aloud as my hands slapped my thighs—half exasperated, half in a trance. Picturing myself driving it seemed completely wrong, but what else was there to do?

She shook her head. "They'll want to go over it again."

When I began to protest, Dolphin Necklace looked at me sternly for the first time, as if to say she knew I wasn't thinking clearly.

And maybe I wasn't.

How could I be?

"People come in and out of our lives," she said, "and there's no explaining it. This is a confusing time, I know."

I could tell she thought he'd left me, that I didn't understand, that she was trying to be kind. I tried taking a deep breath, but it got stuck halfway in. She was going to break the possibility to me gently.

"Let's see . . ." She looked up and away, counting, as if the clouds kept track of her life's facts. "Five years ago? Yes. Five. Down in Florida. I went to a house. A family, two kids." She lowered her voice to make the point that the stakes were higher under those circumstances. Higher than it just being me. She snapped her fingers suddenly. "Father disappeared, like that. We looked everywhere, assumed he had drowned, considered maybe he'd been killed. Or kidnapped, though that never happens anymore. Who knows? He had run some pot, and something went wrong. No one knew. Two years went by, and he turned up. Got pulled over, simple as that. Living about fifty miles away, booked for driving on a suspended. He'd remarried, started again. Called himself by a different name.

No trauma, no nothing. I was there when his wife went to see him. He couldn't explain why he'd done it. He just had to live a different life, was what he said."

She put her hand over mine for a moment, then let it float off. I nodded to convey my understanding.

"But he didn't just leave me," I said. "I'm sure of *that*."

She seemed to try not to sigh but did.

FOUR

My mom, who looked like a slightly smaller, more sensibly dressed version of me, came out to drive me home. I'm not sure I'd ever been so happy to see someone. When I heard her voice, saw her rushing toward me through the parking lot, tears erupted. Beneath the librarian glasses I teased her about, she was crying, too. I held on to her tight, and she let me.

At the dock, Dolphin Necklace explained that I could go, that they'd be in touch, that I'd likely be interviewed again in Nashville. "You'll be hearing from us," she said, glancing at Mom, whose lips clamped together.

Right then, I had the sense that I should have asked what exactly she meant, but exhaustion won out, and I didn't. All I asked was, "What can I do?"—though I knew the answer.

The answer was wait.

Do nothing.

Tolerate powerlessness.

Dolphin Necklace put both her hands around mine as she handed me a card with her name and contact information.

Mom walked me to her car. We pulled away.

When she'd shown up at the marina, it was like some part of Mom knew the drill. Buried within her kindness was a shred of resignation that I was too tired, too crushed, to address. Helpless to convince her that I wasn't cursed.

In my early twenties, Mom had saved me from myself. Soccer, my teammates, and her.

With her teaching middle school and Dad never spoken of, there was no possible way we could've afforded Vanderbilt tuition if it hadn't been for soccer. Being on scholarship at a prestigious school tortured me perfectly—almost daily: my fears of not belonging were confirmed. The notion I'd ever fit anywhere seemed an impossible fantasy. And part of me just *knew*, not so deep down, that I was essentially white trash, a pretender among the privileged.

Not that I was treated badly. I wasn't. What I faced was inside me. I'd been told a hundred times college would be the best time in my life. That was depressing.

Then, the mania started.

I knew it immediately. I'd pictured my grandmother wading out into that rippling water.

What was in her was in me, too.

Was I crazy? Maybe.

Next to me in the car, Mom looked ahead. I folded my arms, the car's air conditioner a chill on my skin.

I was hollow.

"Have you eaten?" she asked, after a while. The police had told her enough on the phone that she didn't have to pepper me with questions, and I was grateful. I wasn't sure I could talk anyway.

"Really no chance that's happening," I mumbled.

She drove to my apartment, waited while I showered. I took two more Ativan and climbed into bed. I didn't care how it looked. A person can only take so much reality at once, and I needed to be away from the world for a while. Not the healthiest coping skill—fine—but it was what happened.

I tried to keep up a ticker of self-appraisal to ground myself, to stabilize. *My name is Emily Firestone. I'm a child psychologist. I have friends, colleagues. My bipolar disorder has been regulated for years. My name is Emily Firestone. I won't lose my mind.*

———

The next day was Sunday. I called work to say I couldn't come in the following day. I paused before I left the message. Was I calling in sick? That wasn't quite right. I certainly wasn't on vacation. Was there a code for *my boyfriend disappeared*?

I couldn't bear thinking of the word *dead*, but the word was all I could think about. Paolo had been so devoted to his lab that it was almost impossible to imagine him not there, pouring over data in the seemingly endless quest to develop an H1–N24 vaccine. But not being able to visualize him *not* there was pure disbelief I knew. Denial.

I called Allie. I couldn't believe she answered. People don't usually answer the phone now. Calling is an imposition. Everyone texts. Besides, she had recently been married. I was sure she had other things on her mind. When she picked up, I could picture her thick, dark hair framing her green eyes. She was the best kind of friend and the worst kind, for exactly the same reason: she was perfectly put together. In college, she had remembered everything on team trips and could be counted on to have brought extra sunscreen or tape that even the trainers had forgotten. As a teammate, she was always on time, or early.

Her voice was quick as a hummingbird but soft as honey, paced in a way that, probably insecurely, I associated with being wealthy.

Later I would regret it, but right then, I told her everything. She listened like she always did.

"Well, I'm obviously not a cop, but I do work at the precinct, so I'll keep my ear to the ground, okay?"

An hour after we hung up, she called back.

She sounded apologetic. "You said they might want to ask you a few questions? They do. A detective named Andre Mason is going to call you. Emily, I'm so sorry. It'll be quick, I'm sure. They can come to you, probably, if you want—"

"No, no," I insisted. I wasn't thinking. I was out of my mind, frenetically pacing my kitchen with directionless eagerness. "I haven't been to your office in a while." How long? I thought back to her being with me the night I met Paolo, then later us parting ways at the bar.

"Text me when you get to the parking lot," she said. She was full of sympathetic urgency. "I'll come out and walk in with you."

Her offer surprised me, but I agreed. I guessed she understood the near-universal discomfort of about walking into a police station. I wondered if she'd considered what happened on top of the parking structure thirteen years earlier, my being taken to the hospital in the back of a police car. I thought of the cold handcuffs against my hot skin, then pushed the memory from my mind.

"Great," I agreed hurriedly. "Thanks, Allie."

"Great," she echoed, sounding relieved.

Detective Mason called almost immediately after I hung up with Allie, his voice like a bass guitar. We went through the business of picking a time when I'd arrive the following morning.

———

My stomach wanted it to be over quickly. At the lake, the police had told me this time might come, but I hadn't guessed how I would feel. It felt like a mixture of *nothing matters* and *get away from me*. People don't generally go to police stations because they're thrilled with life, I reminded myself. Instinctively, I glanced up at the tiny scar on my wrist from where the handcuffs had been tightened just a bit too firmly that night on the parking deck. Then I swished my wrist so that my watch covered it.

Because I'd always wanted a red convertible, I'd bought one I couldn't afford the year before. I drove it uncharacteristically slowly to the police precinct, occasionally checking the clock on the dash. The toe of my shoe pressed on the gas a bit and the engine hummed as I slid past a van going under the speed limit. I'd been pulled over three times in that year alone—enough that I'd come to rethink the wisdom of my purchase.

It was true, I hated to admit to myself; I was still somewhat impulsive.

I found a parking spot, texted Allie, and started toward the front door. I'd been to the station only once before, but it looked exactly the same. Same pressure-washed concrete steps that smelled somehow like both bleach and cigarettes, same Helvetica lettering over the door spelling out POLICE, as if to display the function of the place as plainly as possible. Same weird energy around the building. I pictured the dark cloud that hung over the Addams Family's house. The vibe was like that. The hallway was scratched as if with giant fingernails on either side. Like a monster had made them, I thought—like the Hulk. Fluorescent light from the lobby spilled out through the double glass doors. My bones felt heavy; my mind was still spinning. Would they call about Paolo? Had they found him? His body? *God.*

No, I couldn't think. That was part of the problem.

It had been nearly a year since I'd seen Allie in person. She stood beside the entrance in a loose yellow sweater, hands folded at her waist, and looked like a flower growing out from between the cracks of broken pavement. Behind thin, wire-framed glasses, her eyes brimmed with sympathy that might have cut me if I hadn't been numbed by overstimulation and the neurological blanket of sleep medication. After everything that had happened, what harm was a little pity?

She put her arms around me quickly, then steered me toward the doors, hand on the middle of my back. I could have guessed I looked shredded, but when I caught a reflection of myself in the glass of Allie's door, I was a zombie. Hair unwashed and pulled back, eyes hollow, staring back at me. My face held its summer tan, but I looked simultaneously pale, like I'd faded. I wondered if I should start wearing makeup. Maybe, I thought. I'd start when I had my shit together again.

"No one's with you?" she asked.

"No?"

I started sweating without fully knowing why.

I must have looked bewildered, because she added quickly, "It's fine. There's nothing to worry about. He won't even keep you long."

In the English language, there may be no phrase as uncertain, as anxiety-provoking, as *There's nothing to worry about.*

The chairs in Allie's office were covered with stacks of paper. No way either of us was sitting. She glanced at the clock situated in her crowded bookcase. Her phone rang, but she ignored it. "I hate to think that you have to sit through something like this after everything."

Her dark eyebrows were furrowed. I knew that look; it was her expression when we'd gotten hopelessly behind in a game. When there was no way to win. She used to put her hands on her hips, too, but in her office she stood beside her desk and unfolded her arms. To keep from falling over, I leaned against the wall.

Outside her office, a man in a stained T-shirt, ripples in his huge, muscular back, was resisting as he was led away. His hands were behind him, his shoulder brushing heavily against Allie's door frame, then scraping the drywall.

And I'd thought DHS was rough. We were both a long way from the leafy, manicured, bubble-like Vanderbilt campus. "Just a regular morning at the office?"

"Sorry. Let me get you some coffee," she offered. I didn't object, and before I could say anything, a small cup was in my hands. "Careful, it's very hot."

I tried not to wince as it scalded my lips.

"This whole thing won't take very long," she assured me, looking over my shoulder into the hallway.

I needed to back up for a second. "Am I *missing* something here? Why *would* this take very long?"

Her head cocked a bit, expression softened. "It just won't." Then she circled back to that phrase again. "There's really nothing to worry about."

I knew she was being kind.

What remained of my stomach started to drop.

"Well, that's good," I said, not too dryly, because I knew already, without her saying so, that I was in trouble deeper than I'd understood a minute before.

Paolo's words flashed back to me: *You think you can do anything.* He'd been right. Note to self: Confidence makes you not think. Makes you show up places unprepared.

She squeezed my forearm. "How *are* you?"

I felt for her, understood her confusion. Certainly there were plenty of times in my office when I'd struggled to find what to say. Mostly, I think it's nice to know that someone wants to be comforting; I think that's better than finding the perfect words.

I didn't have time to answer. There was a shadow at the door, then three quick knocks.

Allie looked up. "Hi, Andre."

"Hi." Curt, sharp. His eyes cut over to me, but not right away. They stayed on Allie for a second, and hers stayed on him.

They knew each other, I realized, more than just professionally. Feelings in a room are as plain as the weather. But whatever burned between them had dimmed, probably ending when her relationship with her husband had turned serious—two, two and a half years before. They'd talked about this very moment, this exchange. Her hands were on her hips, resolved.

Dark skin, tall, the posture of a former athlete. A shaved-in part on the left side of his scalp. From under his collar poked a tattoo of a rose, some indelible remnant of a previous life. And right above the rose was a tiny piece of tissue with a central maroon dot.

He'd been in a hurry earlier.

He didn't wear a ring. His eyes flicked from Allie to me. Just then, I noticed that he smelled like some terrible cologne.

"Emily Firestone?" he asked.

"That's me," I said.

"I'm Detective Mason."

He nodded to Allie, then pointed down the hall. "Right this way."

As I passed through her door, Allie patted my shoulder. I tried to ignore the concern in her eyes as she looked away.

FIVE

The lines around Mason's eyes told me he was about forty years old. He wore an oversized triathlete watch, the kind our team trainers used to wear—mini-computers, basically, designed to record and organize multiple sets of data simultaneously. He had a way of smiling a measure too quickly that made me instantly suspicious. He pointed to a room on his left, closed the door when we were inside, and it was suddenly quiet. Just the spaceship buzz of overhead lights. He gestured toward a chair. I pulled it out, sat, knitted my hands together on a table that looked like it had come from a high school cafeteria. The room smelled like a photocopier even though there wasn't one in there. Or maybe like dust. My head felt medication-dull, but the coffee Allie had given me was helping. I downed the rest of the cup.

"Ms. Firestone." Mason glanced down at the paper he was holding. "Sorry, *Doctor* Firestone. Thanks for coming down this morning." He seemed to have been in a rush to get into the room but now was taking his time, observing me. He spoke slowly, like a host on kids' television. He'd learned that hurrying scared people, I guessed.

He took my cup and poured some fresh coffee that I hadn't asked for.

"Want any sugar in this?"

"No, thanks."

Let's get on with it, I thought. "What's happening with the search?"

From his pocket, he pulled a rectangular video recorder the size of a deck of cards and set it on the table beside us. He glanced at its small screen, which I couldn't see. He pressed a button on top, and a red light appeared. Then he folded over a page on a pad and clicked his silver pen.

"The local police had a diver looking for the last two days." This was his on-camera, being-recorded voice. This was the voice, I realized, he wouldn't mind being heard if the recording was played later. Prior to that moment, Mason had seemed uptight in a self-proving, young-professional sort of way. Camera rolling, he faded into the sort of no-personality personality that I could never read. "So far, the only thing they've found aside from a few rusted cans and fishing gear was a corkscrew."

Like the one Paolo had slipped into his pocket, I thought quickly. "You say that like there's nothing much *to* find. They're not about to stop searching?" The question came out as more of a demand than I'd intended.

Mason frowned. "No, but they can't search forever. There's something like two hundred and forty miles of collective coastline. They're going to do their best with the resources they have. My understanding is that the lake's topography makes the currents pretty strange—it's basically a flooded valley. Eventually, the water flow leads to the Elk River Dam, but there are weird back currents."

I knew what he meant. On a map, the lake looked like spiny aloe branches.

"Debris, like a piece of clothing, for instance, could float in a hundred different directions," Mason said solemnly. For the first time, I thought I could hear a hint of accusation in his voice. He held my gaze steadily, as if gauging my reaction.

I could only imagine how I looked on camera: like I'd been in bed without sleeping for most of the last two days. Like I hadn't eaten. Like I should have washed my hair. I touched my ponytail, smoothed the sides, and tried sitting up a little straighter.

"What about his Jeep? Is it still at the marina?"

"His friend came out and drove it back to town. It's at Mr. Fererra's apartment now."

This was a surprise. "His friend?"

Mason hesitated briefly, igniting my paranoia. I imagined his mind working to filter what information was and wasn't appropriate to share with me. "Sure. We've been in touch with Mr. Fererra's friends and relatives for information; his boss, Dr. Silver. Mr. Fererra's friend Calvin volunteered to handle transporting the vehicle back to Nashville."

Cal. He was probably Paolo's best friend outside the lab, super-serious about softball in a way that had always seemed silly, and stoic to the point of being monosyllabic. I'd spent many evenings with his daughter, Olivia, who liked to climb all over the bleachers and me during their games. My interactions with Cal had usually consisted of him casting protective glances in our direction, as if I might just put her under my arm and run off.

Once, I'd asked Paolo what Cal's problem was. "He's just quiet," he'd said.

"Cal drove it home?" I asked Mason, not wanting it to sound as sulky as I did. "I mean, I would have done it."

I noticed Mason hadn't touched his coffee. His mouth slowly worked a piece of gum. Occasionally, the red tip of it—incidentally the same color as his rose tattoo—poked out between his lips like a snake's tongue.

"Have you ever been to the precinct before?" Like he was asking out of curiosity.

"It's been a while, but yes. Last time I was here was to meet with a patient of mine."

"Oh, that's right." He flipped a page on his pad, squinted. "You're with the Department of Children's Services." Soft-voiced, he looked back at his pad.

The vinyl of his chair squeaked. "I want to ask you about your relationship with Paolo Fererra, then about last Saturday night and Sunday morning. Are you okay to talk about those things?"

"Of course."

He kept his eyes down, but his nostrils flared like he was trying to detect a particular scent on me.

As a supervising psychologist, Marty had taught me not to say more than I had to if I was ever testifying in a deposition. In this case, I knew that would be a struggle. Detective Mason wanted to know about Paolo, and I irrationally hoped that by telling him everything, the chances of finding Paolo might improve.

Mason leaned forward in his seat. He glanced down at the device on the table, cleared his throat, shifted his gum from one cheek to the other, dissatisfied. "The police there said you didn't seem to think Mr. Fererra drowned."

"No, I don't."

He coughed. "Where would he have gone?"

Glare from the lights seemed to brighten, but that was from not sleeping.

"That's what you're here for, right? If I had all the answers, I'd go find him myself."

He leaned farther forward. "Let's back up. Two days ago, you and Mr. Fererra went to Tim's Fork Marina. Can you tell me everything you remember?"

"Everything. Everything I remember?"

I heard myself describe the drive down—our laughter, the music playing, the knot in my stomach from hiding the fact that I couldn't swim. I understood suddenly why patients with PTSD don't like to just review details over and over.

"Let me jump in there," he interrupted, the point of his pen lifted off the pad. "You're saying you can't swim. At all?" His hands cut the air, as if severing something, pen catching the fluorescent light.

"That's right." I looked down as I said it, surprised at my embarrassment.

"But you were willing to go sailing?"

I looked at Mason. He obviously didn't understand something important. "We're in love," I explained to him, the way I'd explain it to a kid in my office. "I trusted him."

Mason clenched his teeth around his gum, and the pen returned to the pad. "Sorry. Go on."

I told him about Paolo's plans to fish, the family on the other boat, Paolo diving in after their keys.

He asked if I'd seen the family before, the make of their boat.

I'd been through it all already. My expression must have answered half his questions.

"Hmm, okay." He sounded incredulous, but I couldn't see what was hard to believe. "There are parts of the night you don't remember?"

"I guess."

"Do you remember lying down, going to sleep? Was Mr. Fererra with you when you went to sleep?"

I hated what I was about to admit. "That . . . I don't know."

A curt nod. Then Mason asked, "How often do you not remember things that happened the day before?"

Something about the question made my stomach drop like we'd taken a sharp turn—or like I'd sat down to take an exam I hadn't studied for. Anxiety nightmares about unpreparedness, vulnerability. My hands were slick with sweat. Behind my eyes burned a crimson-colored anger.

Why couldn't I remember? He'd asked a sensible question, but the seeming unfairness of it ate at me. I knew how unreliable memories can be, how they can get distorted and fragmented, and how those distortions can grow into severe inaccuracies. But I trusted my memory—it was a steel trap through the heights of mania and the pits of depression. Likewise, alcohol never took a single memory—even if later I wished it had.

The night aboard the sailboat had been different. I remembered the taste of more wine, the unsteadiness in my lower legs from the boat's gentle rocking. I remembered darkness falling, and then afterward, nothing. It was as if my mind was a computer that someone had hacked to delete one specific file.

"Not often," I answered, finally.

"You two were drinking?"

This again, I thought. "A little wine. A glass or two." Not nearly enough to erase memories, or stop them from forming. I pictured the cords of muscle in Paolo's forearms as he twisted open the wine bottle, and then him casually dropping the corkscrew into his pocket.

His disappearance had to have happened while I was already

out. My stomach sank with the idea. Or rather, with the nightmare I could barely let myself consider.

My hands were sweaty and I could feel my jaw working, grinding. I stared at the tabletop and felt like slamming my forehead against it.

Detective Mason squinted slightly. "You mentioned something to the police at the scene about talking about a previous boyfriend of yours?"

"Oh." My eyebrows crunched; I was midsip with that second cup of coffee. I set the cup down. "Yeah, but that was silly. It was nothing. Not like a real argument."

"Was Mr. Fererra upset?"

I couldn't stop myself from rolling my eyes. "Maybe for a second. Really, it was not a big deal."

"Were you upset?" Mason's eyes narrowed further.

My fingertip found the little handcuff scar on my left wrist. There were no tears, yet; they were still down way below the surface, under the weight of all that forced concentration. "You'd be making something out of nothing if you called that an argument. It was nothing. Do you know what I mean? You can ask me again and again; it's still going to be the same."

A scribble. Another nod. "You're taking some prescription medications. That you brought on board."

I was ready for this one. "I am. Paolo never, ever would have taken my medications. We weren't using them recreationally. He hardly drank. I mean, he works like . . ." I stumbled. "He worked a lot. He wasn't like that."

"The medication was for your bipolar diagnosis. Yes?"

A slap. "Yes. This was antianxiety medication. I've been diagnosed with Bipolar II."

"*Two*? Can you explain that?"

How much to explain? "It means I never really go full manic. No days and days without sleep, no hallucinations. Just depressed. Then sometimes, what they call hypomanic. Revved up."

"Out of control, you mean?"

I shook my head. "No." I'd said enough.

"So, later, you just went to sleep?" he asked, affecting some confusion. "Revved up, but you fell asleep all right? You got used to being on the water?"

"I wasn't revved up—hypomanic—that night. I haven't been in months."

He flipped over a page and went on to ask me about waking up and getting back to the dock. When we finished, Mason leaned and turned off the camera with a small sigh. His terrible cologne wafted toward me. "You know how to get in touch with me. We'll let you know if there's anything else."

He shook my hand on the way out—his grip cool and tight, the grip of someone who wanted to be more than what they were.

––––––––

I strode past Allie's office toward the light-gray rectangles of the front door. Her voice called after me, but I kept walking, not slowing down. Outside, the sun had come up fully, and the lazy light from earlier had broken through the clouds, baking everything.

"What was all that?" I asked, not bothering to slow down. I didn't know why exactly I was so surprised. A part of me knew I shouldn't have been.

The psyche is no good with past, present, future. I was in junior year again. Allie was a freshman—never mind the new truth that we both had gray strands in our hair. I felt like a goalie left undefended. I rubbed my hands together, my body overcaffeinated. Anger, in that moment, tasted like powdered creamer. I squinted in the unyielding light, my eyes scanning the parking lot for the sleek red hood of my car. I couldn't get away fast enough.

I was talking over my shoulder. "He questioned me like I'm a suspect! How did I not know I was, like, *under suspicion* or something?" I swiveled, and Allie was in front of me. "And how the fuck could anyone think that anyway?"

She was out of breath, eyes wet, holding her glasses. Regret for the way I was ranting swept through me, then it disappeared, like an ember floating off a fire. I didn't know what I'd expected of her—to step in? Be my lawyer?

"Let's talk in my office. Okay? Please."

I could see my car out of the corner of my eye. I turned away from her, but my voice softened, just a bit. "Let's talk out here."

I knew she wasn't the one I should be mad at.

We got in my car and closed the doors. I turned on the engine, and the white noise of air conditioning blew over our faces.

Allie looked past me toward the walkway, where a blue uniform moved toward the entrance. She'd pushed up the sleeves of her yellow sweater. "I can't really sit out here for long. I'm sorry you got so caught off guard. Really. I was trying . . . If it means anything, I don't think they'll pursue it."

Pursue it, I thought. They probably won't pursue me. "Well, that's good."

I reminded myself she wasn't a cop, exactly. And that the cops weren't the enemy. They were being responsible, doing their jobs. Questioning me was not a personal attack.

But once the protective/aggressive part of the brain gets activated, it takes a while to start thinking clearly again. I let out a long exhale and held my hands over my hair like I was trying to keep my head from blowing up.

"Emily."

"There's nothing to pursue except finding Paolo."

"*I* know. They just have to—" She shifted as though the seat were hot.

I held up my hands in surrender and spoke slowly. "I know you're in the world's worst position here."

She looked appreciative of the recognition, that I'd gotten outside myself for a second. "He's just being diligent. He'll move on." She touched my arm. "I'm sure."

I was not so sure.

SIX

Over the next few days, I spoke four more times with Dolphin Necklace. When I was in my apartment, her voice sounded like it belonged to someone else—a different woman, someone who didn't match her compact, tan body, or didn't wear dolphin jewelry, or live in a southern state. Were the police there doing enough? I didn't know. Anything less than what it took to find him would always be too little in my mind.

"We're working to identify the other prescription bottles," she said.

"No, no, there was just mine."

She was quiet for a second, then explained, "We've verified yours. There were two other empty bottles in the Jeep's center console that we're working to identify. You said earlier you weren't aware of Mr. Fererra taking any prescription medication?"

"I'm absolutely sure," I told her, a bit too firmly, because suddenly, I wasn't sure.

"Not to treat attention-deficit disorder?" She said the name of an ADHD drug.

"Nothing like that," I said, wanting so badly to be truthful. But it wasn't the truth. Not exactly. I flashed back to something he'd let slip. How long before? Months. He'd mentioned a yellow pill, and then said it was his lab mate's. An intern. That they both took one to work into the night, and that it reminded him of the buzzing, racing productivity of cramming for tests as an undergrad. He'd hurried to cover it, and I'd let it go just as quickly as he twirled me around, playfully dipping me, us suddenly slow dancing in my kitchen. He told me how much they'd gotten done, how important the work was. I'd released the thought to wherever passing thoughts go—until just that moment, when recognition rushed back like a song I'd never wanted to hear again because it had once been irritatingly stuck in my head. It carried the annoying, childlike nausea of simultaneous guilt and misunderstanding.

After we hung up, I stared out the window. Had he been abusing medications and hiding it?

On the next call, the officer explained how Paolo's right to privacy had expired as far as their department was concerned. They'd spoken with his friends, his coworkers. When she told me about being in communication with his family in Argentina, I felt an irrational embarrassment, as though I'd lost Paolo—their brother, their son—like a borrowed bracelet.

She explained that the police weren't treating the case as a homicide because there wasn't enough evidence. They'd gone through his bank records and mine. Everything matched what I'd told them, she said, though accusations curled in her southern voice like a tiny thorn.

I closed my eyes.

"We entered his name into a national database for missing persons," she told me, "in case he pops up somewhere." I hung on her words. I hated to acknowledge that this phrase ignited a crazed optimism in me—some nights afterward more vivid than others—as I imagined him reemerging somewhere: Oregon, Phoenix—with a hangover, a terrible story, and a heap of remorse. Those fantasies were all that sustained me.

I fell asleep for a few minutes, and the present rushed toward me insistently when I woke.

It was some day of the week, but which one seemed unimportant. Mom sat on the edge of my bed and pressed her fingertips together beneath her chin, as if praying I might accept the obvious and come to my senses.

"What are your plans tomorrow?" she asked.

"I have to drive to the lake," I said. "There are some parts of the north side I want to look at."

Mom sighed. She took her hand from my hair and rested it in her lap. "Em, what happened was an accident. A terrible, terrible accident. You're torturing yourself. It's not easy. Losing someone you love."

"Mom, I . . ." I wasn't sure how to be kind with what I wanted to say.

Her voice was soft and cautious. "Have you considered that you may be a little bit in denial?"

I wanted to shout that I was not in fucking denial, but how could I? Not just to the consensus-chorus, but especially to Mom—who seemed, horribly, to relate to what I was going through. To refute her take on what had happened would be to reject her most personal offer—to share in understanding the grief, to join the one-person club she'd started when my father died.

But I couldn't accept it.

I took her hands between mine. "I want so bad for you to trust me."

Her expression, just at that moment, I'll never forget—resignation, disappointment, the temptation to give up. She smoothed the fronts of her jeans and went to the doorway, where she paused and looked over her shoulder at me, wordlessly, before leaving.

The police, Allie, even Mom seemed to accept the idea that he'd died. They were investigating a death; I was investigating a disappearance. I knew I might look crazy, but if their work could help mine, I decided, so be it.

When my phone chimed, I jumped to answer. Detective Mason asked if I was in a place where I could talk, and if I was sitting down.

I stood.

"I have some news. They found a deck shoe, size ten, gray, like you'd described Mr. Fererra wearing, in the water grate in the dam. They can tell it had only been in the water a few days."

I waited, unsure what to make of this new information.

"This sort of evidence . . . is consistent with a drowning. It happens when someone falls over unexpectedly. I'm sorry, I thought you should know."

"So they're focusing on that area? What are you saying?"

In the pause, I could hear a faint sigh. "Emily, they're covering the lake as best they can. As I said before . . . debris can end up anywhere along the shore because of the variance in currents out there. But they don't have the resources for night and day search teams."

"That's bullshit," I said, staring toward the closet where my shoes were. "I'm going out there."

Across the room, Mom's head turned.

"I'm going to ask you not to do that," Mason said calmly. When I began to interrupt, he continued, "It's more likely you'd destroy something useful than find anything they missed."

The lake was more than an hour away. Outside, dusk had begun to fall. I pictured myself sloshing through brush, the cone of my flashlight bobbing over branches. My chest sank as I thanked him and ended the call.

One thing about going through things as a therapist—you have flashes back to what your patients tried to tell you, ways they tried to explain their pain. They all come back to you. You understand something you could never have comprehended before. A new place opens up inside you. And even if it can't be filled, it can contain an understanding of someone else's suffering, even in retrospect.

I finally called Marty. I was on my tiny porch, sipping bitter coffee I'd let turn cold, while crickets buzzed the way they do on late summer mornings.

He listened well. He'd practically taught me how to listen. I could picture his expression—exasperated on my behalf. Even still, I sounded numb to myself, exhausted. I'd made a note to myself to not tell the story again for a while.

"Jesus," he said.

"Yeah. I don't know what to do."

"What could you do? Are you working? Are you able to?"

"I've been in the office, but I canceled most of my appointments.

I don't actually have that much leave. I took it all already. My wisdom teeth came out in February."

His mouth clicked. "Ah, okay. Well, I'm here." And I knew he meant it.

"Thanks, Marty." Some people give you more than you could ever give back.

————

In the shower, I stepped back from the spray, wrapping my arms around my chest. Around me, steam began to cloud. I imagined the sensation of dropping those three or so feet. The water on my nose and lips brought forward the feeling of horror of what falling overboard might have been like—the rush of lake water, and for me, a flood of helplessness. But *had* that happened? Even if Paolo somehow had had more to drink than I remembered and had fallen in, surely breaking the water's surface would have woken him. Surely some muscle memory for swimming would have kicked in—the instinct to survive would have propelled him upward.

And surely I would have heard something, I thought—a splash, a struggle.

But I'd heard nothing. Remembered nothing. Only the silence of dreamless sleep.

None of it made sense. And looking past the fury of my own confusion, I could imagine, easily, that from Detective Mason's point of view, Emily Firestone might seem very suspicious.

Paolo was the one who was gone, but somehow I was the one who'd turned into a ghost. I let this happen, I thought sometimes. I allowed it. One night I'd dreamt the world ran out of air. Anyone still alive gasped for what little remained. Then the world ran out of light.

Then I woke up.

A horrible stab of vindication twisted inside me. The lake, the great sucking blackness, had taken Paolo. I'd been right to fear it all along, and no one had listened.

Getting up the stairs was a feat. Showering was an accomplishment. Makeup was out of the question. So was work. I called in for another week, never went in.

There had been life before my love for him, but it was strange to rediscover it. The relics, the objects that had outlasted him, made me feel naive. In my freezer, I found food I'd bought months earlier. Half packages of it—veggie burgers, two still in their frozen home. I held the cold cardboard in my hands and tried remembering the frame of mind I'd been in when I'd bought them at the supermarket. I'd hoped they would be healthy for us to eat.

A return to thinking that way was unimaginable. His absence made life feel like a house without a floor. At night, a dry wind whipped against the windows, shaking them like someone was trying to come inside. And if someone did, I realized, I wouldn't have found any energy to fight.

I slept beneath a blanket of pills. Some over-the-counter, some I knew I shouldn't take but did. My dreams were hallucinatory: waves that lifted like a giant jawbone; me lost in a museum, somehow both a child and a woman at the same time. I dreamt the sun turned into the moon, then rose so high and bright that it rained a mercury-colored light over everything.

Thursday morning I went downstairs, and the stern, steady voice of a local news anchor filled the kitchen. Mom's eyes were fixed to the screen, her hand absently weaving a spoon through her coffee.

I rubbed a crumb of sleep from the corner of my eye. "What's this?" I asked.

She stared silently, eyes narrowed with disbelief.

"Mom?"

"I'm sorry. This is horrifying," she answered, whispering the last word. "Are *you* okay this morning?" She turned, touched my arm, but I was already looking past her shoulder.

"What happened?" I asked.

She hesitated, a parent's instinct to measure certain explanations. "Someone was murdered. Up on Gainer Ridge." She glanced back at the screen, hand resting on her throat.

Mom lifted her hands from the countertop leaving hazy palm prints, then wrung her hands together. "This would be terrible anywhere. But there? Gainer Ridge?"

"I know," I said, somewhat in disbelief myself. It was not a well-known place—no notable vistas to draw hikers, no water to draw kayakers. Just a rural, undeveloped part of the state—a name you might see on topographical maps in an outdoor store with no pin beside it to mark a destination. For a moment, the news came front and center in my mind, eclipsing the sadness and confusion I felt about Paolo being gone.

Mom said what I was thinking: "What a place for a murder to happen." She shook her head slowly back and forth.

I'd lived in Nashville pretty much my whole life and had only been there once—years earlier, winding around for two hours on country roads to a forgotten-seeming trailhead.

"Foul play is strongly suspected," I heard the newscaster say, "making this potentially the first murder to be recorded in that county in the last five years."

I felt myself shudder.

Was the whole world going crazy? I felt a film of sweat glaze my forehead as images rose: police tape, uniformed officers standing at the rear of a police cruiser, the sharp slope of a wooded valley. I felt sick.

"I'm sorry," I said. "I'm going to lie down again."

Mom followed me upstairs, where her dark shape cut the doorway. Her head was tilted, just slightly, and she rubbed her hands together before sitting on the end of my unmade bed. She glanced quickly around at the crumpled laundry on the floor—shadows in the curtained half-light. She touched my hair, tucked it behind my left ear. I saw her throat move as she swallowed.

I knew she, of all people, understood.

SEVEN

My mind returned over and over to the night on the boat. The memories were like my own personal Zapruder film—I could watch and rewind them again and again, pouring over the details. I told myself I had to be missing something, some clue that would help me understand, but what was it? I pictured his sleek dive from the boat, trying to reconcile how such a practiced swimmer could possibly have fallen in the water and lost control.

Detective Mason's questions came back to me, too, and his skepticism had only made me more confident. No, we'd encountered no one else that afternoon or evening but the family. And no, we weren't drunk, or high. We weren't arguing—maybe that was the most maddening detail of all—until Paolo's disappearance; our time together had been basically perfect. What had I missed? How could so warm and wonderful a time have led to him vanishing, I wondered, a spark of self-reproach flaring inside me for ever letting my guard down—for ever allowing myself to get comfortable in the first place.

———

A week after he was reported missing, Paolo's family decided that there should be a small memorial service and scheduled it for the following Monday morning. The angry part of me wanted to call and chastise them for giving up, for accepting that he was dead— but there was no playbook on how to handle the situation, and I was sure they were as upset and confused as I was.

To have bipolar and function despite it, you have to compartmentalize aggressively. I told myself that even if for everyone else the funeral service represented a period at the end of a sentence—closure—for me it would be a comma. Nothing about Paolo being gone was resolved in my mind, but skipping the service was obviously not an option.

The night beforehand, I slept in short spells, rest coming like shreds of confetti. In the morning, I made coffee and turned on music. Music shepherds your thoughts. And for some reason, what I must've wanted was to picture the opening of the film *The Big Chill*—the funeral scene, specifically, where the characters are introduced as they arrive to say goodbye to Kevin Costner. I turned up the volume. "Heard It Through the Grapevine" kept the silence from consuming me. I pictured William Hurt's character as I found my pills and swallowed the last two. My toes curled into the rug when the bitterness stung my throat.

My phone chirped. Mom.

She was already at a doctor's appointment. "Honey, they're not done with me here. Are you okay? Can I meet you at the service?"

I looked at the time. Somehow it was 9:30, the service starting in an hour. "You're *where*?"

"These first appointments are always on time. They're never this late. I'm so sorry, I'm stuck."

The cup inside my head was full. She would meet me at the church; we would leave together; she wanted to know if that was all right. I looked at the time again. "Sure," I told her, "it's fine. I'll meet you there."

"Right in front."

"Right in front," I echoed.

"I'm sorry," she added, in a quieter voice. "This thing is so unreal."

This thing. I ended the call and threw my hairbrush across my bedroom, where a map of the lake was spread over my bed. *So unreal.* I tried counting the number of times she'd met Paolo, because scheduling an appointment on the morning of his funeral seemed a measure of . . . I didn't know what. Of disinterest.

My phone was still in my hand as I bounded down the stairs. Anticipating the funeral engaged a kind of fearless autopilot in me—a state of being I'd worked hard to grow out of, but it came over me like a fever. Like Bruce Banner becoming the Hulk—that's how a kid had described it to me once in my office—and I'd smiled with complete understanding.

There's only a *thing to do*, and a desire to do that thing. I become an observer. Like a character running in a dream. Depression felt like the shark in *Jaws*—even if it wasn't visible on the surface, I knew it was always there, wanting to consume me. Sometimes doubt would flicker in my gut to warn me depression was approaching like a fin circling through languid waves.

I happened to have vodka in my freezer. Someone had brought it months earlier to make Christmassy drinks. I poured it over ice and colored it with orange juice, sipping it as I turned on the shower. It was cold when I swallowed, pleasantly stinging and numbing my mouth, the ice rattling and swirling in the glass. Bitter. I got why patients cut themselves sometimes. You want your body to match your feelings.

A number I didn't recognize rang my phone, and I let it go to voicemail. People had been calling all week. "Shh," I said to it. I couldn't possibly.

Out of the shower, I drained the glass, returned to the kitchen, and repeated the sequence: ice, vodka, orange juice.

Then I dried my hair and tried to put on makeup. I turned the music louder and slipped on my dress, humming in a purposeful, feeling-suppressing way. The future two hours just seemed like a vague place where I didn't want to go but had to.

I told myself I knew how to drink. I'd been doing it since I was fourteen. By the time my uncle sat on the side of my bed as I was packing to leave for college, wanting to talk with me about alcohol on campus, I'd already been to so many keg parties in empty fields, and held the hair of so many friends, I probably could have taught him a thing or two.

I tested my breath and decided to take an Uber.

My phone rang again. I switched the setting to mute.

Waiting for the driver ten minutes later, I watched the clouds darken. On my phone, the guy was going in circles. My convertible sat on the curb like a dog eager to be walked. It was starting to look like rain.

Finally, he called, lost. "No, it's the other direction," I told him. I hung up with zero confidence he would find me. Overstuffed clouds continued to shift. I was about to get soaked.

I didn't want to show up drenched, so just like that I canceled the ride. I twirled my keys around my index finger as I started toward the curb. It seemed like nothing bad could happen—all of my bad luck had already hit.

I pulled a U-turn in front of my condo as the clouds opened up. Disaster had been averted. I smoothed my hands over my dress.

The church was five minutes away. His mom and brothers would be there. I would sit on the other side of the aisle. I turned on the radio for something to listen to, but nothing seemed to fit—too happy, or angry sounding. Or worse, romantic. I picked up my phone to find music, set it back down. Don't be stupid, I thought. Pay attention. This is a five-minute drive.

At a red light, I pulled down the mirror. My eyes looked like someone else's. Someone who wore makeup. I burped some of the vodka into my fist. Fine, I thought. I look fine.

Then the light changed. The pavement was so bright it looked like it was lit from inside. I crested a hill on Woodmont, and my phone lit up again. "Stop," I said. "Stop calling me." I reached, turning it over on the seat. When I looked up, I heard an urgent horn. There was no time. Cutting the wheel only made it so the collision wasn't fully head-on; their car spun mine, the rear landing in an overgrown ditch, pointing upward into the rain.

The air was smoke. All the airbags had deployed—seeing them blown fed some curiosity I'd never realized I had. *This is shock.* My horn was stuck on, playing a single note that sounded like a low howl, the bray of a wild bird. The windshield was three spiderweb cracks, and through them I could see flames rising from the engine. *Get out. Get around the airbags, look past the black smoke. See what you've done.*

I managed to open the door, but my leg wouldn't work. It buckled beneath me, broken midcalf, and I fell face-first into mud that smelled like gasoline. Pain I'd never felt before. Not like athletic pain, pain you know can be iced down and healed by your young body. This pain was lightning through my leg, a turn and tear and unnatural cutting. Pain like fire inside my skin.

I screamed as my elbows came up onto the ground. I reached toward the other car with my left hand, seeing two of my fingers extending in wrong directions, like tree limbs after a storm. *I'll get there.*

I'm in shock.

Already, I could hear a siren.

I couldn't see into the back of the car because of my angle from the ground. Just the lazy, gray clouds, moving slow and orderly; indifferently raining. With the wind knocked out of me, my yell was a stage whisper.

"Are you okay?" I tried. *Of course they aren't.*

The driver's side door opened and the mother flew out, calling to her son.

The asphalt was steam under my hands, raw against the tops of my legs. In the middle of the road, I heard brakes screech, another horn. I spit something out of my mouth. Part of a tooth. Blood dribbled from my bottom lip, spread in a trail across the speckled blacktop. My eye focused on a piece of glass that caught the sun as the siren became a scream so bright and loud I tried to turn away from it.

Someone said, "Oh my God."

Someone else said, "I never."

A third person dragged me off the road.

"She might have a spinal," the first voice cautioned. "Don't move her too fast."

I might have a spinal. Oh my God, please let me not have hurt that child. Not hurt anyone. Please let me not have hurt. Please not hurt.

"She's out," someone said. "She's definitely out."

I remember that.

EIGHT

Even before I woke, I knew I was in a hospital—the simultaneous smells of sterility, infection, and urine were unmistakable. When I opened my eyes, I saw a tray at the foot of my bed, where a covered plate and a cup with a bendy straw rested.

I tried sitting up, but an IV taped to my arm resisted my movement. I winced at the sting as the needle pulled my skin. In the hallway, a police officer was talking with a nurse. I couldn't hear what he was saying, but her eyes were narrowed. Angry, even. When she looked back over her shoulder, I closed my eyes. I heard the door click, then the officer's voice.

"Emily? It looked like you were awake there for a second. Are you still?"

I knew why he was there, and it wasn't to protect me. I might have done something terrible. Unforgivable. "Hello," I said.

He smiled. He was blond, maybe thirty. "Hi. I'm Officer Chapman. I'm with Metro."

"What happened?" I asked, my voice falling apart through the last word. I swallowed and tried again. "What happened before I . . . came here?" My head and eyes motioned up and around.

I had a memory that was just a flash—more a jolt than an image. The cop looked at me kindly but steadily.

Then I remembered—my hand on the steering wheel, the numb burn of vodka in my throat. Fire. My hand tightened around the top of the bedsheet, so hard that my broken nails began to ache.

Maybe none of it had happened, I wished. But it had. Otherwise, I wouldn't be in a hospital. Talking to a cop. Again.

"You were in a car accident. Do you remember that?"

"Oh my God, were they hurt? Was anyone . . . ?"

He shook his head. "You were the only one injured."

My head sank back into the pillow with immense relief. The thought that I could have hurt someone else was a stab to my stomach. I wanted so terribly to not be reckless.

Then I remembered where I had been going. Paolo's service.

I coughed and it hurt. "Did I miss it? The funeral?"

He nodded solemnly.

I fell back. My stomach felt empty, but also like I might vomit. "What day is it?"

"It's Wednesday evening. You've been asleep for the last twenty-four hours."

Beyond the open blinds was the concrete side of a parking structure lit by the afternoon sun.

"The officer at the scene suspected you'd been drinking alcohol, so a blood draw was ordered."

"I understand."

"You weren't able to sign the citation at the time, and you're in no shape to be served a warrant at this time."

"Served a warrant?"

"Taken to jail."

I had the dizzy feeling of standing on the edge of someplace very tall, of looking out over an expansive canyon. I raised my hands over the bedcovers. Two of the fingers on my left hand were splinted.

"But you're going to be in the hospital for a little while longer." He sat up straight and rubbed his neck. It occurred to me he'd been waiting some time to tell me his news. He smiled again, kindly. "I'll get your nurse."

When he left, I pulled back the cover. My left leg was in a cast from the knee down.

My heart felt like a stone. The nurse returned and didn't say much. I didn't say much, either; I didn't have anything to say.

———

The following morning, when my phone lit up with my office number, I knew what was about to happen before I heard my boss's voice.

"Hi, Emily." His voice sounded prerecorded. "I want to wish you the best of luck in recovery and in dealing with all of your legal issues. Unfortunately, I have to fill your position at this time."

He'd heard about the arrest. Of course he had. I was sure the news had made its way around. I told him I understood. And I did—what choice did he really have? I knew that the inbox for my work email was a mile long by then; I knew people who were already overworked were covering my cases. Intellectually, I didn't hold it against him, but inside, I sank.

He ended the call mercifully, saying that positions opened all the time and who knew what might happen a year from then.

A year . . . God.

I ended the call before I started sobbing and turned the phone over on the blanket. I looked out the windows again toward the visible wedge of blue sky.

The kids on my caseload. All their stories. My work with them, gone. I closed my eyes. I couldn't believe it.

No, losing the job was completely believable.

That night, my mom sat in the chair by the foot of my bed, her red reading glasses balanced on the end of her nose. She'd come to witness another mess. To clean up.

The television was a low mumble. She tucked her hair behind her ears in the alternating light, reading a magazine. I pretended to watch the screen, but really I watched her. I wondered for the first time—and weirdly, I thought, even as I wondered it—about whether I would live as long as she had. Bipolar patients, I knew, had demographically shorter life spans. I wondered what of her I'd inherited, and what I'd inherited from my father, whose name I knew not to speak.

And yet, I almost did speak it. I felt a wave of courage just at that moment, perhaps carried by the momentum of being so low—after all, what else could really go wrong—and I opened my mouth to ask about my father.

But then, all at once, like she'd been reading an article about that very thing, Mom closed her magazine and suggested that I move in with her for a while.

Still, I wasn't sure how much more my ego could really take. I knew she was offering to do me a favor in a way, so I treaded lightly. "I don't know, Mom. I'm thirty years old; don't you think that's going to be kind of weird?"

"That way, you can minimize your expenses," she said, sounding practical. Then she paused a beat as she pushed her glasses back up the bridge of her nose. "And maybe watch Andy if I have to go visit Carol."

Andy was the border collie Mom had adopted the year before. A first-time dog owner, she hadn't accurately calculated the time commitment and responsibility involved.

"Oh my God," I said, too overwhelmed by everything to give my eyes a full roll. The last thing I needed was the additional task of caring for Andy. I felt a quick sting of resentment, then I swallowed it. What Andy needed certainly wasn't his fault, and I knew Mom's offer was fully well intended. But the back of my mind registered frustration—the arrangement seemed like another obstacle between me and finding out what had happened to Paolo.

———

I left the hospital on two crutches and in a knee-high plastic boot that felt like a cinder block—like the nurses who'd heard about my DUI had made it extra heavy. The walkway toward the car was freezing cold as the air conditioners worked against the autumn sun pouring in through the windows. I plodded along, the boot making a clicking sound with each step as it touched the floor, warm sweat on my neck. It seemed like autumn would never come again.

Mom walked with me through the parking garage, where I breathed in the first outside air I'd tasted in two weeks. I balanced my crutches and hopped on one foot while she held open the door to her white Toyota.

"How does your leg feel?" she asked, watching me maneuver around.

"Like I stepped in a bear trap that's still attached."

The next day, Mom dropped me off outside the courthouse while I went in to be booked. Some things you just don't want your mother to see. Our family attorney had talked me through what to expect, and the process went the way he'd described—metal detector, long lines, waiting area like a softball dugout. Then, when my name was called, my photo was taken quickly, and I rolled my fingers one at a time over a scanner with backlit green light.

Afterward, I click-walked back out into the morning, filled with a curious mixture of relief and solitude. The crutches seemed all that was holding me up. The place inside me where feelings were made said I was about to fall into the sharpest depression of my life—the big black. I scanned the metered spaces for the white of Mom's car.

Our attorney called later. "Because of the circumstances, they've made an offer. You plea no contest to reckless driving. One year probation, one year with a Breathalyzer to operate your vehicle. Plus court costs and a fine. All things considered, it's a good deal, Emily; I recommend you take it."

Part of me recoiled at the idea of Paolo's funeral being seen as a bargaining chip; another part wanted every advantage I could get as I figured out what had happened.

And there was relief that I wasn't headed to jail.

The next day, I went to meet with the psychology board about my license.

Boardroom, bright lights, sweating, explaining.

I think because they felt sorry for me, the sanction was light: a year's probation on my license, provided that I could find a supervisor to oversee any work I did.

Only one person came to mind.

NINE

I watched the bottom edge of my bedroom curtains fluttering like the wing of a stingray in the breeze from the ceiling fan. No idea what time it was. The room was so dark it looked like a nightlight had been switched on as my phone lit up, ringing. I sighed when I saw who was calling. Some people never leave you. In fact, they get closer when life gets hard. Marty was one of those.

"Hey, Marty."

"Hey yourself," he began, as if I'd been the one calling him and the phone call was a happy surprise. "I'm checking on you."

I put myself up onto an elbow and rubbed at my eyes. "I'm not . . . at my best."

Depression feels like being at the bottom of a well. You look at the shapes of people up top and understand that, on the surface, there is a world in which you used to participate.

His laugh was gentle as a wind chime. I could picture the kind expression on his face as he said, "You can't lie in bed, my friend."

It was morning, sometime. "I know."

"Emily."

"I know, I know."

"I heard work let you go."

I'd known it was coming, but it stung anyway. You don't get reminded of stuff like that when you stay in bed. "How'd you hear?" I asked.

It didn't matter. Marty knew half of Nashville. It would have been a surprise if he hadn't heard.

We talked through my court date, what the arrest meant in terms of my psychology license. Crazy how transparent your life is sometimes. You think you're the only one who knows what's going on.

"You're going to need to give the board some kind of a plan," he offered, intuitively. "Let them know that you're doing something with yourself, and being supervised."

"Yeah?"

"Yeah. And here I am. Across the hall I have an empty office with no psychologist in it."

I could picture the building—old, worn but stately. A storybook building, a block off of West End. It was practically across the street from Vanderbilt—the hospital where I'd met Marty under much different circumstances.

An office in that building, across the hall from Marty, would be impossibly perfect. I wanted it without seeing it.

"Marty, are you sure?"

Through the phone, I thought I could hear him shrug.

"I don't know what to say. Thank you?"

"Thank me when you get here."

I wiped away the tears in my eyes.

———

I took the first shower I'd had in three days. I stood on one foot like a crane, kept the water cool, and had the feeling that it was clearing a layer of something tired off my body.

I felt lighter. I pulled my hair into a wet ponytail, put on a casual dress, and struggled into my boot. My leg was swollen, throbbing like I'd inflated it. The ache radiated from deep inside—the pain of bone fragments asking to be left alone, trying to heal. I pressed it hard into the wet floor until I knew the edge of what I could stand.

———

My ankle was held together by pins. I'd been hurt before in soccer, but nothing like this. Each step was pain.

A reminder.

I'd taken a walking boot home from the hospital that made a crazy-sounding click every time I stepped. I didn't mind it much the first day. I figured I'd live in my bed, in Mom's house, forever. But since it now looked like I'd be going places, that *click* was going to have to get figured out before it drove me completely crazy.

In the kitchen, Ancy licked at my hand while I made coffee. I told Mom I was going to see Marty. Me driving was about to get interesting because of all the restrictions—and because I now had no car.

Mom was moving toward the door, but stopped short. "You know, you could always use the truck at the cabin." She paused. "Eventually, you know. When things are settled."

"Huh." I cocked my head.

I'd learned to drive in that truck—a black Ford Ranger from the early nineties with a broken odometer. I'd done doughnuts in it through the front field when I was fifteen, slammed the side into an elm once, and even tried to jump it over a ditch with my cousin riding shotgun. He'd chipped two of his teeth when we landed. In college, I'd made out with a boy in the cab and we'd smeared ketchup over the interior dome to make it into a "mood light." There were dried black bits still stuck around the edges the last time I'd checked.

"I'll check it out if I get out there," I told her.

I found a cane that had belonged to my grandfather in the broom closet. The one he'd used pulling my grandmother out of the river. It was wooden with a carved knob on top, and I tested the strength of it under my weight. It might not have been high fashion, but it beat walking with crutches.

Beside it were a half-dozen canvases that I'd started in acrylic. A winter branch on a bruised sky at dusk—dark colors, hot ash, gray earth.

———

At the salon, I told the stylist that I wanted her to cut off all my hair and leave only about an inch.

"Pixie," she said.

"Yes."

She raised her eyebrows. The fluorescent light reflected on her scissors as she went to work.

I ran my fingers over my head when I walked out, and caught a glimpse of myself in the salon window. My hair looked blonder, and stuck up in the way I'd wanted it to when I was younger. Just in that instant, I gave up hope, as they say, for a better past.

I put my hand again through my sticky—and now short—blonde hair and drew a deep and stinging breath. Then I slapped my own face once, hard. Hard enough that I was sure my cheek was red. I angled my cane on the sidewalk and turned my face to the sun and thought, *enough. Enough.* There was a lot that I had to do.

———

Marty had worked in the same building for more than thirty years, having smartly bought it in the midnineties when it had gone up for sale. Someday he'd collect a fortune, but for the time being, he was situated in the center of town.

Along the top of the building, the trim paint had chipped like shredded white cheddar. The hedges along the front had gone free-range, no longer really decorative landscaping. The iron gate was warm as I steadied myself, its creaking like a sound effect from an old movie. Behind me, the afternoon traffic was a chorus of sighs.

I wondered if I should have moved to a different city. After the lake, after the accident. There was still time, I thought. I could find a place where I didn't know anyone—or, more to the point, where no one knew me—and I could start again.

No, I'm doing this.

I gripped the wooden handle of my grandfather's cane and pushed through the gate.

The walkway was brick, raised at angles by weather and roots like a long row of uncorrected teeth. They were loose—they must have been—because when I turned to close the gate, I kept turning. I spun, and the enormity of the ground rose until my elbows collided with the dust and clay.

Stunned, then a sharp pain.

A shadow reached over me. I recognized the crazy outline of white Bernie Sanders hair and the soft clomp of his green-laced, gray tennis shoes.

"You gonna lay there all afternoon?" Marty asked.

A drop of sweat fell from my forehead as I smiled. I pressed my knees together and rolled to sit—trying not to flash West End—and looked at the streaks of dirt up my sleeves and at the tiny cuts on my palms.

"I guess I'd better not," I said.

He sat beside me on the walkway.

"You cut your hair short."

"Looks like you've got a beard going."

He rubbed his hand against his cheek as if to show it was real, or that part of its purpose was for the tactile pleasure. He smiled his Santa Claus smile.

A passing car slowed, its driver curious. Neither of us moved to stand off the walkway.

"Your candidate might be wondering if she's ready for this." I wiped the back of my hand over my forehead, grateful I hardly ever wore makeup. "Or if she should have just relocated. Moved to Brazil or someplace."

"Brazil?"

Or Argentina, I thought. "Or someplace."

"They also say only people who've been wounded themselves can help other people heal," he said.

Nice to hear, sitting on the ground.

I thought about that for a second. "Well, this wasn't the entrance I had in mind. Think we ought to go inside?"

Gratitude can feel obligatory, even anxiety-provoking when it makes you question your worthiness to receive benevolence. But how else could I feel? There's a kind of agony from being the recipient of too much goodwill, and I was reaching my limit.

I managed through the front door and started laughing when I saw the stairwell. I considered a quip about ADA accommodations I chose not to make. The stairs would have been a job with both legs functioning and no cane.

"It's a little tight," Marty acknowledged, having read my mind, again. I followed him to the second level, the clicking of my cane and boot echoing over the old surfaces.

In the hallway, I took a moment to look at the high ceilings and grooved wooden floorboards—the kind that are only in very old or very modern spaces. Marty's actual office—lined with books and family photos—hadn't changed since I'd met him. It smelled like old paper, like a library. I couldn't stop myself from thinking it was what a real psychologist's office felt like.

I sank into his couch and rested my cane between the cushions.

Marty dropped into a chair like we were in his living room. "I'm sorry," he said. "About everything. I'm sure you miss him."

I chewed the inside of my cheek. I didn't know what to say. Conflicting feelings swirled inside me. I felt guilty at the idea of proceeding with regular life while so much remained unresolved, but I had to—both for financial reasons and because I might lose my mind without the ballast of my professional life.

"There's just so much I don't understand. Can't understand. What happened . . . to Paolo." I was trying desperately not to cry, but could feel heat rising behind my eyes. "Before life can go on, I need answers. And yet, everybody seems to want me to forget. Put what happened, and him, behind me. It's impossible."

Marty took a slow breath, the depth of his years of experience shining in his eyes. "That's what's hardest, to go forward even when something is still unresolved. Especially something of this magnitude. You can't be captured by it, but you can't forget it, either. Some part of life, maybe work, has to go on even while you search."

I knew he was right, and that I wasn't the first person in history to have to function while I was—what? What was the word for what I was doing? It wasn't quite grieving and it wasn't quite obsession.

It was reckoning with the fact that part of me had never left the lake.

———

"Thank you," I said finally, clearing the tears from my throat. "I promise I won't mess this up."

"I haven't even offered it to you yet. You haven't seen it yet."

"But in case you do?"

"Okay," he said evenly.

"Okay?"

"Yeah, okay. I believe you." As if there were a reason to. I hardly believed me.

"Why's this happening? Why are you being so good to me?"

"Don't you think everybody deserves a second chance? Don't answer that . . . I know you do. We both do. Otherwise we wouldn't be in this type of work.'

We went across the hall, and he opened the office door. Sunlight streaming in, gleaming hardwood floors. Its emptiness seemed like a set of possibilities. I felt like trumpets should be blaring.

It was beyond perfect.

Also, beyond my budget.

Through the wavy glass, Vanderbilt's red brick tower poked through the emergence of fall colors like a photo from a postcard. Beyond were the steel and glass edges of the medical center. I pictured the shady courtyard where I'd waited for Paolo on a wooden bench beside a statue of a girl reading, back when it seemed like his work would never stop. Four blocks in the other direction was the pale-green roof of the psychiatric hospital.

I traced my finger along the shelving on my way back to the hallway.

"Can I afford this?" I asked. My voice echoed against empty surfaces.

He said a number that was more than reasonable. My hands balled with excitement.

"So what do you think?"

"Marty, is anyone going to trust me with a patient again? With a kid?"

"You're going to turn this corner. You just need a little help right now."

I wanted him to be right.

"Do you remember the story you told me, way back when, about helping people?"

His eyes seemed to shine. I knew the story he meant; he'd brought it up a dozen times. I knew the point he was making and it was well timed. "You were somewhere, a pharmacy—"

"The pharmacy at the medical center." I remembered clearly, because I'd been waiting for my grandmother. I'd been shopping for a card after some round of nonsense she'd gotten into. "Yes," I said.

He smiled warmly, fingertips pressed into his temples. "And you saw a woman out of the corner of your eye. Walking right toward the window, toward that huge pane of glass. She was looking somewhere else. She couldn't see what was right in front of her, but you could."

"Yeah."

"She walked right into it, and it shattered. Went everywhere. You wished you could have stepped in before it broke, said something. You don't have to be perfect to help, Emily."

A memory came back to me—something he'd done once. "Do you remember that magic trick you used to do? The cut string that becomes whole again?"

He nodded. I could see in his eyes that he hadn't done it in some time. "I used to like doing that."

"What made you start doing it?"

He shrugged. "People want something mysterious, something they don't understand. To believe."

"But do they try to figure it out?"

"Some do. Some don't. Kids want to figure it out more than adults. Grown-ups want to get lost in the fantasy. The world can be a tough place. They want a break from it."

I was back on the sofa's edge again. "Will you show me?"

He found a pair of scissors and a string in a desk drawer—a shoelace—and looped it over his hand. He raised his eyebrows as he pulled on it, turning his hand so that I could catch the way he formed a second loop, cut it, and slipped it back down.

Then, he pulled it, straight.

Back to one piece.

He handed me the shoelace to inspect. The tension in my arms and legs relaxed, and I felt the urge to repay Marty for his kindness. He was right; the trick was insanely simple. No one would believe he'd cut it and put it back together unless they really wanted to.

Later, he walked me out into the hallway. I noticed another small flight of stairs at the end of the hall. I couldn't imagine the building had a third floor. I pointed with my chin. "Where do those go?"

"Oh. That's the rooftop. I sunbathe up there in the summer," he added, without a hint of shame.

I couldn't help but laugh. "I'm sure the medical center staff appreciates that."

"Damn right." He laughed himself, his eyebrow impishly raised. "They probably do."

TEN

The air turned lighter as autumn advanced, and the clouds began to look high and wispy, like cotton shredded across a rough surface. Mom drove me out to the farmhouse. I found the family's black Ford truck sitting patiently beneath a scatter of pine needles. I heaved into the familiar seat and pulled the creaking door that could only be closed with a slam. I put my hand around the ripped knob of the stick shifter and pressed in the clutch with my boot. I couldn't believe it started, but it hummed; the smell of dust and cut grass reminded me of learning to drive. I gave a thumbs-up to Mom and watched her turn toward the road. With a fingernail, I scratched at the dried ketchup around the corners of the dome light, then chugged home. On the way to have the Breathalyzer installed, I ground the gears at every stop.

Three days later, Mom came into my room.

"I'm so sorry, honey. Aunt Carol's fallen. I should really go be with her."

In a flurry, I canceled the lease on my apartment and had my things moved into Mom's house. I've heard people mostly describe being overwhelmed by their possessions, but it was surprising how little I owned. Most of it fit nicely into Mom's basement.

As she pulled away, I waved from the porch, Andy nestled beside me. Part of me was sorry to see her go, but another part was relieved at the space from her oversight. As well intended as Mom was, she obviously wanted me to feel a way that I didn't, and to accept what I couldn't—that Paolo's disappearance had been accidental and that somehow his body hadn't yet been recovered. Watching her tail-lights crest the slight rise at the end of her street, I knew her leaving meant more freedom to continue looking into what had happened. Even if it made no sense to anyone else in the world.

———

The licensing board called. They'd approved Marty as my supervisor—a pinpoint of light that flooded my whole life. Hope returned like the familiar smell of your own home after a long time away.

I celebrated by exercising my credit card—at the mall, at a used furniture store, then later at a consignment shop, where I literally walked into the couch and end tables of my dreams. Normally, when I bought three or more things at once, a kind of mania circuit breaker popped inside me, a warning to slow down. But when I thought back to the way I'd spent money in my twenties, I knew this was nothing. These things, I reminded myself, I would actually use.

I rode shotgun beside the delivery driver, the wind singing in through the open window, goosebumping the skin on my arms. He sang along to a country station and flirted with me, telling me my hair was shorter than his but that he liked it.

Marty sent me a few referrals and I put up an ad on a popular website. And, miraculously, it seemed, my phone began to ring. My calendar wide open, I scheduled three appointments for the following week.

I popped open the lids of my storage bin and ran my fingers over the nubby edges of Lego bricks—the solid classic colors and the newer pastel bricks that look like candy—then lugged them to the truck bed. In another bin, I found boxes of crayons in their worn, natural state, and the singular smell of Crayola reminded me of the joy that came from having the coolest job on earth. I got to play with kids and help make their lives better at the same time.

Even being broken myself, I got to help kids heal.

Sweat beaded my forehead. Paperwork, confidentiality agreements, clipboards, pens, I thought. Remember. Remember. That stuff was all up to me now. The licensing board I took a deep breath.

I spent the next morning sipping coffee, going over the forms I planned to use. It was slow work, tedious—I actually had to read it all—but it was also satisfyingly responsible. When I was in college, I'd told girls on the soccer team, with pride, that I hadn't cracked a book until junior year. I don't know why I felt happy to say that, looking back, except that it was my way of owning that I couldn't sit still. At thirty, it was still hard.

Sometimes I was astounded I'd managed to get through grad school.

I did my best to decorate my new office. I repurposed a jar of buttons from Mom's closet, hauled up hardcover books, arranging them in neat stacks on lower shelves. A vase from Mom's kitchen found a home, as did a basket of well-loved wooden toys. I unzipped Paolo's photography case and held the cool weight of his camera like a sacred relic, imagining that the smooth plastic and glass had absorbed his love. I pictured the fish in the lake, invisible, all just below the surface. I put the case and accessories in my desk drawer, then set the camera itself on a high shelf near the window, pointed outward, as though it might enjoy the view.

A feeling that wasn't quite anger or despair played in my heart—a single note that was the breath in my chest. I picked up the camera, powered it on, and clicked back through the stored images. He had startling talent—an eye for creating perfect images that I'd envied since we'd met.

Then, I stopped cold. Something about its shape, the strips of sunlight slicing through a canopy of branches . . . I stepped backward.

I opened my laptop and pulled up a news station's website, then clicked on the icon for the story Mom had been watching before the accident. When the image of Gainer Ridge emerged, I clicked pause, and the screen froze.

I set the camera beside my laptop so that the screens were side by side.

The image on the camera's tiny screen matched the one on my computer. They were nearly identical.

Had Paolo been there the week he disappeared?

Could that be possible? He had shot everywhere in Tennessee, but *there*? And on that date? Gainer Ridge was so far out of the way, and so little known, getting there would require a person to have that specific intention. The photo was one of the last he'd stored. I looked back and forth between the images a half dozen times to make sure I wasn't mistaken. If the picture hadn't been taken at Gainer Ridge, it bore a starling resemblance.

I thought back to the newscaster's words on that day: "Potentially the first murder to be recorded in that county in the last five years."

It had happened so close to when Paolo disappeared.

I tried sorting through the haze of buzzing confusion in my mind for any memory of him mentioning being there. I reached for my phone, called Allie, paced the office as her phone rang. The old hardwood floor had a slight give beneath my footsteps. When the call went to voicemail, I wondered if she'd let the call go because of the awkwardness between us after the questioning two weeks earlier.

"Hey, it's me," I said. My voice was jumpy, abrupt—which wouldn't surprise Allie, surely. "Call me when you get a chance?"

I turned out the light and leaned against the door frame, my stomach unsettled. Night had come quickly, and the furniture looked peaceful in the dark—like large, slumbering animals beginning their dreams in the emerging streetlight.

Just as I turned to leave, my phone lit the dusk.

Allie.

"Oh my God, how are you?" she asked when I answered the phone. "You were in an accident?"

Too much had happened since I'd stood in her office the day I was questioned. I told myself I'd catch her up on the basics later—though she'd probably heard about the DUI charge, so I'd leave that out.

"What can you tell me about the Gainer Ridge case?" I asked, closing the office door.

"Why?"

"Because I'm your best friend, and you know I'd tell you."

"You know I'm not officially telling you any of this," she said.

I thought back to her on the soccer field, always so fastidious in spotting threats, a perfect defender. "Allie, I keep secrets for a living. Team rules. This stays between us. I promise."

Maybe she felt guilty for how uncomfortable I'd been at the station. Whatever the reason, she told me everything, and I closed my eyes as she talked, vivid images in my mind.

———

The murder happened sometime in late September, though no one was sure exactly when. Days had passed before the body was discovered, several of them rainy, which was strange for that time of year in the middle of Tennessee. The body itself was burned so badly that the first people to find it—three teenage boys looking for a place to drink beer and fire rounds from a pistol—didn't understand right away what it was.

They said they'd stopped talking when they found the place; something had quieted them, but they couldn't tell just what—it was as though God, or someone, looked down on what they were doing. They described a kind of emotional residue around the place, too, something that couldn't be touched with hands. Birds and insects must have known it, too; the only sound in the clearing had been the impartial creaking of pines in the scarce midday breeze.

"There was still evil in the ground," one boy had told the police.

They kicked the ashes around with their boots, not understanding that they were destroying evidence, leaving semicircular footprint trails as they speculated. One suggested that it had been a lightning strike, until, backing up, he stepped on a jawbone.

Apparently, they'd hesitated to file a report because they had been carrying alcohol. By the time they arrived at the police department the following morning, it had rained again, further diluting what they'd scattered.

A first-year deputy, just out of the academy, followed them down the two-lane highway to where they'd been. He parked on the slick roadside behind their SUV and tromped through the woods behind the boys. That day's temperature had been in the mideighties, and their backs and arms must have been heavy with sweat as they crossed the empty fields and penetrated the deeper woods. When they came to the clearing, the deputy later said, they all stopped walking simultaneously. His report said that the boys were "bug-eyed" when they returned to the place, and that despite not being a crime-scene expert, he could detect the odor of accelerant—maybe gasoline—when he crouched to the ground.

The three of them circled the body. He told them to get no closer. He made the calls.

Thirty minutes later, three more cars were parked behind his. An hour after that, there were ten more. The deputy followed the boys home, then returned to help block off the road in both directions, angling orange barricades across the steaming asphalt.

The crime scene became archaeological by noon. A medical examiner and a team of forensics experts arrived with cameras and wooden dowels. Some of them wore surgical masks. The team tied a clear garbage bag around a pine tree and filled it with empty plastic water bottles within three hours, occasionally squinting upward at the news helicopter that periodically circled overhead. I imagined its shadow seemed like that of a large, predatory bird.

They found no tire tracks near the scene; whoever had come there had walked. Brass bolts glittered like seashells in the circular ash pile. They turned out to be the hardware of a wooden chair. It had burned almost completely beneath the victim, signifying a fire with a particular level of heat. It had been set to destroy.

Later, evidence of restraint was determined. Bits of plastic zip ties were uncovered, likely having been tightened around the victim's wrists and ankles. If something had been placed over the victim's mouth, it had burned.

Beyond the burned area was the evidence that puzzled the

investigators most: circular indentations in the dirt, forming a tight triangle with points approximately twenty inches apart. They crouched over them, careful to keep sweat from dripping onto the ground.

By late afternoon, the deputies made initial estimates about the distance between the burn site and the road. The initial report estimated half a mile, though some uncertainty was noted. Several paths could have been taken.

The media only ever learned half the story. Just enough that the whole city seemed to ask itself: who would do such a thing?

———

When Allie finished, I thanked her before we hung up.

I thought I heard traces of . . . something in her voice. I puzzled over it like reading a pattern of scratches on flatware.

On the way out of the office, I noticed the second stairwell again—the one that led to Marty's sunporch. I caned down the hall and turned the brass doorknob, which clicked anciently against my palm. Stepping up toward the rectangle of milky night sky, I could hear the breathing of street noise. Up top was a rectangle of tar paper, like I'd pictured, the size of a small garden. I stepped softly, as if my boot in the wrong place might push through the flat surface.

The cool air stroked my cheeks. I could see why Marty wanted to sprawl out there—the view was perfect, as if the city had been designed around that particular spot. The reddening leaves of Centennial Park led toward Vanderbilt's stately bricks. Steam rising from the medical center looked like the exhalation of a giant, while red and white lights blinked where its roof met the sky. With my index finger, I counted floors until I found the corner where Paolo had worked, then turned to the stairwell as my phone began to play its chime.

It was a blocked number. Maybe a potential new patient, I thought.

I pressed the phone to my ear. "Hello?"

"Hi, I'm trying to reach Emily Firestone?" A familiar voice that I couldn't place.

I held the rail, my voice echoing through the stairwell. "This is she."

"I don't know if you remember me; this is Sandy Harrison." She paused. "I used to work with Paolo."

Completely blindsided, I fought to suppress the wave of feelings swelling my chest. I scanned my memory. Did I remember a Sandy Harrison?

So much had happened. Sometimes turmoil clears out memory.

"I work in the lab where . . . he worked. I think I met you a few times, once at a holiday party."

Oh.

Then, I remembered. *The party.*

I could picture the enviable breeze of her hair, curled like cursive letters in a way mine never would. I remembered the rich fabric of the dress she was wearing; I remembered feeling underdressed. She was pretty, with sincere eyes, a little younger than us. She'd said Paolo's name, touched his arm when greeting him, showing a clear connection between the two of them that had made my jaw clench.

I wanted to ask how she'd gotten my number. "What can . . . Hi. How are you?"

"You're a psychologist, right?" She sounded hurried, now; the rhythm of brisk walking.

I wondered how she could have remembered that. "Yeah," I said. "That's right."

"I'd like to schedule an appointment with you. Do you have any openings in the next few days?"

"Just a second." I closed the roof-access door against the night sky and went back to the couch in my office, trying not to sound out of breath. "Sorry. Yes, but I mainly work with kids. If you told me a little about what you're looking for, I could help point you in the right direction. Across the hall is a great psychologist who I've known for—"

"I definitely want to see you," she said. "If that's okay."

Was it? I paused half a beat to think. Accessing therapy can be intimidating, and seeing me wouldn't be breaking any rules. I could meet with her once and then give her a referral if it wasn't a fit.

Through the phone, I could hear her breathing. "Are you still there?" she asked worriedly.

"Yes, I'm here," I said. Something in Sandy's voice told me that she didn't want to talk about what was going on over the phone.

ELEVEN

Sandy arrived early the next day. We'd agreed to meet at noon, but at a quarter till the echo of her footsteps rose in the stairwell. I stood stiffly, working my ankle in a circle to prep it for sitting stationary for an hour. Becoming a psychologist, I sometimes thought, was an odd occupational choice for someone who'd always hated sitting still. I slipped my foot back into the hard boot and met Sandy in the doorway. I held a clipboard with the new-patient paperwork I'd printed for her to fill out.

She hurried toward the door, then stopped abruptly when she looked up at me. I started to say hello but was distracted by the way she inspected the office behind me. Her head was quick and birdlike and her breathing was rapid—more than you might expect from a trot upstairs.

"Sandy?" I ventured. The confident blonde I'd met ten months earlier seemed so diminished that I needed to be sure she was one and the same. "It's good to see you again. Everything okay?"

The sound of my voice seemed to bring her eyes back to me, as if the use of two senses was required to remind her where she was and why she'd come.

"In . . . in here?"

I nodded.

I stepped out of her way as she strode to the couch. After a quick look out the windows, she dropped her purse onto the hardwood floor and momentarily buried her face in her hands. The click of the closing door caused her to look up, and when she did, her eyes seemed tired and afraid. She rubbed at them. "Do you share this office with anyone?"

"No, not this office, but I share this suite. I'm renting space from a good friend." I set the clipboard beside her on the sofa and lowered myself into my chair, trying not to wince as I extended my left leg. "What makes you ask?"

She didn't answer.

"Sandy, I'm not sure where to start. I can tell you're really upset." It felt good to slip on my professional tone of voice. I realized I'd missed the honest productivity of work, the sense that I could make a difference. But I was puzzled by my new patient. I set the clipboard on the desk.

"Do you record these sessions?" she asked.

The question wasn't completely unusual. I shook my head.

She sank back and looked at her nails as if she might find her words there. Earlier, I'd heard Marty's voice carrying down the hall, but now the building was silent in the way of work spaces in mid-afternoon. The faint sweetness of Sandy's shampoo hung in the air.

"I'm sorry," she said oddly before composing herself. "What I'm about to say might be really hard for you to hear, but I have to tell you. Otherwise, I'll feel like I'm going crazy. I already do."

How would it be hard for me? This was maybe the strangest start to a session ever. I raised a palm and lowered myself into the chair opposite where she sat. "Let's just start slow. Whatever it is that—"

"You know about the H1-N24 vaccine." Sandy pressed her fingers against the bridge of her nose, her face half hidden when she looked up.

I tried not to wince. "More than I'd like to get into."

"I know your father contracted . . . And that of all people, you don't need a lecture on vaccine research. You're the only person I could think of away from the lab who would understand."

Understand what? I wondered. I had no idea where the meeting was headed, but some part of me felt set up, ambushed. Talking about my father was the last thing I'd expected. I had a mental compartment where I stowed memories of my father when I needed to focus on the task at hand. My face must have shown my confusion.

"This isn't really a therapy appointment," she said. "I don't know who I can talk to, who's safe. I don't know what he knows and doesn't know."

I thought back to the blocked number that had come up when she'd called.

"What *who* knows?"

I folded my arms and Sandy stiffened. When she glanced at the door, I relaxed my posture. "Let's slow down," I said.

"It's about Paolo. I think he was murdered." The words burst out of her.

My mouth opened, but no sound came out. I leaned back in the chair as if she'd shoved me and could feel my pulse rising, my heart hammering suddenly, the way it had on the dock. The police, the marina, the smell of the coffee all came rushing back. "What . . . do you mean?" I finally managed to ask. "I was with him. He disappeared. Sandy, the police think he drowned." The last phrase came out of me as a whisper.

Maybe we could both hear the disbelief in my voice.

"I know." Her eyebrows shot up. "It looked that way, but there's more to it."

"How?" I finally managed to ask, my cheeks burning.

Time began to slow down as my mind grasped at the possibility of an explanation to the mystery that had plagued me for weeks—even as the clinician in me wondered if Sandy might be paranoid.

"It . . . our lab mate, Matt, is involved. I'm almost certain," she said.

"What? How?"

"I can't quite explain how; that's partly why I'm here. But I know what I saw." Sandy squinted, dropping her gaze to the space between her shoes. "I found something—on a hidden drive—data sets Matt had created."

"Okay," I said. My confusion was beginning to feel like anger, even as fragments of what Paolo had explained about their research began to activate in my memory.

Sandy took a deep breath. "I'll try to start at the beginning. Vaccine research is heavily regulated because it's potentially dangerous. Right now, the lab tests vaccines only on animals. It's called the preclinical stage, which in itself is *extremely* regulated. Each virus sample is cataloged, meticulously, before its use and at the time it's destroyed. Last week, I noticed an order discrepancy—one digit off in a previous order. I thought maybe I'd saved the record I was looking at twice without meaning to, so I logged on to another machine to check our lab record there—a computer I don't normally use. We're supposed to have access to the same records, so if I'd made a mistake, I should have been able to see the correct order numbers on anyone else's computer. But on this one, trials showed up in a separate drive, and when I opened it, it showed completely separate data sets, each one using tiny variants of the protein mutation sequences of the previous test."

My heart hammering, I was getting a little lost in what she was saying. But before I could interrupt, Sandy held up her index finger.

"It was Matt's work. He had saved, then slightly altered, most of the samples he was supposed to destroy. It's like running a completely illegal side project—conducting his own trials, basically, with no one's approval, and then hiding all the data." She let out a breath. "I think Matt's trying to sell the research."

"Sell it? How?"

Sandy edged forward in her chair, fingers digging into the fabric.

"There are groups, countries who would love to know the details of what we're doing. In the wrong hands, the sequences could be turned into biological weapons. Since the logins are all stored, I could see that every one was Matt's, dating back into the summer. Except one. On Friday, the fifth of October, Paolo logged in." She paused to let this sink in with me. "I think Paolo uncovered the data sets from the duplicate tests, and Matt found out."

And then Paolo disappeared, I thought.

"I think Matt wanted to make sure Paolo could never tell."

"Oh my God," I said.

"It's something a person would kill to keep secret," Sandy said quietly. "I just put it all together three days ago. I wanted to talk to you, in case you knew something I don't. And because you . . . well, the police wondered about you."

I knew what she meant. "And you did, too," I said. I meant it as a question, but it didn't come out that way.

Sandy nodded regretfully. "It just didn't make sense. Paolo was so full of life. I don't know . . ." Her voice trembled, her eyes round with fear.

I stood and went to the window, grinding my teeth together. I tried to keep my breathing slow, to stay calm. Her theory was out of the blue—but I knew this much: Sandy seemed authentically terrified, and the way she characterized Matt's jealousy of Paolo exactly matched what I'd observed between them at the holiday party.

I turned away from the window, my shadow cutting a dark shape across the floor. "So why are you talking to me? I mean, I'm glad you're here, but why not just call the police?" I reached toward my phone where Detective Mason's number resided.

Sandy clenched her jaw. "Because there's a chance, I guess, that I'm wrong—that I'm crazy, or saw something I didn't understand. And if I am, starting a police investigation into our lab would be the end of my career. I need evidence to show the police."

"Does Dr. Silver know about this? How could he not?"

"Jay Silver is a fantastic researcher, but he's an absentminded professor in some ways. He's so obsessed with finding the H1–N24 vaccine, he could miss something happening under his nose."

"So why not just tell him?"

"Oh, he'll be the first person I'll tell as soon as I have the evidence in hand. Him and the police. But I needed to talk to someone outside the lab, someone safe."

I took a deep breath and turned. A rivulet of sweat streaked down my side. We were frozen for another second before she motioned for me to sit back down, a pleading look in her eyes.

I passed into my third emotional state in three minutes. There was a release of tension inside me, a sudden pulling back of the curtain behind which had been the wildest, most horrific confusion of my life. After any death, people wrestle with disbelief. Staring at Sandy, my disbelief that Paolo's disappearance, and presumed death, had been an accident crystallized. Subconsciously, I'd been waiting for an explanation for weeks.

An explanation I'd given up on receiving. Until just then.

"But would Matt really *kill* someone over his research?"

My attention was scattered as Sandy began describing the personal dynamics—the jealousy that Matt had seemed to have for Paolo from the very beginning of his work there in the lab.

"Paolo could seemingly do no wrong," she said. "It seemed like there was no limit to what he could accomplish. Everyone knew he was Silver's favorite, but Matt felt excluded. And he probably was." Sandy said Matt's name as though she'd spit it out. "Did you ever meet him?" she asked.

"Just for a second," I said, my thoughts turning back to Matt sulking, sipping from his beer.

"At the holiday party, right?"

"Where I met you." The singe of jealousy I'd felt at the time seemed like a crazy misperception. Suddenly, we were two women on the same team. "And, yeah, Matt was distant and weird, and like, rude, but that was nothing, Paolo said. Just something about a paper. Authorship order. I mean, right?"

"That alone can be pretty serious," she said. "But this wasn't just one paper. The way research works today, we're all hanging on by a thread. But Paolo got assignments that Matt wanted over and over again."

I remembered the way Dr. Silver had beamed with pride at the party, lavishing praise on Paolo.

The analytical part of my brain was trying to cool the emotional storm in my chest. I'd done a postdoc, too. I knew it was different from microbiology, but collaborating could be hard, publishing even harder. Then I remembered a phrase Paolo had used once to describe lab environments: *like working in a shark tank*. My mind spun as I tried to arrange these fragments into a picture. Pieces in a mosaic.

"Think back to when you were in school, in training," Sandy insisted, her tone imploring for validation. "You know how crazy things get when people are trying to make their careers. Universities are like psych wards."

My mind flashed to my own graduate training, to the desperation I'd felt at times, dashing across campus to make meetings, the crazy eagerness to get a committee together, or to locate some obscure form that needed to be signed immediately.

I thought of the statistics I'd read about mental illness among graduate students. I'd suppressed my own mania, pretty often, actually, then propped myself up when depression began to fall over me.

A new narrative started coalescing in my mind.

But there was one obvious problem: I had been with Paolo when he disappeared. When I reminded her of this, she refolded her hands. Her voice dropped. The spidery bare branches of hackberry trees reached toward the window behind her, white as lightning in the sudden sunlight. "Think. Is there *any* way Matt could have gotten on the boat before you left that afternoon?"

"It's possible, I guess. Before we arrived.'

"Or once you were on the water?"

My initial thought was that there was no possible way—but was there? I hated that I couldn't fully remember. "I really don't see how," I said.

"Did anyone board the boat or sail near you?"

"There was a family, on another boat, but it was nothing threatening."

Sandy seemed to consider this. "The timing between Paolo seeing that data and him disappearing can't be coincidental. Matt has access to sedatives for the animals in the lab—they're extremely powerful but not always fast-acting." She stopped and winced. "And compounds for euthanizing. If he was able to get any of that into Paolo's system . . ."

Or mine. Could that explain the blackout of my memory?

But how?

As if reading my mind, Sandy said, "I wondered about that

water bottle that Paolo carried everywhere. That stainless-steel one. I wondered if Matt put something inside it. That night, was he sick? At all? Tired?" Sandy strained for confirmation.

I glanced up at the shelf where Paolo's camera sat like a sentinel. It was hard to hear my thoughts over the hammering in my chest. I thought back to the boat, the drive to the lake; I reviewed the details, pictured the bottle he always carried. "Maybe." I tried to remember. Then I found a piece of the memory I'd been missing before. "He said not to drink after him. That his throat was sore."

Her eyes narrowed.

Had we found something? I wiped my palms against my jeans. Focus began to burn in me.

Slow down. Think.

"But you didn't drink from that bottle?"

"I don't . . ." I thought back. I had no idea. "If anything, I . . ."

"What?" She scrunched her straw-colored eyebrows, lowered her voice. "You what?"

"I fell asleep. Hard." I shook my head, apologetically. "I didn't remember anything. I still don't. I was sick when I woke up."

Her voice quickened, and she put a hand on her stomach. "Emily, you could be gone now, too."

I sat back against the windowsill as if pushed. A tiny voice inside me insisted her idea was far-fetched, that I would have sensed a shred of this before. A biological weapon? Matt's jealousy? But I stopped listening to that voice. I'd heard an idea that made the most sense of anything I'd heard so far. I recalled the feeling in my stomach that morning—the nausea. I could feel it again, like I might throw up. Sweat brimmed my forehead as I looked at Sandy. I felt like the wind had been knocked out of me by a fall, my lungs struggling to fill as if the room's air were being siphoned away. Sandy's theory was an explanation—some hope for finding an answer. But if it was true, it would also confirm my worst fear—that Paolo was truly gone. Dead.

Emily, you could be gone now, too.

I cleared my throat. Drew in a deep enough breath to ask, "So what do we do?"

"Matt works on a laptop that he takes with him everywhere. I'd have to literally steal it away from his hands to try to look there. I need to get back onto the computer I was using before—the one in the lab—and download whatever I can onto a thumb drive. I'll print out screenshots if I can. But I have to wait until he's gone to do it—Thursday at the earliest. They'll be meeting downstairs all morning to go over the travel schedule for the conference. If not then, next week. They're both going to their huge conference in London on Sunday morning. But if this is what I think it is—we can't wait. Until I can get to that computer. I needed someone else to know. I figured who else could I trust more than you, considering everything."

"Then we'll go to the police," I said.

Allie, I thought. Or Detective Mason.

"I'll call you the second I have something," she said.

I picked up the clipboard from my desk and dropped it into her hands. She gave me a puzzled look. "I don't even know your phone number," I explained.

Sandy hesitated, then she set her jaw as she scribbled her information.

My chest felt as if it had been inflated with helium, like my heart might carry me, boot and all, off the ground.

Keep calm. Try.

"Until Thursday?" I asked.

She nodded, then hugged me.

"It'll be all right," I told her, sounding suddenly like a reassuring psychologist. "If you're right, the police will find everything."

Her nostrils flared before she went back down the stairs. The cool autumn air drifted up the stairwell. I leaned against the rail for a minute more, picturing Paolo's smile, remembering the warm waits in my car through his long hours. At the bottom of the stairwell, a sliver of light knifed over the floor where the old door hadn't closed fully. I stared at its sharp shape, imagining. What if it was true? What if the story—all of our stories—were about to be rewritten?

I would remember the moment that way: a cool gust that smelled like dead leaves. My heart beating in my throat. *Did that really happen?*

I entered Sandy's number in my phone and glanced down at her address. I recognized where she lived immediately. It was on the east side, a row of two houses a block away from a bar I'd been to too often after college. She lived in number one. I felt a wicked hint of jealousy; I couldn't help it. Where else would Miss Perfect live?

Stop.

Competition is such a close neighbor to jealousy.

Could any of this be right?

I tore up the paperwork and left a voicemail for Allie, asking if a friend and I could schedule a meeting with her Saturday morning. I said I had some new information. We might just catch a killer, I said.

I hung up and realized I'd gotten worked up, that I'd been ranting a little, and that if Allie didn't already regret telling me about Gainer Ridge, she likely would after listening to my message. I picked up the phone to call back. Set it back down. No, that would make it worse. She'd call me. I'd explain.

Then I realized something else.

There was no way on earth I was going to wait to learn about Matt. Blood seemed to rush through my veins, and a variable, high-pitched ringing began in my ears. I'd thought I had understood the dynamics of Paolo's work life—who among his colleagues was a threat to him and to us and who was harmless. I realized as I opened my computer how wrong I'd been.

TWELVE

It was at the holiday party for Paolo's lab, almost a year before. It was the sort of winter night that starts in midafternoon with clouds so low they look like hazy extensions of the trees. The Jeep's heater was warm on our hands as we rumbled through his boss's leafy suburb.

"Not a boss," Paolo specified. "A PI."

"Like *Magnum, P.I.*?"

He gave me a look. Evidently, the show hadn't made it to his part of Argentina.

"I'm just joking. He was a TV character."

He squeezed my hand, smiling. "Dr. Silver is a *principal investigator.*" Through his accent, Paolo's careful pronunciation made the words sound computer generated. "He directs what we do, secures our funding, gets our dual-use research permits."

"Wait, what's dual-use?"

He twisted his mouth the way he did when he searched for specific words. "Dual-use research of concern. Science and government."

"To make vaccines? Because something could fall into the wrong hands?"

"Right. The vaccine would protect people against an H1-N24 infection."

Of course, I thought.

"But to make one, you have to figure out the specific protein changes, the amino acid substitutions, needed for the virus to be transmitted to humans from birds. That transmission is what the vaccine protects against. But if someone wanted to go to war, they could make a lot of people very sick just by knowing the protein mutation sequence."

I took a deep breath.

His eyes stayed on the road. "Before anthrax got mailed around this country, people weren't aware. Labs did dual-use research without even knowing it. Then politics got involved. And now . . . take a guess what it's like to be from another country, working here, filling out forms to work with a virus. They watch. Every move, they watch you so suspiciously." Paolo's jaw tightened.

He worked so hard, over so many late nights. I put my hand on his.

Had I been in Paolo's place, my emotions would have cracked through by then, but his voice was steady, nondefensive.

"But I get it," he said. "Really. The reason they watch is the same as why we work so hard. One leak, you're looking at a pandemic. Air traffic today, a highly pathogenic virus could spread in no time, go global. So, there are regulations. The more serious the virus, the more tightly they regulate."

He turned down a wide street where patches of snow reflected posh lamplight. I'd grown up in Nashville, but we were way out of my territory. The dry-stack stone fences and elaborate Christmas greenery inflamed my fears of being an imposter, even though I couldn't understand how an academic could afford such an address.

"I should have gone into microbiology," I said.

Paolo clicked his tongue and shrugged, answering my comment self-assuredly. "This work we do," he said, "I'd dreamed of doing something so important. A vaccine—it will save lives, make history." He glanced at me as he said the last word.

I wished I could laugh—part of me wanted to; the other part swelled with admiration, like when I let myself daydream about introducing him to my father.

Dr. Silver's house was nestled between two shadowy oaks. Cars parked three deep in the steep driveway, overflowing onto the roadside. Toward the front door, tidy, underlit hedges rose like statues on either side of the stone steps. I glimpsed shapes in the kitchen. Laughter echoed inside.

The front door opened just as Paolo reached to knock.

Leaning against the door frame was a compact woman with shoulder-length blonde hair who looked directly at my boyfriend. "It took you long enough," she teased, the glint in her eyes making me instantly jealous. "I thought you said you'd be here by eight, you jerk." She gave his shoulder a playful punch.

Paolo staggered a small step backward. "Emily, let me introduce you to Sandy." He turned to me. "Sandy and I work together."

"For what? A full year now?" she asked him.

I extended my hand and smiled as he began to answer. "Hi there, I'm Emily. I'm Paolo's girlfriend."

She took my hand quickly, her mouth barely moving as she spoke to me. "Oh, hi, it's nice to meet you." Then she added, with what very well may have been sarcasm, "I hear your name *all* the time."

All the time? Standing beside me, Paolo shifted from one foot to the other. I pinched his side as subtly as possible as we stepped into the warm foyer. Sandy turned and led us into the kitchen, where a half-dozen graduate students looked up in unison and I was introduced all around. They were drinking sangria; I could smell the fruit as Sandy led us to an open space.

"Dr. Silver was just asking where you were," she scolded him.

I wanted to announce that we were late because we'd pulled the Jeep over to have sex, but I stayed quiet.

"Late start," Paolo apologized.

She wore a distant, unfocused smile. "He wanted to be sure he saw you before he left tomorrow." She turned to me and explained, "Dr. Silver will be in Poland until the end of the month. Paolo knows the lab so well, he practically runs everything while he's away."

"I'm happy to help coordinate."

"Don't be shy about it." Sandy touched his arm again, then asked me, "Why's he always so shy?"

I shook my head. "He's not."

I'd been impressed by the house's exterior, but the inside was even more striking. Dark wood floors, a stone mantel, rolling flames reflected in the crystal chandelier. The artwork was all original, I noticed—each piece luminous in display lighting. Like a place in a magazine, I thought, absorbing the tink of silverware on delicate plates. It could have belonged to the parents of kids I'd gone to school with.

I folded my arms.

A minute later, Sandy went down the stairs toward the living room, weaving between groups, turning heads. Ice rattled in glasses above soft music.

"She was nice," I coughed out, but Paolo was looking the other way.

At the far end of the kitchen, a dark-haired man in skinny jeans and a hoodie pushed himself off the counter toward us. He took a drink from his green bottle of beer and seemed to look at Paolo expectantly. Aggressively. I worked to keep my expression neutral but apparently was unsuccessful, because Paolo laughed out loud. He sounded weary, feigning formality. "And let me introduce you to Matt."

Matt nodded crisply. He tucked his hair behind his ears, showing burning blue eyes. There wasn't a name for their color. They locked on Paolo, and Matt scowled. A slight lift of his chin.

Paolo said, "Enjoying the party, my friend?"

No answer. Matt's eyes narrowed, and his mouth became a smirk. He shook his head. Eyes forward, he strode wordlessly out of the kitchen. As he passed, I caught a whiff of the stale cigarette smoke that clung to his shirt.

Paolo blew air from his mouth, his head shaking back and forth once in disbelief. "Grow up," he said. "Go have another cigarette." He whispered something in Spanish to himself, then said to me, "Seriously, who smokes? That guy might actually get something accomplished if he wasn't taking cigarette breaks."

Matt glanced over his shoulder once more before disappearing.

I hadn't smoked in years, but the tension actually made *me* want a cigarette. I turned to Paolo. "What was up with that?"

Paolo had picked up a wine bottle and was examining the back label. His eyes had a look of devious false-surprise. "What? Oh, Matt?" he asked, as though nothing had happened.

"Um, *yeah*. That was awkward."

He dribbled the wine into a glass, swirled it around, and held it to his nose. The contour magnified his smile and his voice resonated in a tiny echo. "It's nothing. He's being a baby. Authorship order on our last paper. Nonsense."

"You were ahead of him, I'm assuming?" I glanced in the direction Matt had gone.

Paolo sipped the wine and closed his eyes for half a second, nodding. Then he laughed a little, recalling. "Yeah, and on the one before, actually. Matt's kind of . . ." He searched for a word. "A *douchebag*. That's right, isn't it?"

The phrase sounded like a dissonant note—the beauty of Paolo's accent somehow carried the power to also make a word sound especially ugly. When my expression turned inquisitive, he shrugged.

He filled a separate glass and placed it in my hand.

I set it on the countertop. "What are you doing?" I asked.

"What's the matter?"

"Since when are you a wine connoisseur?" I asked.

"You should try this one," he suggested.

Then, a murmur. I heard someone nearby say, "He's about to talk." The room quickly hushed.

Jay Silver had the forward-facing look of a man who seemed destined to arrive at his prime in midlife, wearing round glasses and a cardigan the color of the Syrah swirling in Paolo's glass. His eyes looked warm and gracious as he clasped his hands in front of him like a priest before a homily—perfectly at ease as the center of attention.

He bowed his head slightly before he began. "I want to take a minute to say thank you to everyone for coming here tonight. It's not often we take time from our busy schedules to socialize with each other. I know I'm probably mostly to blame for that."

A gentle wave of laughter rolled through the room like the hush of a receding tide. Silver looked at his shoes, grimacing with feigned apology.

"But stepping away from our benches and getting together is important from time to time. It reminds us of our shared direction and of the larger purpose of our hard work. Together, we're humanitarians here, are we not?"

With his head cocked, he seemed to read confusion in the eyes of the students in front of him.

"Is that putting it too strongly? I hope not. Bubonic plague took two *million* people. In 1918, influenza took fifty million in a single year. That's more than World War I. Smallpox? Five *hundred* million people. It keeps happening. We know this. In fact, it's speeding up. Now, H1-N24. The CDC has counted *twenty-four* outbreaks in the last thirty-four years. We've known about the virus since 1976, but modern air travel could easily take it global in days," he said.

I knew the statistics; I'd heard Paolo say the same figures almost verbatim. But this time made me picture my father detecting his first symptoms. I pictured a map with circles of infection spreading around all the major cities, my stomach hardening with fear. I wanted to run out of the room but realized Paolo was holding my hand. I squeezed his palm, anchoring myself with the sensation of his skin touching mine.

The holiday party still hushed, Jay Silver paused. "I call our work humanitarian because we're working for humankind to outlast us." Silver's voice was catching with emotion. Maybe he'd prepared part of what he was saying, but his eyes glimmered with the promise of improvisation. Around him, the room was still. I realized I was chewing the nail of my pinkie finger. I picked up the wine glass Paolo had filled for me a minute earlier and took a long sip.

"I want to tell you all a quick story about my first experience with H1-N24," Silver continued. "I'm used to talking about the economics of developing a vaccine, but this is a story about the people most vulnerable to an outbreak. I've never told it before. It's about the year I worked in an East African village during my residency. It was a very rural place, and the people there lived simply. If you've never been to Africa, go. See what's there. It's magnificent in many ways.

"I was just starting out, and had a lot to learn about medicine. The first month, I wore a necktie every day to clinic because I thought looking professional was important. Most of my med school classmates had taken more conventional residencies here in the States, and when I imagined the clinics where they were working, I wondered what I'd gotten myself into. If my being in Africa was a mistake. But on my first day, a woman knocked at my door at the clinic and asked if I could help her child."

Silver pinched his fingers together.

"And for just a second, I felt the sting of irritation, nipping at me, biting like an insect. Part of me wanted to go home, to leave even before I got started. But there was anguish in her eyes. I could feel her desperation, and I thankfully snapped myself out of my little moment of self-importance. I had her daughter brought in. They laid her on an exam table, and I began to search for a pulse with my fingertips. I searched her arms, her chest. I expected her to be burning up with fever, but her skin was cold. And after a while, I realized I couldn't find her pulse because she was already gone. I had to explain this to her mother. It was more horrible than you can imagine. I decided then that I would do *everything* in my power to fight the scourge of infectious disease in this world. I took off my necktie. I never put it back on."

Silver quickly wiped at his eye.

"And we should celebrate. Not to congratulate ourselves, but to energize one another. Because we're close. We've gotten very lucky in our work, truthfully. But, tonight, we're closer than ever before to having a vaccine. Because of what *we* do."

Silver swept his hand in a circle as if stirring a cauldron, and a wave of applause washed through the room. In the context of H1-N24, the enthusiasm made me shudder and I felt my feet shuffle slightly backward. I recognized the eagerness in Silver's voice—it reminded me of the way my father had spoken about meaning in his work before he left on his last medical mission trip.

Later, Mom and I had learned that there was a minor outbreak of "flu" in the area where he was working, although details never became clear. He complained of having a fever about a week after he arrived and stopped working, isolating himself, perhaps understanding the possibility of what was happening. Forty-eight hours from when his symptoms first began, he fell into a coma from which he never awoke.

At the age of ten, of course, I didn't know what Liberia even was, or why there was a civil war there, but Mom explained to me what refugees were and how my father had gone to help. He was to help provide basic health care there along with mass vaccinations. She told me years later that he'd planned to speak on the attacks against hospitals and feeding stations when he returned.

Of course, being my father, it would only make sense that he would volunteer for the most dangerous mission trip. I wished I'd been old enough to have the words to ask him why he went. He had a sadness about him—hopeful, but with some resignation—at least that's what I remembered. Years later, I'd wonder if he ever struggled with depression, like I did.

After Silver spoke, soft jazz returned, then the hum of conversation. I felt like I was on the set of a movie. Paolo placed his hand on my arm, and I realized it felt uncomfortable.

"What?" he asked.

"Nothing," I said. Not wanting to get into where my mind had truly been, I changed the subject as deftly as I could. "What's up with Matt? And Sandy? Is she like your work spouse or something?"

He leaned his head back like I'd said something funny. "I've never heard of a work spouse. But, no, she's a friend. Come on, I was trying to introduce you. Matt . . . I don't know what to say about that guy. I'm sorry if he made you uncomfortable." I didn't hesitate as Paolo refilled my wine glass.

Just as I began sipping, Jay Silver appeared. Resting his hand on Paolo's shoulder, he gave it an avuncular squeeze. "Who's uncomfortable? No one's allowed to be uncomfortable at a holiday party." He grinned, mock-offended.

Paolo sighed, his expression somehow both embarrassed and relieved. He raised his glass. "Dr. Silver. Let me introduce you to my girlfriend. This is Emily."

The amusement in Silver's expression softened into sincerity. His head cocked slightly. "I'm glad you're here," he said. "I know your name very well, of course. I was glad to see you at the fund-raiser."

My thoughts spun back to that night—pulling Allie away from the University Club before the ceremony had ended; later, the colored light from the bar reflecting in Paolo's eyes as he stood to greet us, the spell he seemed to cast.

Paolo squeezed my hand as I leaned against him.

"So, you're the one who drags my best researcher out of the lab at a decent hour?"

"I'm that one," I said like a smart-ass, which didn't seem to faze him.

"Well, then I owe you a gracious thank you." He had a very slight accent that I couldn't place. "When Paolo first started in the lab, some of his lab mates thought he must not have a place to live. He was there when they arrived in the morning and stayed on after they left. One night in the first month, I put my hand on his shoulder"— Dr. Silver squeezed Paolo's shoulder again—"and he didn't seem to feel it. I had to say his name before he turned around. Now that's focus."

"It's true," Paolo admitted.

"Do you remember what we did then?"

Paolo laughed shyly, evidently having endured the story many times. "Dr. Silver took me out to breakfast."

"It was five o'clock in the morning," Silver explained. "I thought I was getting an early start, but he'd been there all night. I took him down to a diner where the nurses all go when they get off work. Then I told him to order whatever he liked, and he asked for three plates of pancakes." Silver leaned toward me as if to not further embarrass his mentee and revealed, "Then, he ate them *all*."

I thought back to the times Paolo had made dinner vanish

inside his slender frame. There was something American about his ravenousness—or maybe his desire to assimilate. To be successful.

"That doesn't surprise me," I said.

"I want this young man to stay healthy and have some balance in his life. I don't know how much he talks about what he's doing for us, but he's incredible. Brilliant. I'm sure you're very proud."

I wasn't sure what to say. Had I been proud enough? Actively proud?

Silver smiled at me. "I know your father lived here. Do you have other family in Nashville?" he asked.

"Emily's family's been in Nashville for a long time," Paolo interjected. "They have a farmhouse on a lake, south of here."

He slipped his arm around my waist. I felt like elbowing him in the ribs.

Dr. Silver smiled inquisitively. "A farmhouse, on a lake?"

"Oh, no, it's neither," I said. "Just a little cabin, and less than ten acres. Down the dirt road after the Concord exit."

"Emily did both her degrees at Vanderbilt," Paolo added, completely out of nowhere.

Something about the pride in his voice, his overeagerness to impress, made me want to slip away from his embrace.

"Challenging programs," Silver said with raised eyebrows. "He tells me you're a psychologist."

"I am," I said, my shoulders loosening slightly. "That's true."

"How fascinating. You know, I think psychology is really the most important of the sciences. I say that all the time. Did it always appeal to you? You have to tell me how you got started studying it."

There was no way I was telling him how exactly I'd gotten "started" in psychology.

"I picked it in college," I said. "Seemed like a natural fit."

"For a brilliant mind, I'm sure."

I might have actually blushed. I was starting to understand the magnetism Paolo had responded to in Dr. Silver. I noticed no one called Dr. Silver anything but *Dr. Silver*, which seemed laughable, but at least he wasn't starting a fight with my boyfriend, or hitting on him.

Silver looked at me deeply, there seeming to be no end to his curiosity. "And are you researching at all, or in practice?"

"I work for Human Services. Mainly with kids."

"Tremendous," he offered, seeming to mean it. "The difference you must make in the lives of those kids is unimaginable."

"Well, yeah, thanks. I like what I do. And I hear you're off to Poland?"

It's always easier to talk about someone else. Psychologists do it to hide in plain sight.

"Poland was last month. This week is California. Not quite as exotic." He lowered his chin, and I had the feeling that I was talking to Jay Gatsby—like he might find in his pocket a picture from his days at Oxford to show me.

"Although Paolo likes it out there. There's an annual conference we all get to. You have to come."

This new side of Paolo's life was so entirely different. It made him more full, more real.

In that way, I liked being there.

I caught Sandy glancing over from the too-loud conversation she was having, once looking as though she might drift over, then turning away.

"Well, come on in. Anytime," Dr. Silver said. "We'd love to have you. It'll give you a chance to meet the rest of the team."

Back at the kitchen counter, Matt looked on. His figure was silhouetted by the light behind him. He tucked his hair behind his ear again, sipped from his slightly illuminated green beer bottle.

Later, I cornered Paolo, digging about him trying so hard to impress Dr. Silver. "He clearly adores you already," I said.

Paolo frowned, as though my not understanding the value of good impressions saddened him.

"I'm serious." I poked him. "You don't have to try so hard."

His hands rubbed up and down my shoulders. I felt my muscles relax.

"I'm sorry, baby," he said. "Really."

The rest of the party was so dreamlike that later I'd wonder if it had really happened, if I could have been that person, doing those things. I wasn't sure.

I remembered the feelings.

I remembered watching Sandy's flowy hair out of the corner of my eye, hearing her dangerous laughter, sensing her theatrics—working so hard at being polite. She wanted something.

Matt wanted something, too. Buried in his hoodie, surrounded by expensive things, holding a half-empty beer bottle. His hair like brushed coal ash in the mercury kitchen light.

Once, when Paolo laughed, I noticed Matt's eyes flick toward him and then fall away. Just in that instant, I wondered what he might be thinking.

THIRTEEN

Keeping it together in my office was easier with Sandy there. Alone, my mind had free rein. The echo of her footsteps down the stairwell had hardly faded before I was hunched over my laptop, pulling up search possibilities. Surely she knew I would look. How couldn't I?

Who was Matt? Had she been cagey about him? I couldn't tell.

I needed a last name.

She was barely down the sidewalk, but I found her number on the paperwork and called. Straight to voicemail. I called again—voicemail. I remembered the nervousness in her voice as she talked about maintaining some discretion and decided against leaving a message.

She wants you to look, I thought. Maybe she planted this like a seed. *You could be gone now, too.*

I forced a deep breath. My stomach could remember the nausea of the morning he went missing—the heat and lazy rocking of the boat and the crazy, taunting horizon. It was the sedative. It had to be. I'd taken just a little, from his bottle, maybe, or from his lips. He'd—I stopped for half a second—he'd fallen overboard, I thought.

You could be gone now, too.

I knew exactly what I was going to do, however long it took to find out more. That it didn't completely make sense didn't matter. My hands shook over the cool keys. I tensed and relaxed the thumb that had broken, stretched my mending foot forward.

Stress brings mania, stress and mania. *Relax.*

Relax was not an option.

She knew you'd do this. Paolo must've told her how you are. Maybe they were closer than . . . No. They weren't.

On my laptop, I pulled up the Vanderbilt Medical Center site. It let me search by first name if I included a last initial—beginning, obviously, with Matthew A. This took a minute. The city's third-largest employer evidently employed a fair number of Matthews. With a first name and last initial, I found a list of departments, some of which had their own pages. I happened to know there was no website for their particular lab because I'd tried looking it up in a frenetic fit of curiosity the week I met Paolo.

Nothing from the Matthew As.

Matthew B. Two computer guys. Nothing.

I struck gold on Matthew C.

Matthew D. Cianciolo. That even sounded right. My trembling fingers misspelled it twice, but then up it came: Microbiology. Post-doc, fourth year. Four years, and so very eager to publish. Four years of accumulating desperation. A *shark tank*, Paolo'd called it.

Back to the main page, another search, and up came his photo—a slightly younger version of the man I'd met. Shorter hair, combed neatly. He was tan. He'd probably had his photo taken during some orientation, I figured, back, when—four years earlier?

I studied his dark eyes.

Poison, she'd said. *Poison.*

I tried Sandy's phone twice more. No answer. Again, I left no message. Clearly, she didn't want to talk that way—my phone to hers.

I texted her: CAN YOU CALL ME? I was messing it up, I knew, breaking her trust. I couldn't stop myself. I told myself it wasn't like that; that she had come to me. Anyone would understand.

I typed MATT CIANCIOLO into the search engines—Google, Yahoo, Bing. The entries where he was named seemed highlighted on the screen by my intuition. Of what there was, most were closed loops linking right back to his job. Then the lists dribbled into randomness, other people with the same first or last name. There was a Matt Cianciolo who played minor-league baseball in Arizona

from 1997 to 1999. And a Tom Cianciolo with multiple rental prop-
erties. I copied what I found to a desktop file.

On to Twitter, Instagram, and Facebook. Nothing on the first
two that was even close. I supposed he could be hiding, working
with a ghost profile. I knew kids who did that to avoid monitoring
or to get around the websites' age restrictions.

He was on Facebook. My heart skipped when I found his picture. Mouth dry, I ground my teeth. The photo was a few years old,
probably taken about the same time as the one from the medical
center. Sunglasses covered his eyes, but it was definitely him—same
hair, same chin. Same expression that he'd had the night I met him—
angry, defiant. I recognized his look from kids I'd worked with. It
said everything was unfair, rigged against them. He had put up little
else, or he had locked it so that you'd have to be a friend to see it.
His "friends" list wasn't viewable; just the basics. As if he wanted a
page just to keep up appearances. I copied his page to a folder and
moved on.

Outside, wind rattled the old windows. I heard Marty's footsteps down the hall occasionally. Otherwise, the only sound was the
whisper of heat coming up through the creaky vents, fighting the
season's first real cool weather. Occasionally, a metal-on-metal clink
came from inside the walls like a wrench knocking a pipe. Old
building, I thought.

On to the pay sites that check backgrounds, which I knew
existed, yet they were new to me. I glanced at the screen to check
the time, then at my purse where my medication was. I knew it was
time to take a Lamictal, but there was no way to pause. Some people
board trains. I *was* a train. I was a boulder that wouldn't rest until it
reached the bottom of a hill. I rubbed my eyes, found a credit card,
and popped my wrist to soften the ache.

I paid to use three of the sites. The information pretty much
overlapped between them but gave me what I needed. Middle name
(Daniel), last three addresses (which included two grad-school
apartments in College Park, Pennsylvania), and a list of relatives that

I knew I would Google, cross-check, social media–check, and probably background-check later.

I pulled up a map and found his current address. I knew the street, less than three miles from where I sat. The soccer team had run down it in a pack on summer mornings when I was in college. Mostly apartments and a few rented homes.

I pulled up a map and found the address; I pulled up a satellite map to be sure.

I knew right where I was going.

———

I backed my Ford Ranger into the lot opposite Matt's apartment and cut the engine. It was still before five—no way he was home yet from the lab. Paolo easily worked until six thirty on a light day, seven thirty when it counted. But nine, nine thirty was never out of the question. I had plenty of time to explore.

Don't.

There was no way not to look.

Wait.

My cane knocked against the metal-framed concrete steps up to the second floor until I found his door. No mat, no decorations. Just basic black paint, coated again and again. I glanced down into the courtyard in the back, at the path to the propped-open door of a laundry room. This was where he lived. *Paolo's killer.* From where I stood on the landing, I could see across the street to the Ford's faded hood. I touched the row of silver mailboxes until I found Matt's, then I went back down to wait.

And wait I did. Six, seven, eight. I was starving. I finally took my medicine, three hours late, which I knew would destroy the timing of going to sleep, assuming that, under the circumstances, sleep would be possible at all. Over the years I'd reached a delicate neurochemical balance—like an alliance within myself—but timing and dosage were essential. When I altered the schedule of my meds, it could take days to readjust. I sighed, decided to cut myself some slack.

Nine o'clock came. Car lights passed. I cracked the truck window, and a breeze whistled in. I pulled up my collar and slumped in the seat, watching the dark window.

This is crazy.

The whole thing only halfway made sense, anyway, I knew. Sitting there at all—and the two Internet hours that preceded it— had gone way past being analytical. I knew this. I fell into the place where thoughts and dreams and imagining are the same thing. I found flashes of the last year, then jolted back awake, my fingers bent into angles, highlighter-orange fire rising from the hood of my car. The wreck. The people I could have killed. My head slammed back against the seat.

I turned the key to check the time on the dash. Ten twenty in blue digital lines. Still no light in Matt's window. I knew the waiting could go on all night and lead to nothing.

I had an appointment scheduled at 8:00 AM with a new kid, and I would be there—rested, ready to do my best work. I would be there. There was no doubt.

I put my lips to the Breathalyzer, blew, and started the truck.

———

I went somewhere else. I think I was dreaming. My mind filled with pictures from the summer before, when Paolo and I stood on the porch of my family's cabin at the far edge of the neighboring county. We'd known each other a month then.

The cabin, my uncles called it. It was a shack, really. But I loved it. A one-bedroom place with creaky floors and a rickety porch on both the front and back, loose steps, and a pond in the front. My family had owned the cabin and surrounding land for I-didn't-know-how-long. I had no idea. Nor did I understand—since we had no money—why no one ever talked about selling it. It was a good bit of property—maybe twenty acres. I think owning it felt pleasantly weighty to Mom and my uncles, like the comfortable feel of expensive silverware in a palm. Owning land said to our family that we were somebody.

Something about that place had always stopped time—the high, exposed wooden beams on which I'd tried to land paper airplanes as a kid, the wood paneling. A dirt driveway extended a quarter mile from the highway up to the gate, and a white fence traced the road like a slender brushstroke.

One late summer night at the cabin, I'd run out to pick up dinner for Paolo and myself. Being together was hypnosis against my will, like learning I'd been slipped the best drug imaginable. Fear and fury constantly scratched at my insides, even as I bounced on my toes, a lunatic. It was different than being manic—love was the best kind of out of control.

"I'm back," I called, grocery bag hung over my arm. "What have you been up to?"

He hid his grin in a way that made it contagious. Then I saw what he was looking at.

"Oh my God, no," I said, laughing. "That yearbook! I used to have terrible hair."

I tried to take it from him and he switched it from one hand to the other, then back again, until I fell against him, laughing. He laughed too, arms around me, so full of warmth.

Later, I told him that the lights on the highway reminded me of the scale of everything, about watching them as a girl. I pointed when a pair appeared on the horizon, moving steadily. A ship at sea.

"They're like fireflies from here," I said.

He put his arm around me.

Thunder called from the distance.

"It's about to rain," he said.

I'd had the same thought a second before; I'd hoped the rain would tap and whisper against the windows and roof. When the first drops fell, they were reluctant—dotting the dusty porch steps— as if they might be all that came, or as if the clouds knew not to show too much too fast. A minute later, they were quarter-sized, dampening the dirt.

Then came a flash. I saw and heard it at the same time, like the tail of a giant wasp stinging the earth. We stood, as if commanded, the swing knocking against the backs of our tanned legs. I gripped his hand. Near the road, fire rose immediately from an elm. The flames reached toward the clouds, their desperate smoke like a prayer to be retaken by the sky.

I watched, transfixed. *This is happening.*

The screen door slammed behind Paolo as he ran inside. He was yelling over his shoulder. "It's been too dry. It'll all burn if we leave it." He was right. The grass was long and the leaves were the color of wheat.

He cursed his phone, which had no signal, dropped it, and found mine.

"You literally have to lean against the windows," I told him, some small part of me finding the whole thing darkly funny. Mom talked sometimes about getting a landline. Never happened.

Eventually, the signal hit his phone and his voice was loud into it. "Lightning hit a tree and there's a fire spreading fast. Baby"—he hollered at me—"Baby, what's the address out here?"

I didn't even know. "Highway 96, south from the Concord exit, about three miles down."

Embers floated above the pond, then disappeared into its dark mirror. I rubbed my sweaty hands together as another tree caught, bursting into flames like it had been waiting to. Fire the color of sunset silhouetted the low, determined edge of the storm as the smell of charred pine reached us. Along the road, the rows of headlights stopped. A thousand motes filled their beams—the embers raining sideways, making it seem like everything was under water.

"I wait until the fifth date to let things get exciting," I said.

Ash landed on the rail. He brushed his hand over it, blowing urgently. Between the two of us and the trees, the wind carried hundreds more.

His accent sharpened. "They'll be here any minute."

I looked over the living room. Everything was wood; it would be gone in minutes if the fire touched it.

Over the hill that rolled west toward town came the first hints of a siren.

———

Wednesday morning, Halloween. Another Lamictal, water.

Breathe.

How do you act normal, as if nothing out of the ordinary is happening? I'm terrible at it. I had a thousand questions. I needed to meet with Sandy again, if only to cure the unreality that had set in.

I tried calling her the following day but hung up when it went to voicemail, thinking back to the suspicion in her eyes and her skittish, birdlike way. As much as I needed confirmation, a bigger part of me was afraid of scaring her off.

My thoughts ran rampant—a mind full of echoes, I caught myself staring at nothing.

Making a sandwich, I cut halfway through my index finger while slicing a tomato. I didn't realize what I'd done until I felt a warm drop of blood on the top of my bare foot. The tomato-blood mixture was a Rorschach print over the white cutting board. I ran the faucet cold over my hand until the bleeding slowed.

Shadows shifted across the old hardwood floors all that afternoon from bare branches in the wind. Mom's windows were gentle waves of glass. Even under the circumstances, I wasn't used to her being away. Her house felt enormous compared to my apartment, and it would have seemed empty if it hadn't been for Andy, who slept in bed beside me at night and tolerated the glacial pace of our morning walks. I couldn't help but wonder who was living in my apartment by then, if anyone. Who slept in my old bedroom and prepared food in my old kitchen? Someone. A presence like a silhouette had taken over that part of my life. I ran my fingers through Andy's soft black coat, the Band-Aid around my index finger collecting fragments of his fur. His hair, I thought, smiling, was longer than mine.

I was grateful for Halloween—it gave me something to focus

on, something to do. As it turned out, like it has again and again, I was no good at waiting.

Daylight savings didn't end until the following week, but it was already nearly dark by five thirty. Down the street in both directions was a flowing network of costumes and iPhone screens. I filled a wooden salad bowl with bite-sized Hershey bars and leashed Andy beside me on the porch. It happened to be a warmer evening, and my hooded sweatshirt brushed heavily against the sides of my neck. Mom's neighborhood had sidewalks on both sides of the street and was understandably popular for trick-or-treating. In her neighbor's yard, plastic tombstones poked up from the evergreen lawn. A skeleton clawed its way out of the ground.

My phone chirped; Allie was calling back. "You left a message the other night, after we talked," she reminded me, sounding reluctant.

I was rethinking everything. Telling her too much seemed like a mistake. I needed to be sure. Credibility, in this case, was not my strongest asset.

"It's just going to be easier to explain everything on Saturday. It's kind of a crazy story. I want to make sure it's right before I get you involved."

In the background of her call, I could hear the murmur of voices, a telephone ringing, someone yelling, displeased. "Are you at work?" I asked, incredulous, but with a tug of professional envy. "Are you really this productive of a human being?"

She laughed, or sort of laughed. "I'm leaving now, really. Halloween party with the Mr."

Married life, I thought.

"Are you going out?" Her voice was encouraging.

I rolled my boot back and forth on the concrete porch. When I heard the phrase *going out*, I could still feel the faint traces of excitement that remained from when I'd been wild. I could almost taste the sweet sting of vodka and feel the sticky, dark smoke in my throat that had signified being out of control, burning bright. Most people, I knew, could celebrate without climbing rooftops or taking boys whose names they didn't want to know into the shadows of backyard elms. They hated, and then loved, to see someone else lose control. They watched from a distance. That was what *going out* had meant before.

People want to see what will happen when they sense anything could.

"Nah," I said. "Staying put tonight."

When I ended the call, I spun the phone around in my fingers. What I really wanted was to pace the kitchen and bite my cuticles, alone with my thoughts. I petted Andy's back and extended the salad bowl filled with candy as the first group ascended Mom's stairs. Two vampires and an indecipherable.

Up and down the street, shadows followed by larger shadows bent toward rectangles of steady light. They moved in packs. Most wore costumes and masks. Playing pretend, not who they really were. Occasionally, groups would halt, then seemed to be released by the eruption of a flash. Having not lived in the neighborhood for years, I knew none of the kids, of course. Some of the parents wore puzzled expressions when they approached the porch—the disrupted expectation of seeing my mom. The role of mom, I thought, will be played tonight by her twitching, preoccupied daughter. In other faces, I saw a sort of muted politeness, even a wariness. Those were the parents who'd driven in.

Later, I called Mom for some company and could practically hear Destin in the background—the plink of wine glasses and silverware above the lazy, rolling tide. Seventy-five degrees, she told me.

"Why don't you bring Andy down?" she asked, as if I could. Retirement had wiped the conventions of a workweek from her mind.

It took everything not to spill the meeting with Sandy to her. I knew opening up, telling her would only make her worry, maybe enough to cause her to drive back. So, lying by omission, I told her I had to keep focused on building my practice and that Marty had asked about her, the guilt of doing so feeling like a dull pain in the

back of my throat. I was listening to her laugh when I saw a familiar face approach, tugging a smaller, also familiar face like a shadow
beside him.

This, I could hardly believe.

Had he come looking for me?

"I'll call you back," I told Mom.

FOURTEEN

Cal moved with the same half-beat-slow caution of the other parents who had sought out my neighborhood's long sidewalks. One night a year. But Nashville wasn't exactly a metropolis. Some part of me was surprised I hadn't run into him before now.

The timing—my God.

A few of Paolo's friends had called me after he'd vanished, but not Cal, with whom he'd been closest. Without realizing it, I'd decided I'd never see him again.

He looked the same: his cropped brown hair combed neatly to the side and his green, sun-strained eyes striking against his tea-colored skin. I could smell the Irish Spring soap as he stepped onto the porch.

He stopped when he recognized me, and his face tightened. His hand fell onto his daughter's shoulder.

Olivia pulled free and planted herself beside me, wondering aloud what I'd done to my hair. "You cut your hair!" she observed.

"Yeah, I did," I said as she began reaching into the bowl. I stopped myself from informing her that she had gotten taller and instead touched the joyful tangle of her curls. The spray of freckles across her nose had darkened, with green eyes that matched her father's.

"Olivia . . ." Cal began a vague sort of warning. "Just one."

He'd never been jolly, but his standoffishness now seemed more pronounced. It made me want to tell her to never mind, to take as much as she liked. Or dump the bowl into her flannel pumpkin bag until it overflowed. I smiled up at him and lavished her bag with chocolate.

"I didn't realize you lived here," Cal noted briskly. It was all he seemed prepared to say on the subject.

"It's my mom's house. I'm just staying here for a while. You're nearby?"

He shook his head.

Olivia interjected. "Dad's house is *waaaaay* out. Mom stayed in town when they split up, but Dad likes *peace and quiet*." She made finger quotations for this phrase. "So we have to come into town to trick-or-treat."

"Oh."

Cal looked over his shoulder toward the street. "Olivia."

Andy stood and circled her, nudging her hands as she squealed with joy.

"That's Andy," I informed her. "I think he likes you."

"I like *him*! Hey, do you still like to go watch softball?"

"No, that was just for last year."

"Why just *last* year?"

I looked at Cal, who seemed resigned to hold his breath until our encounter ended. He looked at my cane, my boot, saying nothing.

My thoughts flashed to watching Olivia climb on the warm metal bleachers the summer before, when I'd explained to her that the "birds" circling the field lights were actually bats. "Like Stellaluna," I'd told her after she'd made a face. The next time I saw her, I'd brought the famous book from my office for her to look through. We'd bonded over how playing softball was less boring than watching it.

After attending my fifth game, I'd put my hand on Paolo's arm on the drive home and asked what he thought about having kids. He'd shaken his head, picked at the baseball clay under his fingernails. His smile had been sly. "Of course. Don't you think we should get married first?"

"There's the old charm," I'd teased. He had taken the doors off his Jeep for the summer, and when he stepped on the gas, it was like being inside a tornado. I'd kissed his neck as he shifted gears.

It seemed like a different life.

"I had a friend who played on your dad's team," I explained to Olivia.

She smiled, satisfied. Her eyes illuminated with an idea. "*May* I have a drink?"

"No, baby," Cal mumbled.

"Of course," I said at the same time.

When I turned, she was crouched beside the door as Andy barked, nose pressed against the glass pane.

But Cal took another step toward the sidewalk, avoiding looking at me directly. "We really should keep moving." He had the permissive tone of a parent rapidly losing ground.

"Dad, I'm *thirsty*. She said I could have a drink."

"Cal, I'm happy to bring something out."

He was basically pinned—there was no way to deny his daughter a glass of water, and he knew it. Cal shook his head, and Olivia pushed into the living room, laughing as Andy began licking her hands. I gently took Andy's collar and Olivia skipped past me into the kitchen.

"She's had some candy," Cal explained.

"Two Butterfingers, one Kit Kat, one Hershey's Kiss," she sang, "and one bag of Sour Patch Kids."

"Kit Kat is my favorite," I confessed.

"I'm in dance now. I can pirouette!" Olivia exclaimed. "Watch."

I poured water from Mom's glass pitcher as she twirled. She spun once, twice, then stopped to clear her dizziness before spinning a third time.

"Excellent. How long have you been taking lessons?"

She looked at Cal, whose arms were folded over his chest. "A few months."

"I usually live with Mom, too, but she's been on the road, so I stayed with Dad *aaaaall* month."

I placed the glass in her hands, then looked at Cal. "Can I get you anything?"

"No, I'm good."

Olivia returned to Andy. There was no separating them. Cal's silence was so awkward I couldn't take it, needed him to speak more than three words to me. "Playing softball this fall?" I asked.

"Just ended." He refolded his arms, regaining his Marine Corps posture, and scanned Mom's living room as if searching for an object worthy of investing his interest for the next few minutes.

I stepped in front of his face. "How've you *been*, Cal? I didn't get to see you after everything happened."

"I need to go to the bathroom!" Olivia said, standing. She had been kneeling down, petting Andy, letting him lick her some more.

I directed her down the hall, and when I returned to him, Cal's lips were pulled tight, as though he was summoning patience from some deep inner well. He wasn't going to talk.

I was long past being able to wait something like this out. "So . . . what's your . . . problem?" I lowered my voice so that Olivia couldn't hear. "You're acting like a dickhead."

His head tilted slightly, as if mechanized by stoicism.

"Yes," I said, "a dick . . . head. You're acting like a dickhead. I never did anything to you, Cal."

"I never said you did." His eyes were gentle. They flicked back toward the door. Calmness can be infuriating.

I kept talking in a kind of stage whisper, part of me horrified at the sense of my own guilt I was revealing—fears I'd never put into words. "You think I'm the bad guy? That I'm responsible for what happened? Take a number. But I didn't kill your best friend."

He shook his head.

The encounters with Detective Mason and Sandy had left me raw. It was all bleeding out of me. I couldn't stop.

"Look, you didn't like me from the first time you saw me. But really, I was never anything but good to Paolo. And you."

"You really want to have this conversation?"

"Yep. I do."

He raised his eyebrows.

I wasn't going anywhere. Olivia was well out of earshot. "Ab-so-lutely," I said.

Cal shrugged. "Okay. I'm sorry to say it, but I think you're bad news, Emily. And I actually did think that the first night he met you. Just my opinion." He looked relieved to have finally said it out loud.

"What makes me bad news, *Cal*? In your opinion."

"You're a nut."

The word bounced off of me. *A nut* was the best he had? I shot right back. "Well, as long as we're getting clear on things, I think you were just jealous because I stole your friend away. He spent more time with me than you."

He made a face like this was preposterous. "Please," he groaned.

"No, I think that was exactly the problem. Right during your divorce, I stole your best friend away, and you started sulking."

Cal nodded as if he was actually considering the notion, then he countered by saying, "It wasn't the timing. It was that during that time, you got him addicted to the pills that killed him."

This I had not expected. Down the hall behind me, I could hear the water running and Olivia singing, her voice muffled by the closed bathroom door.

I leaned in. "What did you say?"

"I'm not trying to start a fight with you in your house."

"It's not my house," I insisted, as if it mattered. "But too late."

"Thank you for letting Olivia use your bathroom and for giving her a glass of water."

"Um, no. No way."

"Never mind." He straightened. "It really doesn't matter, Emily."

"Fuck you it doesn't matter." We were going to have this out.

He raised his eyebrows again, drew in a deep breath, set his jaw. "You heard what I said. I don't need to say it again."

My hands moved to my hips. "I heard *something* you said that made no sense. Maybe you could explain." I took a step into his personal space. Cal was still as a tree trunk.

He took another breath, and for an instant, I glimpsed the extent of what he'd gone through, a wave of empathy for his loss washing over me. Being consumed by Paolo's disappearance put me at risk for being self-centered about my grief.

Cal continued, "You're saying that the night he . . . that the pills—or whatever—came from somewhere that wasn't you?"

I felt like screaming. I wanted to break my cane over my knee. I wanted to tell him about Sandy. "Yes, you're dead wrong. If he took anything, it damn sure wasn't mine."

His voice hardened again. "He made bad decisions after he met you. Period. I knew him for a *year* before. I met him right when he came to this country. Before everything changed."

It was taking everything I had not to cry. "Bad decisions? Like?"

"Everything about him changed. Drugs? Late nights? You tell me."

It sounded completely unfamiliar. *Drugs*? Did he mean the ADHD medication?

"I take one medication," I said. "Sometimes a second. But I don't do *drugs*." Yet I came off sounding defensive.

Cal's eyes narrowed like he was watching a highlight reel of fielding errors in his mind. "He was exhausted. All the time. He started showing up late to everything after you two met."

"Cal, he was always late, to *everything*. He worked sixty-five hours a week."

Cal shrugged, threw another dart. "He came to games drunk."

I frowned. I knew the *one* time he was talking about. Paolo and I had spent the afternoon on a blanket, surrounded by the emerging green buds of spring. It was his first time off in a week—and I'd opened a bottle of wine. "That was one time, Cal. And I wouldn't have called that drunk."

He gestured like he was letting go of something. "Either way."

"Either way, what?" I stepped forward again.

"In the two months before he died, he no-showed me I don't know how many times. That wasn't him. Something was up, so I called him on it. Know what he said? He said he was taking care of you."

It felt like he'd slapped me. Olivia emerged from the bathroom then and took another sip from her water glass. She looked at us quizzically, set the glass on the counter, and resumed playing with

Andy on the floor. Cal and I instinctively stepped into the living room.

I must have looked as baffled as I felt. "Um, what?" I began. "Taking care of me?"

He sighed. "I just don't believe that the smartest, most ambitious person I knew—a guy who grew up around water—would just randomly . . . without something chemical"—he paused, then expelled the word he'd been avoiding—"drown. It doesn't sound like the guy I knew. And I'm sorry. Really. I know you've been through a lot, and I actually really didn't want to ever say this. But, since you're asking, if I'd had to guess—and I did—about where those chemicals might have come from . . . it doesn't take a genius to think they might have come from his girlfriend, whose purse was like a *pharmacy*."

"That's shitty to say. And actually, stupid, too."

"That was how he described it."

I stopped. "He said my purse was a pharmacy? But even if . . . that had nothing to do with . . ."

"Nothing?"

I could have strangled him. Keeping my voice down was nearly impossible. "Look, I've fucked up. I've fucked up so many times in so many ways I stopped counting. I fucked up after he died—got in a car and drove drunk. But I'm not a pill-head. Paolo never took *anything* of mine—"

The sound of glass breaking came from the kitchen. Cal and I rushed in to find Olivia standing in a puddle.

Her eyes were round and afraid, her voice already shredded with the pressure of tears. "Andy jumped and I . . ."

Adults emerged from our petulance. Immediately, both of our voices changed.

"Honey, it's fine," I told her as she buried her face in her father's shirt.

With Olivia attached to his side, Cal motioned toward the pantry and I nodded. He went in and retrieved Mom's broom and dustpan. "If you take Andy out, I'll get this glass up."

I supposed that this was what the Marines had been like—everyone did their part. I took hold of Andy's collar and went back to the porch, where I checked his paws.

When I came back inside, Olivia was sitting at my kitchen table and Cal was laying a dish towel over the side of the sink.

"It's all taken care of." He had returned to professional mode. "You may want to go over it once more later, just to be safe."

"Will do." My voice was weirdly formal sounding as I sat beside Olivia. She'd laid her arms and head down on the table.

"I'm really sorry," she said.

"It's really, *really* okay. Just a glass," I assured her with a shrug. Then an idea came to me. I moved Cal aside as I found some string and a pair of scissors in a kitchen drawer. "Besides, I have some magic dust that puts things back together. I'll just sprinkle a little on it later if I get around to it."

Olivia was smiling in anticipation, watching my hands as I returned. "What do you mean?"

"Sit." I motioned toward a chair.

She sat. Andy looked on, tongue wagging.

Depression is so horribly self-absorbed. Working with kids is exactly the opposite. You just focus on them, completely. Olivia straightened, smiled. It had already worked.

I did what Marty had shown me and looped the string. I found the "dust" in my pocket, closed the scissors, showed her the cut, worked the magic. Then I put the string back together.

"How'd you *do* that?"

"I told you." It was my turn to sound calm. "Magic. Really nothing it doesn't work on."

She looked at her father, who rolled his eyes.

"Show me again!"

I did.

"We actually really should get on," Cal said, finally.

Olivia sprang to her feet, thanking me and petting Andy on the way through the door.

"I'll be right there," Cal called after her.

He looked at his shoes for so long that I almost spoke up. Finally, he said, "You're right."

I started an angry stammer, then stopped.

"What you said was right," he continued. "Your prescriptions are none of my business. I jumped to conclusions. And I apologize."

Now I was really surprised. "Wow, okay. Thank you."

"Emily, I shouldn't have—"

"Oh, shut up with all that." I said. "Don't be so weird and formal. I just don't get it. *Taking care of me*? That's what he said?"

Cal nodded, squinting at me.

"What?"

"Actually . . ." He searched for the words. "It makes even less sense now."

I couldn't have agreed more. I ached to tell him about Sandy, but how much of her story would be it responsible to share? "There's something . . . that might be happening . . ."

He turned. "Something?"

I handed him my phone. "Put your number in here. Now's obviously not a good time, but can I call you this week?"

He held my phone like it was an animal that might bite him.

"I'm not going to prank call you, Cal."

Seeming to consider this, he jabbed his index finger roughly against the screen and handed it back to me.

Watching him and Olivia start down the front steps, I couldn't help but want to fast-forward time to my meeting with Sandy. The desire to see her, to know what she'd learned, burned like hot coal in my stomach.

FIFTEEN

Eighteen months before the lake, I met Cal the same night I met Paolo, at a fund-raiser for medical research. I'd dragged Allie along as my date.

"Remind me why we're going to a *fund-raiser*?" she asked as I sped toward the frozen-in-time University Club, with its imposing curtains and sturdy silverware.

There was enough incredulity in Allie's voice that I smiled to not feel offended.

"It's for H1-N24 research. It's been almost twenty years since . . ."

The air between us changed as she understood. The mention of a deceased parent does that. Allie's eyes conveyed warmth, even pity, as her lips pressed together.

"It's not going to be *bad*," I said, knowing this only because I'd asked specifically about the content of the presentations before RSVPing yes. No way was I making either of us sit through a slideshow about the disease itself—the symptoms, or various forms of partially effective treatments. I knew plenty about H1-N24 already. First signs showing within three days of infection—mild fever, headache, muscle pains, followed by vomiting. Later, bleeding from the mouth, nose, and gums. Low blood pressure eventually causing organ failure and death.

I'd made the mistake of attending a presentation once where grainy images flashed of microbes on slides, followed by photos of patients with exhausted, horrified expressions. There's no academic curiosity when it comes to a loved one's suffering. Imagining my father, I'd run out of that conference room with a hand pressed over my mouth.

But this one was different. Easy. Just talk about the research itself and its funding needs.

The University Club was exactly as I'd remembered it from Athletic Department banquets. My job was to stand on stage during one of the presentations beside a dozen other people who'd lost family members to the disease. For this, my name tag was adorned with a star. The clink of glasses and flatware punctuated the rumble of conversation. Allie leaned forward as the speakers took the small stage, digging her elbows into the white tablecloth—obviously missing campus more than I did.

"You're okay?" she asked before I went. The earnestness of her friendship made me feel vaguely guilty.

"All I have to do is stand up straight. And for that, I've consumed the perfect amount of wine." My words blended slightly. I winked.

When it was time, I climbed the wobbly stairs with the rest of the group and smiled into the obscuring light. The speaker, a researcher named Jay Silver, began an impassioned appeal.

My eyes brimmed with hot tears.

Don't think, I said to myself. *Go somewhere else.*

Then applause began. I was heading to the restroom when a voice behind me spoke. "Your father has been an inspiration," it said.

"Thanks," I said, irritated. I hadn't needed to know that. What I would have liked was the eighteen years with my father I'd missed.

"I mean it." He extended his hand. "I'm Paolo." His eyes seemed warm beneath the dark tangle of hair.

The hallway was dim, my vision still blurred by the confounding stage lights. "Emily," I said, accepting the handshake. I was caught off guard but for some reason had stopped walking toward the restroom.

"You're leaving?" He looked vaguely concerned.

I nodded. "In a minute. My part is over. Plus, I brought a friend who I probably owe a drink at this point."

"I know it's a little offhanded," he began, "But I'm meeting a friend after this too. Why don't you join us? I'd love to buy Sydney Firestone's daughter a drink."

As long as you stop mentioning my last name like that, I thought, feigning indifference.

Later, I pulled Allie out a back door before the dessert was even served.

"You want to go *where*?" she asked, stumbling after me. "Shouldn't we stay for the end?"

She was right, of course, we should have stayed. So, why the rush? Maybe reminders of my father made me run. Maybe the weirdest pickup line I'd ever heard intrigued me. Probably both.

"Would you have any fun at all if it wasn't for me?"

"Emily."

"It'll be an adventure," I assured Allie, who'd folded her arms but couldn't fully stifle her grin.

———

Minutes later, we were in midtown at the Red Door Saloon.

Allie nudged me as Paolo stood. Behind him, his friend Cal—bearded and serious-eyed, the sort of outdoor-type guy I never seemed to relate to—shook his head. Suddenly, I was back in middle school.

The bartender placed a cold glass in my hand and condensation ran icily down my forearm. Though I started to refuse him, Paolo rushed to buy it—and one for Allie, too, whom he hadn't even met.

The drink was strong, perfect. I pointed at Cal. "Your friend looks like he's having an awesome time."

"He'll be fine for a minute. I'm talking to a beautiful girl right now."

Oh my God, I thought, I know better.

And yet, that was the start of it.

————

Later, Allie cornered me at the far end of the patio while Paolo pretended not to watch us. In college, the soccer girls used to tease Allie about being a mother hen, but she'd always had a way of being sweet and direct at the same time. Her black hair caught the red and pink bar lights. She rubbed my shoulder.

"Leaving with those guys is a bad idea," she informed me. I could barely hear her above the roil of conversations and the thumping bass line through the speakers. I could feel the reverb in my chest.

I respected that Allie was trying to protect me, but that didn't mean I was going to listen to her.

"Emily, remember the time you went hiking by yourself? With only, like, a tarp and some bear spray?"

I did remember that. I'd come back covered in scabs. Our assistant coach had asked if I'd been homeless. "Yeah. I don't know what I was thinking there."

"Or the time the team flew to New York for the Memorial Day tournament and you went off in a cab with people you just met on the plane? Strangers, basically?"

I had to smile—albeit involuntarily—about that one.

"It's funny now because nothing happened," she said.

"We won that tournament," I reminded her.

She shook her head. "Me and two other girls spent the first day searching all over the city for you."

She was right. I could be a major-league pain in the ass, especially back then. Meds, therapy, career, and support all kept me coloring inside the lines.

But what I saw in her eyes was the heartbreaker—that my selfishness and compulsiveness could be so hard on people around me. It didn't feel like selfishness to me; that's what no one seemed to understand. It just felt like doing what I needed to do. The part of a person that knows the difference between what they want and what should happen was, in me, broken. *Disregulated* was how my first therapist had put it.

I could be very hard to care about.

Allie could see on my face that I was going. She dropped her hand from my shoulder.

Thirty minutes later, Allie was long gone. My head spun as Paolo and I tangled together like teenagers in the back of Cal's Volvo. Even drunk, the car seemed oddly anachronistic. Cal didn't say very much, but based on his hunting jacket, I pictured him as the sort who drove an enormous SUV.

"Where to?" I was asking. "It's early." It was not early. I'd never meant to go *out* out, but once I get started, I'm a spinning top. I knew that.

It was stupid, a throwback to earlier times, but that didn't seem to matter.

Cal's eyes were straight ahead. "Home. I'm taking you home."

Paolo and I jointly whined from the back seat.

The Volvo moved along at a safe but very deliberate pace. Up front, Cal's head turned toward the center of the dashboard, where a small digital clock—which looked like it had been attached by Velcro—emitted a dusky green glow. Like a bomb timer in an eighties action movie.

Paolo teased, "Cal's just up past his bedtime. I don't know how I talked him into going out." He put a hand on his friend's shoulder. "Lights out is at what, nine thirty?"

"Ten on weeknights, Friday and Saturday it's ten thirty."

They had the easy camaraderie of teammates. Cal's hand patted the gearshift.

Paolo stage-whispered, "He eats the same things, at the same times, every single day."

In the rearview mirror, I caught the faintest upturn of a smile. "Like that's a bad thing," Cal muttered.

"Cal's a vet," Paolo explained.

"Like small animal?" I piped up.

"Marine Corps," he clarified quickly.

They seemed nothing alike. "Wait, how do you two actually know each other?"

"Softball," Cal said simply.

I turned to Paolo. "Somehow, you don't strike me as a softball player."

Cal struck me as a softball player.

Paolo struck me as just a player.

"You like being in the lab?" I asked him.

"I *love* being in lab." His voice was soft, a gentle rumble in my ear. "You know about the research, of course." I felt the muscles in Paolo's stomach tighten as he sat up behind me.

"Of course."

"Emily, where did you say your place is?" Cal asked, turning the wheel. The engine growled as he accelerated through a yellow light. I was still watching Paolo's eyes in the rushing streetlight.

———

The next day, I sketched a picture of a test tube with a wide-eyed, smiling face and texted it to Paolo.

Lol, he texted back. What are you doing tonight?

Later that night, I waited for him to get off work.

His text appeared: I'll be late.

Days later, jittery, hypomanic, I stood in the concrete aisle of a used bookstore, tiny puddles squeaking under each of my sandals, a spring thunderstorm pummeling the roof. My hands trembled as I paced, smelling the slightly sweet, vaguely hypnotic smell of decaying paper, looking for something, looking for something. The new relationship had me buzzed. My phone vibrated in my pocket, somebody calling. No way could I contemplate answering. Reading was impossible; no way was I sitting still. I knew that. But book shopping was something I could do. I needed a book to find me.

When it did, when I saw the one, I took it from the shelf and opened the cover. Tucked in the pages was a plane ticket the previous owner had used as a bookmark. The flight was from Nash-ville to Argentina. The carrier was United.

This is crazy, I thought. This is crazy.

This was the language of God.

I floated above, saw invisible things.

I closed the cover, bought the book, and called Paolo from the parking lot.

His voice echoed off his lab's hard surfaces.

I asked him, "If you came with a warning label attached to you, what would it read?" This was after we'd had sex for the third time. As if anything he'd say could change the way I was about to feel about him.

He laughed quietly. I pictured him cupping the phone with his other hand. "Why do you ask?"

"Because I want to know. I want to know you. At the begin-ning of relationships people usually know what the problems will be, but they minimize them."

"Is that a psychologist thing or a bipolar thing?" I could practi-cally hear him grinning. "Or both?"

"I guess you won't say," I said.

I heard the sound of a door closing, his voice adjusting to hav-ing more privacy. "I don't get it. You want me to tell you what problems I'm going to cause you in the future?"

"Yes, I do."

In the background, someone spoke, and Paolo sounded eager to return to what he'd been doing. "Probably . . . my worst quality is the best one, too. But you know, stubborn people persevere."

"I hear you on that," I said. "I do."

You don't even know, I thought.

SIXTEEN

My thoughts, after Cal left, were organized into two basic categories: worry about the dragging of time until I met with Sandy again, and worry about what exactly Cal was talking about.

A drug addict? A pill head? I'd been called a lot of things, but those were new.

I thought back to the prescription bottles the police had found in Paolo's Jeep. Unanswered questions, his right to privacy.

Everything turned over and over in my head. I couldn't sleep, wanted to take a pill, didn't, laid awake. I picked up the phone to call Cal, stopped myself, and turned over in bed again.

Cal had activated my worst fears, brought the worst time in my life right back to the surface.

————

Twenty years old. The parking structure was ghostly empty except for a few cars. I'd been up there before when I couldn't sleep. It was close to campus, lonesome at night; attached to some kind of medical building. I didn't know for sure. None of that was my world yet. When you're twenty, you have only an outline sketch of how life works on which to base your plans.

I could taste vodka on my lips, my tongue still numb from it. I walked the ramps counterclockwise upward, hands shaking, jammed into the pockets of my jeans. Floor three, floor four. My chest pounded like we were halfway through practice drills, though the soccer season had ended months before. I laid my palm on my chest to feel the hammering, then wiped the back of my hand across my cheeks.

Inside me was the big black, the blob that ate everything it touched. The only way to not lie in bed was to stay out, to walk. To keep walking. I'd known it before, but it had never been quite so bad, so consuming. I thought of it as The Nameless Dread.

Eventually, I'd fall asleep. At least, I prayed I would.

It was still early enough that the only sound was the faint *clink clink* of metal from somewhere, like a rivet hitting a flagpole. It surprised me that cars were there, one every other ramp or so. There was a dented subcompact the color of mint ice cream, then a white pickup with a dusty bumper covered in pro-gun stickers.

Floor five, six. Wind leapt off the concrete, shoving me in the back. My head hadn't touched a pillow for three days. I was humming songs to myself like there was a radio inside my head—fragments of tunes, rhymes, looping on repeat.

Floor seven.

A bird called from somewhere in the treetops below, and my head swiveled toward it. The animal in me wanted to hear its shrill voice again. My hands trembled in my pockets. My head found, then looped a song I hadn't listened to in years. No idea where it had come up from. Where did I . . . ? No one would ever understand this feeling, like a shot put formed inside my chest. Around it, my heart beat.

Maybe I'd sleep . . . later. Or maybe I'd do it. It would only take a few seconds; then everything would be over. The carousel could stop.

Another car. Goddammit. Red hatchback like a drop of blood on the pavement. That's funny, actually, I thought.

Was it?

I wondered if I would do it.

Eighth floor was the top. Streetlights like a star map spread across the city floor. I climbed onto the ledge, dangled my feet over. The concrete under my palms was rough and dirty, though the air smelled clean and felt warm and good surrounding me. I was looking down. All the way down. The backs of my shoes bounced forward off the concrete wall. I started to lean forward, too, to look down, but wobbled and felt my fingertips dig into the rough wall. My nails bent back until they hurt.

"'Scuse me." The man's voice behind me was so soft. "I didn't want to startle you, but why don't you come down off of that? You're making me a little nervous."

"I didn't know anyone was here." I sounded drunk. I started turning toward the voice, felt my balance give, stopped. My eyes focused on the blinking red of a far-off radio tower.

"Why don't you let me help you come off of that?"

"No, thanks."

"I really think—"

My shoes bounced. My bottom slid forward.

"Whoa there." I could hear him shifting from one foot to the other. "Just hang on there, all right? Hang on."

I watched the red radio tower light. The shot put in my chest had become like a bowling ball.

"You're scaring . . ."

Me. He'd almost said, *You're scaring me.* But I turned my chin over my shoulder and locked eyes with him before he could finish. Dark skin, with soft, tired eyes. Maybe forty-five, maybe fifty. The age I imagined my dad would be. Was this him? Finally come back? That was crazy. I knew it was.

What he said was, "I saw you from my window." He pointed at the building. "I saw you walking, then climb up on this . . . thing. I thought maybe you needed some help."

There were no words inside me.

Then, tires grumbling, a police radio. No lights, I noticed. No one wanted to spook me.

You can't spook a ghost. I was already dead.

But not all the way. Not dead enough that hands couldn't grip my shoulders, couldn't pull me backward off the ledge and onto the concrete.

Then the lights came on, blue and ever bright—starbursts of color, announcing something . . . what was it? The big black, the blob they couldn't see had been detained. I spit on the floor of the cruiser. The handcuffs chilled my wrists. The man with the tired eyes disappeared down a flight of stairs. A metal door banged behind him.

My head was full of . . . something. Something that made sleep inevitable, irresistible. Like the aliens say, I thought before my eyes closed, resistance is futile.

When they opened again, I was in the company of another middle-aged man—Marty—who guided me through my first hospitalization. He had a kind smile and a piece of yarn in his palm, trying to show me that things that were broken could get put back together. He was no good at the trick, not yet. Years later, he'd throw away all his best judgment and recommend me for my graduate program.

In the hospital, I knew what my diagnosis would be before anyone acknowledged it because I'd feared bipolar for as long as I could remember. I'd feared it looking back over my family history, picturing my grandmother wading into that glassy river at sunset. I'd had dreams where she'd turned and her face had been my face, her terror had been mine. I pictured bipolar laying latent, genetically, waiting for its opportunity. The way a sleeper cell does. Or cancer.

The harder I tried to ignore my mood expressions in middle and high school, the less I could. Every down day became the beginning of my descent. Every time I laughed too long or stayed up too late made me wonder if I was just about to go careening off of the edge.

But in the hospital, I knew. I knew definitively, even if I didn't know how to think about it, except as a monster inside myself. The tormenting Hulk, the mutated DNA in my blood, inextricable, permanent, my deepest and most personal flaw—the dark half of my identity. Who wouldn't be afraid? Until I snapped, it was like waiting for a bomb to go off. I knew when the whisper of my thoughts turned loud, and violent, and unyielding—before the parking garage and the cutting, cold handcuffs.

Clinically, no healthcare worker seemed to want to say the word *bipolar*. But Marty didn't bullshit me. He drew a line on a piece of paper and explained my mood as a continuum. He numbered the line one to ten. A one was very depressed, a ten completely out of control, manic. We talked about how much fluctuation I had, and the rate in which it happened.

He taught me a word: *euthymic.* That was the state between four and six. Euthymic sounded like another planet, or the name of somewhere exclusive, a club I couldn't get into, or would be kicked out of after being revealed.

But that was where I wanted to go—and stay—mostly. It would take therapy and meds, which narrowed the range, clipping off the extremes. Marty explained that most bipolar patients stopped taking meds after a while because they felt muted through their week-to-week lives, mainly devoid of energy. The sevens and eights felt vibrant and satisfying.

What I needed was to minimize the ones and twos—days of complete blackness, no perspective, no ability to see my hand in front of my face. Those were unsustainable. More than that, they were intolerable. It's like people say—no one kills themselves because they like dying. They jump from burning buildings because the fall hurts less than the fire.

Fire's hard to live with.

I wanted a life—not to follow anyone into a river.

There's a self-centeredness to poor mental health that I absolutely hated; I wanted to be someone I liked. The teammate, camp counselor, daughter, friend.

That first week, Marty raised an eyebrow at me when I tilted my head back and swallowed three pills at once. I told him I'd try anything. I wasn't going back up on that parking garage.

———

On Thursday morning, my phone lit up with a text from Allie: CHECKING IN ON YOU. STILL OKAY?

THANKS FOR ASKING, I typed, picturing her surrounded by paper piles. I was lucky to have a friend so caring. HOW ARE YOU?

The ellipsis on her end of the conversation breathed while she evidently touched her screen—sitting at her desk, I imagined.

YOU WANTED TO MEET ABOUT SOMETHING ON SATURDAY? I
DON'T KNOW IF I CAN. MY SCHEDULE IS OFF THE RAILS, THE WHOLE
DEPARTMENT IS IN A FRENZY. IT'S ABOUT TO BE ALL OVER THE NEWS—
THERE'S BEEN ANOTHER KILLING. ANOTHER BODY FOUND.

I felt pain in the back of my throat as my head dropped back.
All I could picture was Sandy's terrified expression as I replayed the
hours after she left, all my texting and calling. My legs tightened,
ready to run. My hand shook. I typed, A WOMAN?

At that moment, I didn't care if Allie wondered why I was
asking.

A sweeping stretch of time before her next text came. Beads of
sweat on my lip.

VICTIM WAS A MAN. THEY THINK HOMELESS. WE COULD BE
LOOKING AT A SERIAL KILLER.

I set the phone down and covered my mouth, swallowing hard.
Don't, I thought. Don't take solace.

Go to the news.

———

The body had been found at dawn the day before—Halloween. A
local artist, moving through the dry brush, made the discovery.
She wore the decade-old overalls in which she taught community
ed, her late husband's field jacket hung over her shoulders. In the
dawn light, her breath had been a series of tiny spirits.

She'd set out early to capture a peak autumn landscape in acrylic.

Brushes jangled inside her canvas backpack. As she stopped to
tie the jacket arms around her waist, coffee sloshed inside her ther-
mos. When she looked up, she recognized the black, twisted vines
in the modest clearing as a body. She understood that the surrounding pines had been bewitched in ash, and she dropped everything to
the ground.

She placed her horrified call. Police arrived within minutes.

These remains were less than a mile from the site of the previous murder, four months earlier. The circumstances were similar.
Like before, the victim had been zip-tied to a metal chair. This

time, the chair had been chained to a tree. The killer had ensured that the victim wasn't going anywhere. But since everything was scorched, the cause of death was indeterminable.

No one understood at the time why the victim had been kept in the same place for days. Or why his last days, but not death, had been recorded.

As with the first murder, two sets of footprints led toward the clearing. Only one set led back toward the road.

Late in the afternoon, the police found a Zippo lighter in the brush that was assumed to have ignited the blaze.

A murder like that, if it could be understood at all, couldn't be comprehended emotionally. The killer had to be someone who had no feelings at all. I turned this over and over in my mind—the fact that Paolo seemed to have been to Gainer Ridge before the previous murder, Sandy's conviction about what she'd found out about Matt. Was this murder connected to the previous one? Allie sure seemed to think so. But could Matt possibly be involved?

I called Sandy again, then texted her. WE NEED TO TALK.

————

Waiting was torture, trusting that Sandy was going about collecting whatever evidence she could. It felt helpless, out of control. To discharge whatever anxiety I could, I returned to my lifelong strategy: exercise. Working out always got me out of my head. I needed to be out of my head. Sports had been my go-to since elementary school, when I'd gravitated toward PE more than any other girl I knew. In high school, it got serious; and at soccer, I got seriously good. Then my college team had been a sort of sweet torture, testing the limits of love versus overexposure.

At twenty-one, Advil had turned into a vitamin. My body became a machine. A machine that performed until what I felt like stopped mattering. I willed myself to move in unnatural directions, to tolerate the passage of boredom, to anticipate directional changes fifty yards away.

That evening, my truck creaked over speed bumps in the

parking lot of the Green Hills YMCA. The parking lot was nearly full, but I found a spot near the back. The seat fabric felt cold on my neck. As raindrops began to dot my windshield, I watched car lights splash in and out of the parking lot until my breath began to fog the glass. After daylight savings in Tennessee, it feels as though it's dark all the time.

Another body. Horrific.

The case was something I couldn't look away from, even though knowing about it ached.

I realized my hands were gripped so tight that my fingernails were marking crescent moons into my palms.

Go on, I thought, get up there. You came here for a reason.

Inside, I hung my sweatshirt and leaned the cane under the row of hooks. I situated myself on a recumbent bike beneath a television so large it seemed satirical. I took my left foot out of the boot, slipped on a running shoe matching the one on my right foot, then started turning the pedals.

This wouldn't really be working out, I thought; this would be a warmup. This wouldn't be sprints till I threw up.

I set the timer on my phone to chime after thirty minutes, then turned it facedown in the bike's drink holder.

In no time, sweat beaded my face. My hands turned slick on the grips.

A dull ache pounded my left side.

Keep going.

I could picture the screws flexing inside my ankle. It felt rigged together, like some kind of contraption that might fall apart. I reached for my phone but stopped myself.

Don't think about time. *Keep going.*

I focused on the wall opposite me, ignoring the television flashing overhead.

Then my phone was chiming. My gaze snapped back into the room. I wiped at my face with the front of my shirt as the shock of pain I'd willed myself to ignore burned my left side, heel to hip, like that whole section of me had been ripped open.

My mind flashed like a scream to the image of a burned body in the woods. Why? Like everyone else in the city must've wondered: why?

I unclenched my jaw.

The chime sounded again. Time was up.

I turned over my phone and realized there were four missed calls, all from Sandy. There was a voicemail from her number. I checked my texts, my fingers making sweaty prints on the screen. Three from Sandy, their time stamps like punctuation points between the calls. Some part of me knew, even as I hobbled off the bike, that these would someday be examined by a detective.

They read:

I WAS RIGHT. I FOUND MORE.

I HAVE TO GO TO THE POLICE.

I'M SORRY.

The air was full of electricity. Still panting from the bike, I started the voicemail, but the whir of machines made listening impossible. I shoved back into my boot and grabbed my cane, took the stairs down two at a time until I was back out in the breezy parking lot, where lights reflected off the wet asphalt. Sitting on the wooden bench beside the entrance, a new whoosh of air flew over me each time the doors opened.

I pressed the phone against my damp cheek to listen.

She sounded terrified, hushed but echoey, as if running—footsteps pressured her speech like a metronome swaying too quickly. I pictured her looking back over her shoulder, blonde hair slashing back and forth across her tiny shoulders. I pictured her pretty, perfect teeth as I heard her voice.

"It's Sandy. I hope you get this tonight. I need to see you as soon as you can. I found more. Much more. You can't trust anyone, can you? Nothing matters now. I'm never going back."

Something great and terrible started to swell in me, familiarly.

I replayed the message. Her thoughts were raw and unorganized—fear had disallowed any pretense.

I called back. Her phone rang to voicemail.

My heart pounded. I moved to the truck, grabbed the cracked steering wheel, the Breathalyzer, and blew. I knew I was going to her apartment, that nothing was going to stop me.

I started driving and called again. Five rings, then voicemail. I didn't leave a message. What would I say? *Call me?*

A line of cars formed in front of me along Woodmont, someone waiting to turn left while headlights streamed ahead.

I was going to bang on Sandy's door until she answered.

Had I taken medication that morning? Yes, surely, I thought.

This wasn't manic, I told myself.

But the only things that existed were Sandy's apartment and getting there. My mind raced to guess the distance. Two miles? Three, maybe? Distance was time. Time needed to pass.

On the interstate, traffic slowed again then it stopped altogether. I changed lanes. The truck's turn signal made a sound like cracking plastic. Some kind of construction ahead, or something, that I couldn't make out—just a grinding line of brake lights and wispy tailpipes. An orange light flashed somewhere up ahead.

"Goddammit," I screamed, beating the steering wheel. I pictured Janet Leigh's expression in *Psycho*.

Except I was the psycho.

Rain fell steadily. The windshield wipers strained to smear the frozen bits. Sleet touched my forearm. I reached for my phone, flashed to an image of my wreck. I could picture the other car, twisted. *No.* I didn't need GPS anyway; I'd known where Sandy lived the second I'd seen her address.

I glanced back at the glove box. Was Sandy a patient? Of course not. I considered calling Marty. Someone needed to know, and I imagined his voice—calming and reassuring.

Then I talked myself out of it, knowing how erratic I'd sound. Marty had taken a chance on me. The last thing I wanted him to think was that I'd already gone off the deep end.

I craned my neck. Still nothing to see beyond the line of cars stretching out under the low, Mylar clouds reflecting downtown. The car in front of me lurched ahead, then taillights blazed again.

Through the rear window, the hazy light of a pale rectangle—someone leaning over a screen.

"Go, dammit! Go!" I laid on the horn. In the rain, it sounded like a pathetic request, like someone coughing at the back of a crowd. A pair of hands raised in a shrug, as if to say, *What do you want me to do?* I didn't care. I hit it again.

Eventually, I crossed the river and found traffic was no better on the east side. I cut through a church parking lot at a slow intersection. My headlights found a closed gate, chained and locked in the center. I pictured my cousins and me shredding a field twenty years before. The engine rumbled as if to catch its breath—as if to remind me of its age—then growled reluctantly as I turned the wheel toward an opening in the landscaping and gunned through a ditch onto a side street. Air whistled in. Bare branches swayed in a canopy overhead as I tore past sleepy houses, the seat belt laid tightly against my chest.

I ran two red lights, almost hoping icy-blue lights would appear behind me. I imagined this whole thing as a scene from a movie, a higher purpose justifying my reckless driving.

I counted the addresses until I found Sandy's townhouse at the far end of the row. Neat, new construction, the front lawns on either side still covered in straw.

I slammed the truck door. Freezing rain instantly soaked through my tank top.

Sandy's upstairs lights were on. Along the row, the other windows were dark.

I could hear the strain of her voice on the recording in my mind. What had she found? What had stopped her from saying? An instant passed in which my head told me I didn't actually know Sandy very well, that I could be frozen in the cold, sobbing rain because of a misunderstanding, histrionics.

But I knew—*knew*—I wasn't wrong.

My chest felt full of helium. Something had happened. Something devilish.

I rubbed my bare arms. I could hardly feel the rain. One thing about mania, even hypomania—you burn inside.

I rang the doorbell, knocked. Down the row, the door fronts stayed dark. I rested my finger on the round button beside her front door, pressed it again. The chime sounded vacant even ironic, like I should have understood its futility already. I stepped into the landscaping for a look into the window, the soaked mulch spongy beneath my feet. Inside was like a charcoal sketch, just outlines. The edge of my boot caught the ground, and my ankle screamed in pain. I'd pushed it too far already on the bike. It didn't matter.

Rain pelted me as I limped back to the street. Upstairs was still and ghostly lit. Maybe she'd left the lights on, I thought; maybe she'd gone to the police, or was calling me back to say it was a mistake and that everything was all right. I limped back to the truck, found my phone, and trudged through the muddy side yard.

The light above her back deck was out, but even from below I could see the door pushed in, swinging open. My ankle gave and splinters ripped into my hand as I gripped the slick wooden handrails and pulled myself upward.

"Sandy?"

The cold metal of the back door sent a chill up my arm when I pressed it open. I glanced at the tiny cuts on my palm, the warm trickle of blood already washed away in the rain. I shoved my hand into my jacket pocket.

"Hello?" My voice seemed to drop off, like I was yelling into space.

Water had blown into the kitchen and reflected dimly on the tile. A gust of wind yanked the wet doorknob from my hand, shoving my shoulders. I called her name again as the rain dripped off me, puddles swelling slickly around my feet. I'd rushed over, but inside her condo, on the stairs, a wave of reluctance washed over me. I shouldn't be here, I thought, but I had to be.

Call the police.

My mouth was dry. The door slammed behind me with a gust, and the blinds scraped as they swayed back and forth. I took my hand from my pocket and let it guide me up the stairs, toward the only light.

The bedrooms were dark. A long triangle of light stabbed out from beneath the bathroom door. My stomach knew already that she was inside.

I pushed open the door. Her blonde hair was half floating, a wave beneath the water. The hem of her white shirt rose to the surface, her dark jeans like black weights around her legs.

Sandy's eyes were empty, dead.

Still, I dove for her, letting out something between a scream and a howl as I struggled to hoist her. I dragged her onto the tile, part of me knowing it would be no use. I went through the motions of CPR. Around us, the floor flooded. Her head fell back coldly onto my knees as I pinched her nose, breathed into her mouth.

Gone. Nothing was inside her.

Her skin felt a way I didn't know skin could feel—not warm and not cold. It felt like water the temperature of your own body. Like an ocean you disappear into. Or dissolve in.

I was in an out-of-body spell.

This was shock.

When my phone fell out of my pocket, I wiped it off and dialed 911.

"5411 Boscobel Street," I cried. My head hit the hard side of her sink as I slipped. "My friend has drowned."

Whatever she'd learned had killed her.

But I needed to find out what it was. Immediately.

SEVENTEEN

"You need to get up." A rough hand on my shoulder, then one under my arm, pulling up. Uniforms behind me. Then static, voices through small speakers.

"How long had she been in the water?"

"I don't know. She was in the tub when I got here."

"How long ago was that?"

"Ten minutes?" I guessed. Time was distorted. I thought back to the rain, the splintery handrail. "Maybe fifteen."

Maybe I was dragged backward; maybe I floated. Footsteps splashed behind me, navy-blue shirts filled the room and hallway. Lights turned on abruptly—the hall, the bedrooms. A voice giving directions. Another asking me questions. I couldn't look directly at anyone. *I'm not here. This isn't happening.*

When I stood, I paced the hallway, wild-eyed and shivering, glancing at Sandy every few seconds, like she might sit up, spit water from her mouth like a fountain, and cough. Like she might end the nightmare.

A blue shirt appeared in front of my face, blocking my path. A light shined in my eyes until I pushed away the hand that held it. I was acting crazy. I knew that.

They might think I was crazy, I considered.

Or they might think I killed her.

Then someone muttered the word *drugs*. A voice asked me directly, "What have you been taking tonight?"

I swallowed, shook my head. I wondered what they already

knew about me. I pictured Cal's expression. I started to find words to describe what I'd taken that day, to say it was just for symptom control—a mood stabilizer—but they were drowned out by the reverberation of a singular idea: *Sandy had drowned*.

I realized I was trying to think up a path toward a place where what had just happened . . . hadn't.

I bit my cuticles, walked a tight circle.

Water everywhere, puddles under shoes.

There had to be something to do. That was the problem— helplessness. There was absolutely nothing to do.

I couldn't think about Paolo, not yet. But the great expanse— of he and I, and the way he died—was rising inside me like a bubble from the bottom of the ocean. It was only a matter of time before it reached the surface and became a part of the atmosphere.

How did this happen? Matt's name, his hoodied shape, his smoky trail at Dr. Silver's holiday party, were sharpening in my mind.

Then there was another voice, light reflecting off metal badges, and the scratch and crackle of a radio. There was a hand suddenly on both of my shoulders. "Excuse me, Miss." These weren't questions, I ascertained; they were directives for me to stop pacing. My shoes squeaked to a halt. When my eyes found the face from which the voice was coming, I understood it was not an EMT. This was a cop, somewhere in his late twenties, crew-cut blond hair wet from the rain.

He asked, "Did you place the call to 911?"

"Yes. Me."

"Oh. Hi," he said. A wave of recognition washed over his face. "I need you to come on downstairs for me. Okay?"

In Sandy's kitchen, he half rotated a chair and pointed at it. "Just stay here for right now. Okay?"

I looked at him without looking—dark-blue uniform with even-darker blue splotches from the rain. He had young, inquisitive eyes. He took the chair between me and the door. I couldn't place him, but he looked familiar.

My heart continued pounding.

Police were smart, I thought. I'd tell them what I knew, and they would go find Matt. If I could just think of his last name, then they'd go get him. I lit up my phone.

The familiar blond cop turned to me. "You'd better set that down for now." He sounded helpful, like a hardware store employee pointing me in the right direction.

I set down the phone.

My hair, arms, and legs dripped a mixture of gym sweat, rainwater, and bathwater. An EMT draped a blanket over me. Even shivering, my cheeks burned as I glanced around Sandy's condo—a calendar on the cabinet with notes in her handwriting for appointments she wouldn't keep, a ceramic bull on whose horn she'd hung her keys, its eyes resigned, mournful. Her family photos sat, waiting like lost children.

I touched the crescent-shaped scar on my wrist, fighting the feeling that some giant hand seemed resolved to knock my world off its axis again and again.

Lights flashed through every window. The blond officer sat with me while the others lingered around the door frame, taking turns pointing at the sky. I could hardly sit still, unintentionally rocking in the chair. The nontemperature feel of Sandy's cold body crashed over me like a determined sequence of waves; when one hit, another was eager to follow.

The blond officer checked something on his phone and assured me, kindly, that more people would arrive to talk with me very soon. He beat on his knees with flat palms in a fast rhythm, some old, nervous song from inside himself.

"Listen." I tried not to sound wild. "I know who . . . I know some things, some important information."

"If you'll hang tight for just a minute more—"

I stood. He stood, too. He lowered his palms. We both sat again.

More police arrived. One mumbled curses every few seconds. He reared his fist back like he was about to strike something.

"The rain'll complicate things," the blond officer volunteered.

"It destroys evidence," I said quietly.

His body straightened. He glanced back at the doorway, then at me—a slight hesitation. "Maybe so, yeah."

"I need to talk to . . . somebody. A detective." I reached for the cop's arm.

He pulled it back just as a stout woman in a yellow raincoat appeared. She slipped covers over her shoes, gloved her hands, and ascended the stairs.

Cool air blew in from outside. "Medical examiner's here." He nodded very slightly and pointed his chin toward her.

"Look, I'm on your team here. I need to talk to . . ." My mind searched for a name—pink gum, razor nick. A rose on his neck. "Detective Mason! Andre Mason."

I'd said the magic words. Semi-magic, at least. His head swiveled. He looked at me for a doubtful second, began to stand, stopped, then completed the movement. "Stay here?"

I agreed.

He went to the others by the door, downpour raging behind them. They alternated turns glancing over at me. One raised his phone to his ear.

On the stairwell, a flash erupted like lightning—two, three, four times. They were taking pictures of her. I pictured Sandy's body in the lewd, forensic light and shook my head to clear the image from my thoughts—the blankness in her eyes, the lack of reflexes that should have cleared the water and hair from her mouth. The vacancy of death. I fought a protective impulse to run upstairs, take the blanket from around my shoulders, and cover her.

I fought the impulse to think about Paolo, too, what his expression might have been like in the water.

When Mason arrived, his eyes found me from the doorway. He covered his shoes and strode over with the familiar blond flanking him.

With a quick nod to me, he turned a chair around and sat, glancing down at that training watch. "They said you called about twenty-five minutes ago?" His voice was calm clarity, unimpeded by gum, uncomplicated by whatever conventions had lingered between him and Allie.

His way of smiling a beat too quickly, I noticed, was gone.

I forced a deep breath into my lungs to interrupt the sudden crying jag that was about to hit me. "Yeah. I found her. I tried . . . I pulled her out of the water and I tried—" A part of me needed him to know this so he'd understand I was a decent person; another part was trying to tell him I was innocent.

He seemed to be thinking something else entirely. "It's okay. I need a lot of information from you, and I'm going to get you out of here so they can work. Do you need to stop at home? Change clothes?" His chin gestured at the wet patch of floor beneath me.

"You need to find a guy named Matt—Matt Cianciolo. He works in the same lab as—"

Palms up, assuring eyes. "Emily, do you want to stop at home?"

"No," I said.

He turned to the familiar blond. "Can you drive her?"

"Drive Dr. Firestone?"

Something about the way he said my name made Mason's eyes narrow. His voice broke with a juvenile sort of disbelief. "Do you two know each other?"

"Well, sort of, yeah. I mean, kind of." He sounded all golly-gee, and right that second I remembered where I knew him from. "She did my psych eval when I came out of the academy."

Shit, I thought.

I knew that didn't sound good, as I watched Mason's expression harden. Like a twist in a bad movie, I realized the omission of this fact made it seem like I was covering something up. That there were deeper, and maybe devious, reasons I'd obfuscated knowing about police work.

When was I going to stop looking guilty?

Mason's eyebrow rose, only slightly. He checked that triathlete watch once more and carefully pulled a stick of gum from his pocket. His voice slowed back to interrogation pace. "Why don't you stick around here? Help them out. I'm fine to drive her."

Then he looked at me like he intended to never let me out of his sight.

"Are you about to question me?" I asked, my voice breaking.

"Yes, I am," Mason said. The smell of his cologne hitting me as he turned me toward the back door.

———

I left my cane behind. It was somewhere outside Sandy's apartment. Or inside. I didn't know. At the precinct, I stumbled down the claw-marked hallway and past Allie's office, each step a pang in my ankle. I had this minuscule fantasy that some officer, maybe the blond one from Sandy's condo, would burst through the door and say that Matt had been detained. That the search was over.

Nausea stabbed my stomach. I covered it with my hand, keeping my eyes on Mason's collar as he led us through the hall with his ballplayer stride.

The room was the same—same cafeteria-style table, same coffee urn, same Walmart-at-two-AM lighting. Same photocopier smell. This time, it seemed smaller and damper.

There were more chairs around the table, but for the moment he and I were alone. Mason's video camera had been set up when we walked in and was pointed at the chair where I'd sat before, with its steady red light like HAL from *2001: A Space Odyssey*. I considered how I looked.

When I ran my fingers through the still-damp strands of my hair, the splintery cuts from Sandy's stairwell stung.

"Coffee?" Mason asked.

He's put something in it.

Don't be crazy, Emily.

I set my palms flat on the table. "No. Thanks. I know why you brought me in here like this. I should probably be calling my lawyer right now."

Unflinching calm. Energy leaked out of me, but Mason's pulse was probably resting at fifty-eight. He glanced out at the hallway, at Allie's dark door. "Now's the time, if you want to do that. We'll get started in a second, but it can wait."

"Look, we're wasting time. I'd only call just to not be stupid, but I don't give a fuck because I've *done nothing wrong*. If you don't start listening to me, I'm gonna scream."

Mason didn't blink at the profanity; his expression said, *Go ahead and scream, then*.

"How long did you do those police evaluations?" he asked with a provocative evenness, eyes flicking down at the video camera, daring me to call a lawyer.

I straightened defiantly, stared back at him. Willed my voice to slow down. "All during my postdoc, then for about a year afterward. If you're asking, yeah, I learned a little about police work. But I'm not a cop, obviously. I'm a psychologist. I mostly work with kids, Detective."

But he knew that. Since our last interview, he'd learned more about me than he was going to let on, I was sure. He'd read my booking sheet from the crash, knew about my blood alcohol content. He'd seen my mug shot.

There was a knock at the door as two more people, a man and a woman, entered with the purposeful efficiency of the pre-subpoenaed. Mason introduced them, but my eyes washed over their blank, well-trained expressions. The man wore a white button-down shirt, and the woman carried a portfolio case and wore her hair in a high, serious-looking bun.

I shifted in my chair. Three detectives made you more than just a person of interest.

"You understand that everything you say becomes a part of the official record of this case," Mason began.

It wasn't really a question, but I nodded anyway. "Yeah, of course."

That previous meeting had been like preseason. Now we were in the playoffs. "It's obviously been a very intense night. I want to talk to you about Ms. Harrison and about what happened earlier. Are you okay to do that?"

I nodded.

"Sorry, is that a *yes*?" Slightly aggressive.

I could hardly keep my face composed; my heart was thunder. "Yes."

"How did you know Ms. Harrison?"

"She was one of my . . . she was a coworker of my boyfriend's."

"She was a coworker of Mr. Fererra's?"

"Yeah."

"And how long had you known her?"

"We met at a party about ten months ago. I want to tell you about a guy named Matt Cianciolo. Can I do that?"

This was a barrier to my understanding the legal trouble I was suddenly in: the person who most wanted to discover exactly what had happened to Paolo and now to Sandy was . . . me. I couldn't tell if the police questioning me wanted to wake me up to a different reality, or if they took my eagerness to redirect them as some sort of ruse.

It felt like impatience was going to burn through my skin.

White Shirt looked at High Bun, but Mason looked straight ahead at me. He nodded in the patronizing way people address the elderly when they seem to not understand. Slow-blinking, deep chin dip. My chest had reached a rolling boil.

"We want to hear every part of what you have to say, but we want to keep the order straight. We want to not get confused about just how things happened earlier. I know that may be frustrating. So . . . let's back up. Tell me about the holiday party where you met Ms. Harrison."

I seriously hope Allie never went to bed with you.

"It was a holiday party." I tried not to sound as exasperated as I was. "At the head of their lab's house in Belle Meade. There were maybe forty people there. I met her for all of about three minutes. I didn't see her again until the day before yesterday. She called me and said she wanted to schedule an appointment for counseling, and—"

"You said you work mainly with children? Did I get that right?" He flashed genuine confusion.

I held up my hands. "She called me. I've worked with adults, too. But it didn't matter because she didn't really want therapy. She wanted to talk to me about one of their coworkers. She thought he killed Paolo."

Real perplexity swept the room now. Tight Bun made a note.

I leaned over the table. "That's what she wanted to talk about. She wanted to tell me about Matt—"

"Another coworker?" Mason asked.

"Yes! Named Matt Cianciolo. She thought he'd developed . . . I don't know. She thought he somehow slipped something to Paolo before we went onto the boat. They work with sedatives, drugs for euthanizing animals. I didn't understand, but in a way it all actually makes sense. I was sick, too; I woke up sick. She said maybe I ingested some of it. He lives at 1440 Chestnut Street, Apartment 2C. I know I sound—"

I knew exactly how I sounded. I sounded like Sarah Connor in *Terminator 2*, trying to be convincing about robots from the future. Not that I could stop myself.

"We'll look into Matt Cian . . . ?"

"Cianciolo." I started spelling out the name. I noticed Tight Bun set down her pen halfway through.

This pace, I thought, is going to kill me.

"You said Ms. Harrison called looking for a therapist. Did she actually schedule an appointment with you?"

"Well, yes but no. She came to my office, but it was clear that it wasn't an appointment from the very beginning. She wasn't my patient."

"She didn't fill out any paperwork for you? No intake form, nothing like that?"

"I mean, she wrote down the basics. Her name and phone number. Her address."

"Why nothing else?"

"I'm telling you. She didn't really want therapy."

"But she came to your office and filled out forms? Why would she do that?"

Right. Why had she? I thought for half a second, needing them to understand that I'd not just shown up at a patient's home. My thoughts were a dizzying swirl. "Because I needed her phone number. I didn't have it. I'd only met her once."

White Shirt spoke for the first time, abruptly. He squinted like I was bright. "How did Ms. Harrison contact you, initially? To schedule the meeting."

"She called my phone."

White Shirt's eyebrow arched over the frame of his thick glasses. "Your cell phone?" he asked. His voice dropped an octave on the word *cell*.

"Yeah."

He and Mason glanced at each other. "Your cell history didn't record Ms. Harrison's number?"

"It came up as UNKNOWN. She said she thought it would be safer."

"She called from a blocked number, so you didn't have her contact information. You had her write it down on your office paperwork."

"I had the paperwork on my desk, sitting out for when she came."

Two uniformed cops sauntered by, unabashedly curious as they passed. If I never defended myself in front of another committee in my life, I thought, that would be okay.

The clock was ticking. Who knew where Matt had gone. I pictured the frustrated expressions at the scene, a downpour washing away evidence.

Tight Bun spoke. She had exacting eyes. I could tell that she wanted to get everything right. It wasn't personal. I understood. "Did Ms. Harrison consider herself to be your patient?"

"Absolutely not."

"She came to you under a pretense, then?"

Slightly different angle, reiterated as a consistency check.

"That's what she said. She was scared. She said she'd seen something on one of the computers in the lab—Matt's computer." My memory searched for a record of Sandy's exact words. "Something like orders for chemicals to create a poison."

"And then?" Mason asked.

"Then we agreed that she was going to go back to the lab and find it again, print it out, and we were going to bring it to you." My eyes locked on Mason.

"Why didn't she print it the first time?"

"I don't know."

White Shirt's head was cocked. "You mentioned a few things about the coworker." His southern accent was like the crackle of fire. Slow and low. "His address. How did you come to know it?"

"I found it on my own."

"Through an Internet search?"

I felt like answering *That's how it's done these days*, but I said, "Yeah. I searched online—not too hard to find the basics."

Something about my brevity made White Shirt squint harder, like he was trying to tell what I'd left out. "That's not far from your office," he observed. "Have you been by there?"

Looking worse every minute. I alternated glances between the three of them.

"Yeah," I admitted, "Of course. Of course I was curious. I wanted to know where he lived. Sandy wasn't lying. I believed her."

Detective Mason switched his gum to the other side of his mouth. He asked me to tell him everything I knew about Matt Cianciolo, and so I did. Their expressions hardly changed through my soliloquy; they stayed so still and frustratingly unblinking that the truth felt like something I was making up. High Bun scribbled a few more notes. Mason checked some data on his watch.

Finally, White Shirt cracked the knuckle of his thumb and made an expression halfway between a wince and a wink.

He and Mason glanced at each other subtly, and Mason clicked his pen again.

"So tonight, earlier—"

"Wait," I said. "What happens now about Matt?"

"We'll handle the investigation." Mason's tone was a stop sign. White Shirt was a rounded mannequin behind him, arms folded over his barrel belly.

I shook my head. "Sandy told me she suspected a guy she worked with was a murderer. The same guy she thought killed my boyfriend. And now she's dead. Now . . . I mean now, as in right *now*, don't you . . ." I was caught between naivety and exasperation, searching for the words. ". . . need to go pick him up?"

"This is helpful. I assure you we'll follow every lead in this case."

I stared at Mason.

"I assure you," he repeated. "I want to get back to earlier . . ."

Run.

". . . when you got the call from Ms. Harrison."

Deep breath.

White Shirt squinted like he was calculating the time.

I explained how I was at the gym, away from the phone when she called.

"Any message?" Mason asked.

"Yes." I reached for my phone; their necks all craned. Then I laid it on the table and Sandy's voice from two hours earlier filled the room.

First, soft static, like a fire going out. Then her voice. Her terror seemed to expand the room, pushing the walls outward. The buzz of the overhead lights sounded like anticipation.

White Shirt spoke first. "What did she mean when she said, 'You can't trust anyone'?"

"She was talking about Matt."

"And you drove to her"—Mason rubbed the back of his neck—"on your restricted license?"

A brief hesitation. "Yes."

"Because of the DUI arrest."

I guess he had to say it, but it felt excessive. "Yeah."

"You thought you could help her?"

I started to answer but faced another question before I could.

"You knew her address offhand?"

I willed my voice back to calm. "When she wrote it on the paperwork, I knew where it was."

"Had you ever been to Ms. Harrison's home before?"

"No."

"Had you ever met her before, outside of work?"

"Just at the party with Paolo."

More writing. "How well did they know each other? Ms. Harrison and Mr. Fererra?"

I started to shrug.

"Were they close?"

"No."

"Had they been involved?"

My head cocked. "What?"

White Shirt's look said *You heard me.* His jaw was set, patient.

"No," I said.

"No?" His eyebrow arched over his glasses.

Oh, I realized. I could tell by the way he asked. They'd gone through everything of Paolo's. *They had been involved.*

Tears pressed in on me. I thought I might fly through the roof and keep ascending into the night sky. Disappear forever. "No," I said, "I really . . . I don't think so?"

I was now a jealous ex. A murder suspect—the only obvious link between two murders.

I looked at Mason and asked, "Can I go?"

———

They let me go out the front door.

The barrier that stabilized my life had snapped. Usually fortified by medication, support, responsibility, and fear, it shook away like a dead leaf on an autumn blanket. The lifelessness of Sandy's eyes had dismantled it. They'd looked up, persistently up, toward nothing, toward the unseen place for which she'd departed this earth. Maybe she'd met Paolo there.

I wondered if his eyes had looked the same beneath all that water.

The *whoop whoop* of a car alarm called. From lower Broadway, the stomp of country music flew past the war memorials, through the haunted elms. It was the middle of the night. My ankle howled in pain, but I didn't care. I was going to find Matt, find evidence against him. I was going to see him arrested for the murders I'd just been accused of. I'd bring this to an end—even if it meant not trusting a soul or myself, not sleeping till it was over. Even if it meant Paolo speaking to me from somewhere that wasn't real. I'd finish it.

Someday, my eyes would be dead, too. But not before I became a runaway train. If that's what it would take, so be it.

Despite myself, I knew who I was about to call.

EIGHTEEN

I was the first person in the West End Starbucks after it opened on Friday morning. The smell of strong coffee, the feel of it scalding my mouth. The nausea of zero sleep.

Lamictal? The day before. *Right? Right.* Later, I'd take two, I thought. That'd be fine.

Cal's Volvo rumbled into the lot, a wisp of exhaust rising from the tailpipe. A minute later, he sat down across the table from me like the chair was hot, looking back over his shoulder. Neat beard, iron eyes. The blue collar of a dress shirt peeked out from under his brown field jacket.

"Okay, you got me," he said. "I'm sufficiently curious. I'm here. What's so—"

"Do you know Sandy Harrison?"

A tiny hesitation. "Yeah," he answered. "Sort of—"

"She's dead," I reported, stopping him. "I found her last night."

His lips parted slightly, a glint of fear crossed his eyes like a spark on the iron. His hands rested on the table as if they might push off.

It sounded otherworldly, I knew, the script of a life that was never supposed to happen.

"How?" he asked, head snapping back. "How'd she die?"

"She drowned. Drowned in her bathtub. She called me right before it happened." I rubbed at my raw eyes.

"She called you?" A slight catch in his voice.

I told him the story, what I'd told the detectives—about the records Sandy found, how she'd come to me, what we'd planned. "We were going to meet again today," I said. "This afternoon."

"She thought Paolo . . ."

"That's right." My voice cracked with disbelief. "No one wanted to mention to me that they'd been dating? It was a hell of a way to find out."

His eyes were downcast.

"Was I the only one in the world who didn't know? How big of an idiot was I?" It felt crazy, under the circumstances, but I had to know.

Cal's sigh was barely perceptible, but it was there. I could tell he hated spilling the beans on his best friend, even if he was gone. He squinted, resigned. "I'm not going to bullshit you. Yeah, they had a thing."

I looked past him, past my lonesome truck, out to the distance. Not for an answer; for somewhere to go. My stomach—which I thought couldn't get any heavier—had turned into a shot put. Blood ran hot in my veins.

How had I not known? This was everything at once. Too much. Calm and conflict were reduced to numbness. I caught my reflection—a ghost in the window looking as ragged as I felt. My hands tightened around the white cup in front of me.

"It wasn't serious," he was saying. "Probably blinking out already when he met you. There might've been some overlap, but I don't think it went on long." His voice was deep and measured and gentle.

I appreciated it.

Cal sat back and went on. "I only met her . . . twice? Maybe three times? I don't put myself in anybody's business."

"Right."

"But you asked, so . . ." Cal lowered his chin. "They think you killed her," he said suddenly. Law wasn't his world, but he was quick to the bottom line.

I started crying again. I hated it, but I did. Wherever I went, it felt like the walls were closing in on me. "They didn't say it exactly, but I know I'm a suspect."

There was a new distance in his voice, a sudden and stark practicality. "You've . . . called a lawyer?"

My eyes dropped. "No," I admitted.

"Mmm, okay. Well, you should. I know a guy. I'll send you his contact info."

Cool air blew in as the door opened and closed. Someone getting in line. Cal snapped to look over his shoulder.

"I know a lawyer, Cal."

"Right. Of course. Because of the accident," he said.

I could tell he hadn't meant to sound mean.

"Look, I'm really sorry to hear this is happening. And I'm sorry you didn't know about the other . . ." He meant Paolo and Sandy. The wooden chair squealed across the tile floor as he stood. "I hope things work out, Emily. I'm sure you'll be all right."

"I need your help."

Cal's lips were tight. He shoved his hands in his pockets. "I don't think so. I'm definitely no legal expert, and—"

"Cal, sit down. Please."

He looked at me. Another bolt of fear crossed his iron eyes, a quick ghost. But also, kindness—or at least the desire to not be a dick. He was measuring me. Could he help? Should he help? I must've looked like chaos across the table. I could tell he wanted stability, a professional life. He wanted no part of this. Paolo dying was more than enough turbulence; what I was saying went way beyond.

The door whooshed open again. The breeze nudged his collar. He looked at the entrance, then turned back to me.

"Please." My voice was all tears. "Sandy came to me to tell me Paolo dying wasn't an accident, that he was murdered. That he drowned because he was poisoned. I know it sounds crazy, but now Sandy's dead, too." My peripheral vision registered a head turning, but I didn't stop. Couldn't stop. "And there's a detective right now who thinks I probably murdered two people. But since I know I didn't, and you . . . you know this, too, don't you? In your heart you know I didn't?"

"Yes," he said.

"And we both know what that means."

Cal took his hands from his pockets and rested them on the chair back. He couldn't help himself, either. He pulled out the chair, sat back down. Despite his best intentions, his desire to leave me to live out my fate, I don't think he could help what he was about to do.

"We both know what that means," I said again, wiping my sleeve over my wet cheeks. "The person who killed Paolo and Sandy is out there"—I motioned toward the window—"and I've already found where he lives."

Cal lowered his voice, but his eyes looked awake, even hopeful. "You told the police, I'm sure. They won't waste any time."

I shook my head, rubbing my cold hands together. "I don't know."

He asked me the same questions Detective Mason had—how I knew where Sandy lived, what the deal was with her coming to me as a patient. I told him the whole narrative, including my unsettling meeting with Matt, as well as Sandy's full story. What I knew of it, anyway.

His eyes pinched up a little. "The police are good, Emily. They won't play. They'll jump on this." Cal's eagerness made me feel slightly less insane. He was leaning forward now, chest pressed against the table. "They're probably talking to him now."

"I don't know."

"You keep saying that. What don't you know?"

"Cal, think about it. I have Sandy's story, but that's basically it. She's not here to tell it. And it's a story about a jealous coworker? A few equations and order forms on a lab computer? They have a washed-out crime scene that I walked through. The strongest connection between the two of them is me."

Cal responded like he hadn't heard the last part of what I'd said. "They have enough to look at Matt."

"*If* that's what they were thinking." I held up my palm. "They have me with a cut on my hand as if Sandy and I had a fight, touching everything. Touching her." Sandy's empty eyes charged my thoughts. I fought the images, wiped the newest round of tears, tried to stay in the coffee shop. "They have a different story right now."

His head leaned slightly. Deep and intelligent, his combat-shocked voice understood. "They have a story about an affair."

I nodded jerkily. A bird's nod.

"The more obvious motive."

I continued ahead, so he wouldn't have to say the rest. "A more obvious motive for a jealous, crazy person, a pill popper with a criminal record. A psycho who's been hospitalized."

Cal bit his lip, wincing on the truth. He scraped the tile with his brown boot, looked at his watch. "No, if you're not involved, they'll clear you fast. Right? This isn't your life under investigation."

"Cal, of course I'm not involved." I put my hand on his, a reflex.

Not sleeping had lowered my boundaries.

He squeezed it, pulled back.

I plunged on. "But how long will they wait? Until after Matt destroys any evidence? Sandy wanted to go slowly so he wouldn't know to cover his tracks any better than he already had. With this, now, he's scared. I need . . . to find what there is on him."

Cal bit one of his nails, shook his head.

"I'll say this another way—he's leaving the country Sunday morning. He's going to that conference with Silver. Do you understand? He leaves and he's not coming back. Two days. Cal, even if the police find something on him later, once he's gone, he's gone. A potential double murderer gets away."

"Emily, it's not—"

"Two days. Cal, help me."

"Emily, let the police work."

He looked at his watch. I dug in deeper. "You won't help me catch the guy who killed your best friend?"

Cal raised his chin, dropped it again. "I can't. Really can't.

I'm—look, I should be in my office right now. I have Olivia. I hate that this is happening, but it's not my place. I can't get involved in this." He pressed his hands back on the table.

I stared at him.

"Emily."

"What time do you pick up Olivia?" I asked.

"Look, I'm not your doctor, but you should get some sleep. The police will—"

"Cal, what time does Olivia get home from school today?"

A slow, hesitant blink—a part of him reluctant to reveal how available he was to help. "She's with her mom this week."

My hands were fists. "Cal, please."

He looked again at the door; then he unzipped his jacket and rubbed his hands over his forehead. When he looked up from his hands again, his expression was disbelief, near-complete incredulity. "What would we even do?"

"All you have to do is watch out for me."

"Uh-huh. Watch out how? Where?"

I dragged my fingertip through the meek condensation on the window, creating a dewy line through which a fraction more of the outside world was clear. Then I smeared it all with my palm, droplets forming and running down toward the baseboards. "Just make sure no one's coming when I steal a computer from the lab."

———

Cal agreed to meet me later. "In the meantime, get some sleep," he'd said.

I lied and said that I would.

I texted Allie. *I have to see you.*

No response.

Like that was going to stop me.

I drove to her office. I'd wait.

It was almost possible to believe nothing had happened—that Sandy was still alive, even that Paolo was. Tacit normalcy—the texture of wet gravel beneath the soles of my shoes, the hovering haze of cloud cover, midmorning traffic sounds. The steady light inside the Burger King sign. All normal, oblivious, encouraging in a strange way.

Thinking this way meant I was tired.

The rain had cleared and cooled the air. Shallow puddles rippled on the rain-slick asphalt. I leaned against Allie's car in the same precinct parking lot I'd left ten hours earlier. It was a four-door Honda Accord. A married person's car—in that inoffensive champagne-silver color that was pleasant enough but no one noticed. I rested my hands on the hood, wondering if I would ever drive anything like it, live the way Allie lived.

I watched the shifting, cerebral folds of the clouds, my fingernails tapping the cool metal, until I heard Allie's voice behind me.

"Um, no," she scolded. "No way. Jump up off my car 'cause I am not talking to you. Not right now."

This voice she was using was brand-new to me—not a teammate holler across a sun-bright field, nor her confessional whisper in the fleeing-ghost highway lights of a team bus. And not her supportive, professional voice. This tone was ripe with intolerance—a voice for inmates. Or for someone ignorant requiring firm redirection.

Again, the feeling of unreality.

The car's signal lights flashed yellow as she used her remote key to open the Accord. She strode toward the door like she had no intention of stopping.

My arms were folded. I didn't budge off the hood as she reached past me. "Come on, Allie."

"I mean it—no. Don't put me in this position. A, I can't legitimately even talk to you, and B, what are you even doing here? You should not be here."

I'd thought initially that Allie's voice was a voice for arrestees but realized right then it was from burnout. It was the tone used by people who had helped me too much and had stopped caring. People

I'd worn out. I hadn't heard it from anyone in years, but the sound was the same. The content hardly mattered—the tone told me a person's involvement had departed, and that it was entirely my fault.

"Where should I be?" I asked, really wanting to hear her answer.

She twisted her lips, as if tasting something bitter.

My hands were glued to her car. "Just tell me one thing: are they going to find him? That's all I need to know. Are they going to question Matt?"

She glanced over her shoulder as a crisp-uniformed officer clicked along the sidewalk, smiling as she gave him a quick wave. The smile dropped as she turned her face back to me. Her voice lowered to a forced whisper. "Emily, I'm not a source, okay? I'm not giving you the inside scoop. But you know that, right? You didn't want to mention all the hiring evals you've done for Metro?" Her eyebrows were up, accusingly.

Word traveled fast, apparently.

It was my turn to roll my eyes, even if I was too jacked-up and exhausted to explain. "That was years ago, and it's getting blown out of proportion. I may have picked up a few procedural things here and there, but—"

She held up her hand. "Enough. Really. You know more than enough about police work. Finding that out made me look stupid after I protected you. You don't need my protection."

"I need you to listen."

"I need you to go home. Emily, you don't look good."

"What I really need," I said, "is for you to trust me."

"I'm not in a position to do that." Allie backed up a step, hands on the hips of her skirt. "Not now."

I knew there was no point in acting indignant. Three months earlier, I would have kept the same distance if our roles had somehow been reversed, served my patients and my department, trusted my professional colleagues to do their jobs. "Do you really . . . really think I . . . ?"

"No, it's not my job to think one way or another. My job is to communicate with the public. That's it. And that includes maintaining a wide professional boundary from anyone under active investigation. Which is why I'm asking you again to get off my car."

I stood but remained between her and the door. "Allie—"

"No. Don't start." She was shaking her head, eyes closed. "Nope, no. There's no *for old times' sake*, no *team rules* anymore. I've already said and done too much."

"You have, and I appreciate it, I do. I just need to know one thing. Just one *yes* or *no*."

She opened her eyes. I could feel the old-friend conflict behind that mask. She saw two Emilys—the one she knew and the one she suddenly couldn't trust. If anyone understood feeling suspicious, it was me.

"Just one *yes* or *no*. You're speaking to a concerned member of the public."

A car splashed past. Neither of us moved. Autumn's last sun-yellow leaves clung to wild-angled gray branches like reluctant angels behind her. She nodded.

"Is Detective Mason, or anyone, going to go after Matt?"

Allie took a deep breath and held it in her chest. Then, finally, she confirmed exactly what I'd suspected. "Several interviews were conducted. At this time, there is only one person of interest in that particular case."

There seemed no real path back toward usual adult life; just a pursuit in the general direction of justice, which now needed to happen. My own drop, my fall from the path, had been so sickeningly steep, I wondered what would unravel next, what even remained that *could* unravel. I'd been a soon-to-be-engaged child psychologist. Now I was a double-murder suspect. My stomach felt achy, purposeless, like some ancillary organ my body no longer required. Despite her death, a small part of me struggled to make sense of Paolo and Sandy having been together, of what I'd missed, and of what it had felt like for her to hide their relationship when she came to see me. How significant was it that they'd been together? Could I trust what she'd told me? Or did it make her even more trustworthy?

I dropped my hand onto Allie's wrist and she let it rest there, just for a second, before yanking it back. I touched her shoulder, then abruptly, she left. Allie's taillights bobbed as her Accord dipped out of the parking lot toward who-knew-where. Toward away from me.

In my truck, I set my lips on the cold, plastic Breathalyzer. I knew already what I was about to do was probably a very, very bad idea. But that awareness in my thoughts was like a whisper, drowned out by the roar of what I meant to do.

NINETEEN

I turned the ignition and texted Cal: LEAVING THE POLICE STATION, HEADED TO THE LAB.

Knowing Cal thought of me as crazy offered a kind of bleak reassurance. No need to worry about it. I pictured him squinting irritably at the message or stone-faced, disinterested. My fingertip hovered above the screen, then typed: NOT TO BREAK IN.

I paused, then added: NECESSARILY.

An ellipsis appeared immediately, as if he'd been looking at his phone.

Cal: COME PICK ME UP. SAME STARBUCKS.

Had he thought of something? He'd seemed so reluctant two hours earlier. A quick drive across town, during which I realized I'd never really expected his help, and that I'd resigned myself to going it alone. Of all the people, I thought, of all the partners, it had to be the guy who hated me; the monosyllabic Marine Corps vet with whom I had basically nothing in common. Then, a fleeting but acute sadness for not having known my father, for life presenting such unexpected companions. That was no medication talking. That was no sleep.

Cal showed himself to be a man of few words, but I didn't need a lengthy explanation for why he'd responded to my text. I could feel the change as the passenger door creaked open. He climbed in beside me, a whiff of Irish Spring soap and cool air. He glanced at my uncle's gun rack behind us. "It's just two days till he leaves?" he asked, abruptly.

"Two days," I echoed.

"So, if there's anything to find out about this guy, we'll know pretty quickly—forty-eight hours."

"That's right."

Cal fixed his jaw determinedly, as if it was just then that he'd truly decided to help. "Okay, I'm in. Let's do this."

I started to thank Cal, but he shook his head. I could see no real thanks were needed. With the pieces in front of him, he needed the same answers I did. I held back from overselling and pulled into the drive-through line, which advanced at a glacial pace. I remembered him telling me earlier that Olivia was spending the week with her mom. Even hardly knowing him, it was plain I was now interacting with a previous version of Cal—a military guy, a devoted friend. No cynical pragmatism of daily professional life. No parenting responsibilities.

Cal scratched contemplatively at his beard. "So, how are you planning on walking in and out of the lab without that guy Matt noticing you took his computer?"

"That's where things get hazy." I hated to admit it.

"So there's basically no plan?"

"I'll improvise."

The drive-through line advanced and we moved forward another place in line. Cal didn't have to say the obvious: improvisation wouldn't work.

His hands were folded in his lap. "Um, maybe we should brainstorm?"

"Did you want some coffee?"

"How long since you've slept?" he answered.

Sleep. I kept forgetting. I had to think. "Night before last, some."

He extracted a canvas wallet, began peeling apart the Velcro. I waved it away, ordering into a crackling speaker for us both. A minute later, steam rose from our paper cups. I knew the coffee would scald my tongue and it did—the pain graciously jolting me, caffeine to follow.

Cool air flooded the half-open window as I drove.

"You work in IT, right? We need Matt's computer, bottom line. Once we have it, can you hack in?"

Cal sighed a little. "Truthfully, yes. I probably could get in pretty easily. But we can't just march in and commandeer the thing. Do you know anyone else in that lab?"

"I don't think so." Only fragments remained in my memory of the other lab mates—stories I'd half heard, general descriptions. No one who would remember me, let alone believe me or grant an extremely self-compromising favor. "If that lab was a normal place, I'd say there'd be no telling who was even there working today, who would have stayed after finding out about Sandy. But they're a different breed up there. They work even more when they're burning off stress. Do you know any of them?" I asked. "Like from softball?"

"Nah."

"I met Dr. Silver . . . once."

Cal's eyebrows crinkled.

"The PI." His image came to mind—his tight gray beard and curious eyes. Warm, welcoming voice.

"Ah. That's right."

Cal began scrolling through the medical center website on his phone, navigating the directory.

Worry reawakened from a moment earlier. "What if Matt has deleted or destroyed everything that would incriminate him?"

A hollow whistle rose from Cal blowing into his plastic lid. Down West End, the skyline cut the clouds like a black line on an Etch A Sketch. "I wouldn't worry about that part," he said. "Anything can be found, trust me."

I was staring at him, trying to drive. Air pressure rocked the truck in a curt whoosh. I looked up as the doppler-fade of a horn screamed in the other direction. Taillights. A near miss.

Pay attention.

Cal looked at me.

"Sorry," I said.

An accident would be checkmate, even if no one was hurt. Even manic, I knew this. Cal's finger reached the final name on the list, halting at a hyperlinked email and phone number beside it. He started to speak as I plucked the phone from his hand, my finger touching down. This was right. We were calling the person I should have called first, even before Cal—the person Paolo most admired and trusted.

The truck engine growled irritably over the ringing. I was forming something like an introduction when I heard his phone beep—a medical center number calling in. I pressed green.

A slight pause before Jay Silver's voice came across the line, inquisitive but not impatient. I could only imagine the chaos there, and what it might be like to lose two coworkers within a month. "Hello?" he said.

I launched into what I'd meant to leave as a voicemail. "Dr. Silver, this is Emily Firestone. Sorry to just look you up like this. Paolo Fererra was my boyfriend. I need to talk with you." Wound up, I felt like I sounded about sixteen years old, words rushing like water. "I know—I mean, I can't imagine everything going on right now . . ."

"Oh, hi," he said, eventually. He sounded worn, like an exhausted family member acting polite. I pictured his round glasses propped onto his forehead, him rubbing his temples. "I remember, of course. Firestone. Well . . . okay. I just don't know when. It's a bad time. I'd planned to present a paper out of town, but some things have happened . . ." He started with mid-December dates when he might be available. He might as well have suggested waiting a decade. I flashed to Sandy's eyes staring up through the ceiling, the steering wheel slick under my palm.

Slow down.

"It has to be today. It's important. I'm sorry."

I could practically see him checking his watch but noticed he wasn't saying no. "It's almost lunchtime, and I have a meeting at one. I could meet for a few minutes, maybe on the way. Can you walk with me?"

"Great." I gave a thumbs-up to Cal.

"How well do you know campus?"

"Just say where," I said.

Cal reached over and flipped the truck's clunky signal as we headed down the hill. We parked and walked. It had been years since I'd been in the central campus but little had changed. The brick facade of the athletic dorm, where I'd lived for four years, rose familiarly above the trees. In the courtyard, I leaned against a statue of a bronze coed who stared off inscrutably, a book resting lazily in her lap. I smoothed my clothes.

The courtyard itself was vintage picturesque Vanderbilt, an arboretum arranged beneath a dome of unreality. Undergrads called campus the *Vander-bubble* for a reason. It insulated them. Inside existed the Disneyesque sense that wealth and beauty simply forbade bad things from happening. Waxy magnolia leaves fluttered as if preprogrammed. Beyond their canopy, the gray sky towered limitlessly. Even the vague imperfections seemed like calculated elements of charm.

I heard Silver's footsteps before we saw him. Sunlight flashed on his glasses, giving the appearance that they were lit from within. The energetic, paternal man I'd met a year earlier slumped, a hint of a skeptical smile tugging at his lips as he descended the stone walk. I wondered how much I might have alarmed him with the urgency of my phone call earlier, but then I guessed he was used to harried researchers working deadlines. I wondered if he'd registered my absence at Paolo's funeral. We went through the business of introductions between him and Cal.

"I'm sorry," he said. "I'm very off. We had a terrible tragedy last night. I'm reeling, frankly. I don't know which end is up. A tragedy after a tragedy." Only then did I hear the full weight of what had happened in his voice, ribbons of emotion cutting through. He touched his wristwatch, head swaying exhaustedly as he turned to walk.

My boot tapped the path, his pace obviously slowed to accommodate mine. Beside us, a wave of leaves glittered like a school of fish.

"That's why we're here," I told him. "I was the one who found Sandy."

It stopped him abruptly, the surprise. He looked at me, blinking. "I'm so sorry," he said. "I didn't know you knew her."

"I actually didn't know her very well, but—"

"We go around the clock to deadlines—it's a lot of pressure." He shook his head. "There's a conference we're all going to. First trip as a group in a long time. I begged her to go. I thought she needed it—a break, a chance to come together. She wouldn't consider it." He sounded close to crying, his voice trailing off. "She told me she was taking some medication. I knew she'd been . . . down. I could see it. They said she was in her bath."

"Yes," I said.

"But it wasn't an accident," Cal chimed in behind us, almost startling me.

"She didn't commit suicide, Dr. Silver," I said, struggling to find the exact words, the professional language Sandy had used. "She told me three days ago about something she'd seen in your lab. Data, tests that had been run twice with some slight variations."

"I'm sorry?" Silver seemed lost suddenly, as if he'd retreated into fatigue and grief.

I reached for his forearm. "Sandy came to my office earlier this week. She told me she'd seen something that made her think Paolo had been murdered. Last night, she called me terrified; now she's gone."

He winced, hand on his stomach, like I'd knocked the wind out of him.

I retold the story of Sandy's visit, realizing that each time I did, it sounded more implausible—like a lie I needed to expand to keep covering the gaps. Then I said his name: "Matt Cianciolo."

Silver's head cocked, just slightly, when he heard it. I told him what Sandy had seen, what she'd wanted to get back to.

"I think he killed her," I said, jumping to the only conclusion that made any sense to me. "She found something in Matt's work. Double records. She thought he could be selling the research."

From the clock tower, the hourly chime rang. Students began to pass between buildings, mostly gazing into their phones. A small group approached, and we cleared the path, stepping onto the soft, emerald-colored grass.

Dr. Silver lowered his voice, defensively. "Take my word for one thing—there are no double records in my lab. I'm absolutely sure of that." He paused, seeming to recall something before returning to his protective tone, like I'd pushed too far with so direct an accusation. "I hate to think about what Sandy was going through before last night. Maybe she was more depressed and overworked than anyone realized. It makes me feel terrible. The police also asked about Matt. I'm assuming you told them about him? To look into Matt Cianciolo?"

"Yes—" I said, barely able to temper my impatience.

"I told them what I'm telling you." He again dropped his voice, his eyes taking a slightly scolding glint. "There is no way Matt would harm anyone. Zero chance."

I could feel Cal's presence behind me and was grateful he was there. His shadow felt like a guardrail keeping me from spinning off course. Insistence poured out of me. "It's not a coincidence that both she and Paolo died, Dr. Silver. She thought Matt was doing something illegal—" I began to stammer.

Dr. Silver recoiled. "There are a lot of personalities in that small space. I . . . maybe I shouldn't say any more. I don't know why I'm being so open." He glanced suspiciously at Cal, then back at me. "You must be very good at your job, Dr. Firestone, but I really should go."

I ignored the jab—I was used to the weird and squirmy ways in which some people thought of psychologists. "Was Matt at work last night? Just tell me that."

Silver's lips tightened.

I pressed on, "I—somebody has to find out what's in his computer and get it to Detective Andre Mason. He knows all about it, all about it." My words were starting to rush, to pressure ahead, like typos in a sentence typed too fast.

Dr. Silver's brown, professorial shoes retreated slightly, his heels meeting the rolling shade cast by a magnolia tree. Behind him, swaying leaves let through bursts of sunlight; camera flashes from an old movie.

I stepped ahead, erasing the distance he'd just created. I was practically pleading. "How would someone access that computer?"

His eyes dropped, eyebrows raised, as if searching for a trivia answer. "The only person who could would be me. We're on a closed network, but I can look at anyone's work." He paused for a second before starting away, adding, shortly, "And I will, thank you. I'll look. I'm in touch with the detective, Mason."

I reached out as if I were hooking on to him. "No, look, I need to know what's there."

Silver stumbled, nearly tripping backward. "And I need to protect my lab," he informed me. "Look, I'm sorry for what you've been through. I didn't know you knew Sandy, too. But I'm not drawing any conclusions. If there's something on Matt's computer, I'll know."

I had the sensation of forgetting how to talk. Cal looked on silently.

"I'm sorry," Silver said, "but I really can't imagine him doing anything like what you're suggesting. And now, I'm sorry again, but I have to go."

He disappeared into campus, his pace expressing regret for having met with us.

Birds calling from the fire-and-apricot-colored trees. Then, a second of silence. The walkways quiet again after the class change.

"That went well," Cal observed, his facetiousness barely perceptible. "Think he'll just let us in?"

"Oh, shut up."

"I don't think we completely freaked him out—not completely. Pretty close, though."

I replayed what Silver had said in my mind. I turned toward Cal. "Sandy told me Matt takes that laptop with him everywhere."

"Okay . . ."

"That means he takes it to his apartment."

"No." Cal shook his head. "No way."

"I know right where it is," I said, grabbing the sleeve of his jacket as I started toward the truck.

TWENTY

Cal insisted I try to sleep. Walking back to the truck, he looked into the fever dream in my rabbit eyes and said I'd crash without it. Said he'd seen sleep deprivation in the field, soldiers eschewing judgment for impulse, real paranoia.

"If you want to get this done," he told me, "you have to shut down. This isn't a straight line." Mission strategy.

He's in on it. He's distracting you.

Still, enough of me knew he was right that I agreed.

I closed my eyes, but it wasn't real sleep—not the kind when your mind winds down, or flicks off, or goes wherever it goes. This sleep was the kind where your eyes close but your thoughts persist like a rolling boil. The ceiling fan blew over me, curtains holding back the gray midday tide of fall. Only a dull awareness remained that I hadn't really worked in more than a month and that I had a checking account that was basically empty.

When I couldn't take any more, I texted him. I fed Andy, showered in a scalding rush, swallowed six Advil for my ankle, consumed an overripe banana, and sat in a sweatshirt on the front steps until Cal's royal-blue 240 Volvo appeared—the kind that looks like a cross between a tank and a shoebox.

"Seat belt," he said.

"Cal." I shook my head.

"Fine. Are you open to an idea that doesn't involve us breaking in anywhere?" His tone sounded hopeful that a few hours' sleep might have provided me some wisdom.

"*We're* not breaking in," I informed him. "I am."

"Uh-uh, not smart. Think about that, Emily. You can hardly walk. You're not ready for special forces tonight. Sandy said he carries the laptop around with him, right? What we're looking for is an opportunity. Maybe it'll be easy; maybe he's careless."

He doesn't believe you. It's a trick; he's wasting your time.

Just then, I realized I'd forgotten my Lamictal.

I shook it off.

Take it later, I thought. We have forty-six hours.

I sighed. "So, you just want to be what—like, on a stakeout?"

"Yeah, if we—no, if you—just smash and grab, anyone would just call the police. If you actually want to get this done," he said, "we're going to have to follow him out of the lab. And then wait. Patience."

Patience: something I was known to not have.

Cal shifted the manual transmission into gear and the engine hummed reluctantly, as if cautious about what it was being asked to do.

"Am I imagining things," I ventured as he drove, "or is this a different boxy Volvo than the one you were driving the last time I saw you?"

Cal seemed content not to elaborate as we passed the street-parked cars and neat houses in Mom's neighborhood. "No, you're right. I have a few."

I knew I had to trust Cal. I was in free fall, in an incomprehensible amount of trouble. Everything at once was too much to think about—I couldn't. But when I considered Mom, Marty, what they would say if they knew, the sensation was vertigo.

"Okay," I said. "Let's watch for a while."

I directed Cal to a metered spot on the road that lined the medical center parking lot. I knew that area very well, having waited hungrily there many times for Paolo to finish his day. For half a second, I swooned for the incomprehensible luxury of leisurely waiting for my boyfriend with a paperback on my lap, the challenge of reading by variable streetlight my most pressing problem.

In my memory, I could still hear Paolo's voice as he leaned into the car. Him asking teasingly, "Would you mind giving me a ride? I don't live far from here."

The Volvo chugged to a halt. Cal cut the engine, took his phone from his pocket, quickly checked his messages, and laid it on the dashboard. He scanned right, then left, then looked in the rearview mirror a long time.

"Anyone who leaves the lab comes out that exit." I pointed to the silver, space-age overhang, curved like an enormous frown. "That's the only obvious way in or out."

"You'll recognize him?"

"Of course," I said. I hoped.

Of course you will.

We waited. People passed—purposeful shadows moving between cars—unaware of being watched. Cal settled into silence that he seemed content to maintain. The seat belt made a metallic clicking noise as I released it and settled back into the seat. I looked around. For an older car, it was impeccably neat. I thought back to the crushed cups on the floorboards of the truck I'd been driving, the spiderweb crack in the windshield, the exterior that had maybe never been washed. The Breathalyzer, for God's sake.

Half an hour passed. Occasionally, Cal popped a joint—his thumb, his shoulder.

I was too wound up not to talk. About something, anything.

"You seem to have a thing for Volvos," I said.

He answered evenly, "I started with just the one, then I realized I just kept working on it after it was fixed. So, I bought another one, parked it right beside the first. I kept meaning to sell one. Didn't get around to it. I kept going from there."

Something told me getting around to selling the cars wasn't a high priority.

"Have you done it long?"

"No, just since I got back."

He meant from the war.

"It's relaxing." He shrugged. "I don't know. I hung around the mechanics a lot on the FOB and learned a few things. It's like solving a puzzle. Satisfying when you finish one. There's something to show for your work. You fixed something. Somebody gets to drive away because of something you did. Besides, they're very safe cars," he informed me, as if this was a brand-new idea.

My eyes glued to the building's exit, I tried to recall whether I'd ever successfully fixed anything approaching the complexity of a car. "It's impressive, for sure," I said.

"I know it's not really conventional—living out on a farm, fixing up old cars. Most people think it's pretty weird."

"You should hang around me more." I laughed. I had to. "I make everyone around me seem *pretty* normal."

Talking like this was what we could do to not think about Paolo, or too deeply about what we were doing. We were quiet again, watching shadows. Fifteen minutes. Twenty.

"Sorry," he said. "I'm quiet. I'm not used to being around people that much."

"Well, we're here. We may as well talk."

"I don't talk much. I mainly keep to myself."

"Then you probably have a lot to talk about."

He looked at me.

"Humor me. Come on, waiting is making me want to crawl out of my skin."

He thought for a second. "Are you gonna bill me?"

"Totally," I said. "Okay, so . . . the Marines. How long were you in the Marines?"

"About eight years. Straight out of high school to pay for college. Which it eventually did, just not the most efficient route."

Only then did I notice the clear cord wrapped around the outside of his ear like a thick thread of fishing line. A hearing aid.

"Where were you stationed?" I asked uncertainly. I'd done a VA rotation during my internship year but had been in a hurry to get to my work at the children's clinic. What little I'd learned about military life and terminology had departed my memory like the forgetting of a dream.

"Fort Hood, Fort Campbell, mainly. Then training—North Carolina, Georgia. But you're asking if I deployed. Twice to Afghanistan."

His window was cracked, but he rolled it down farther. The bottom edges of the windshield had begun to fog.

I wanted him to keep talking but didn't quite know what to ask. "What was it like?" I said, eventually. I was prepared for him to snap back at me; I half expected it. But he pursed his lips thoughtfully, popped the knuckle of his index finger. I had the feeling that Cal's resting pulse rate never rose above sixty beats per minute anymore.

"No one's ever asked me that before," he answered.

"Um, that can't be true. Weren't you married?" The question sounded impossibly naive the instant it left my mouth. I wanted it back, but it was too late.

A fraction of a smile, like a crescent moon. He shook his head almost imperceptibly. "I'd rather talk about Afghanistan," he said. "Which was . . . crazy and mundane and everything all at once. It's hard to describe to someone who wasn't there. I know it's strange, but in a way, I miss it. I don't mean I want to go back. Really, I don't and I wouldn't. I mean, I have Olivia, but life there is simple. You survive. You follow orders. It's one day, then the next day, then the next day. You do your job. It's a lot easier than civilian life in a lot of ways. People out here in the civilian world are insane—there are no rules."

I didn't want to say so, but I couldn't help but think about what he was doing right then in that context. A part of me wondered what it was like to live day-to-day without feeling really alive. Another part didn't have to wonder.

"You had some hearing loss?" I asked.

His eyes closed for just a second as the memory seemed to hit him, just a very long blink as it came back. He turned his head, gritted his teeth. "Yeah, I did." Hard for him to admit, I could see.

"Then you went to school after all, when you got back?"

"Right into computers. The work was easier than what I'd

already done. Sitting in the classrooms was hard. I was always watching the door, couldn't talk to anyone. One day, one of the kids—because they looked like kids—he was maybe eighteen? Started saying everyone who'd served in Iraq and Afghanistan should be tried for war crimes and thrown in jail."

"You lost it?" I guessed.

"Yeah," he admitted, shyly. "I knocked over his desk, grabbed him by the collar. He looked terrified. I was in a blind rage; I'd never felt like that before. The professor called campus police. Nothing really happened—I explained what he said and they dropped it, gave me a warning. I sat in the back of the room for the rest of the semester, tried to finish as much as I could online after that. I'd reconnected with Olivia's mom by then."

"I wasn't going to ask."

"She's something else. It's definitely all about her. High school girlfriend, reconnected on Facebook. Amazing singing voice, and she knows it. There's a reason we're not married anymore. Two reasons, actually. Part of it was her wanting to tour all the time, and part was me, definitely. I try not to let little things get to me, but it's a little like having two kids sometimes. Actually, softball used to be my place to just relax."

Hearing that was a surprise. I remembered how seriously he took every part of the game. Paolo and I had laughed.

"But she's basically a good mom when she's here. I just stay ready all the time because she flakes out. We split the time with Olivia. My ex lives in a condo off Thirty-First Street, maybe two blocks from your office, I think."

It was practically across the Alleyway.

"After we split, I went back out—toward where I grew up." Cal motioned westward, saying the name of a neighboring county near my family's cabin.

I could imagine him on a porch on summer mornings—warm, sunlit grass rolling in airbrushed waves around him.

"It's a ways out there, isn't it?"

"It suits me," he answered simply. "And Olivia's got the best of

both worlds—there are ten acres and a stream behind my house; she
runs around the woods on the weekends. And then she's close to her
friends when she's in town with her mom. That's a nice thing about
Nashville," Cal added. "Ten minutes outside of town you can still
be out in the woods."

When he said the country road he lived on, I realized our property was less than a mile away. "We have a place out there—my
family," I said. It was the first moment I thought Cal and I weren't
basically polar opposites of each other. "Hickory Road, halfway
between Cedar and Poplar."

"Oh, sure," he remembered. "Out by where that big oak got
struck by lightning last summer. Flames a hundred feet high."

"That's it, that's the place. The driveway is a hundred feet past
that point. That's our cabin. I was there . . . with Paolo the night of
the fire. We watched it burning from the window. He was the one
who called the fire department."

Hearing Paolo's name made Cal's head turn, the way a dog's
ears perk toward a distant sound. "I remember that night. Really?
Your place?"

"Yeah."

It did seem like a crazy coincidence. Then again, Nashville
could feel like a tiny town the longer you lived there. Revisiting
that night from six months earlier felt like hearing about someone
else's dream. I pictured the embers, the shotgun over the mantel,
the fear in Paolo's eyes. I'd had a sense then that anything could
happen.

Cal seemed to be considering the memory, and the idea of my
family's land. Or maybe the mention of Paolo's name had quieted
him. Beside me in the car—reflective, frustrated, anxious in the
tangerine streetlight—he looked like what he probably was: a man
deep into his thirties, creases cut around his mouth, life's losses
haunting his eyes. He wasn't sitting outside the medical center out
of curiosity.

Then he said, "I can't tell if you think he's dead."

"Do you?"

Outside, the wind blew, and the shadow of the branch above the car moved over the dashboard. Then it was still.

Cal looked me in the eyes and spoke quietly. "Yeah, I do."

Inside, I felt something collapse, like a small paper bag being crumpled. I knew what Sandy thought had happened to Paolo, but Cal had the objectivity of having never met with her. Cal would not tell me something untrue, I realized then. I trusted him.

"I'm sorry," he said softly. "It's what I think. It's why I'm here. I want to find out what happened to him."

"No, no." I started wiping my eyes. "Don't apologize. When I'm in a different role, when I'm a psychologist, I tell people things they don't want to hear because sometimes they need to be told." I thought of Marty's words to me, years earlier, urging me to be careful and kind in dismantling a person's supports, even if they were false.

"And I'm sorry I ever blamed you at all," he said.

I rested my hand on his shoulder as we watched in silence then as people passed under the frown-shaped entrance. I understood Cal's wanting to remediate the helplessness of loss. Anger comes from feeling powerless.

"What's he look like?" Cal asked, suddenly refocusing. "Matt?"

Just as he asked, a person emerged from the far end of the parking lot, their shape visible in flashes between the parked cars and hedges. The person I was about to describe—his hair, his slouch—strode quickly along the walkway.

I grabbed Cal's arm. "That's him!" I pointed. "There he is."

The building's upward lighting cast a shadow twice Matt's size over the sharp lines of steel and glass.

Cal sat up, turned the key, shifted the Volvo into reverse and waited until a set of red brake lights appeared through an ashy puff of exhaust at the far end of the lot.

We followed him. Cal kept one car length between Matt's and ours but never lost sight of the tail end of Matt's American sedan, even as he turned into the parking lot of the supermarket where my mom shopped. Somewhere during that drive it had become nighttime—the late afternoon giving way to darkness. Lights atop towers washed out the parking lot in that not-quite-blue, not-quite-white unnatural color there's no name for.

Cal seemed to know better than to ask what I was doing once we parked. I heaved closed the Volvo door, supposing he was going to wait, my cane and boot scraping along the flawless supermarket asphalt. Better I go alone, I thought, my eyes focused on the back of Matt—his gray hooded sweatshirt. Was it the same one he'd worn at the party? That seemed too coincidental to be possible, like a careless repetition in a stage production.

Maybe because I associated the store with my mother, or because he seemed to be wearing the same clothes I'd seen him in nearly a year before, we both seemed out of place. I stopped and peered inside his car, seeing nothing that looked like a computer bag. Was he carrying it with him? I supposed it was possible. Would I just grab it if he left it in a cart and run out of the store? Even I knew that was crazy, but I needed to look, anyway. I needed to watch his movements, to know what he was buying. I needed to observe this person who'd derailed my life and ended two others. Who'd killed my love.

Inside was ultra-bright. My eyes adjusted hazily; my hands turned the cold handle of a cart I grabbed as a prop. People passed as if on tracks—automatons.

I followed the back of Matt's head, moving swiftly past orange and yellow balloons, among the impossible citrus pyramids, ignoring the sense that someone was watching me as I watched Matt, peering out from behind counters and cardboard displays.

You're paranoid. Concentrate.

The even sobriety of Cal's company from only a few minutes before was suddenly absent—as if I'd been tethered before and on my own I'd gone adrift. The proximity to Matt was an intoxicant, dizzying. What would I do if he turned and faced me?

I pictured the obviousness of my dawdling.

He'd moved when I looked up, half hidden by a display. I slipped into an aisle, picked up a box of something—cookies—and pretended to read it. People pushed past like the flow of water, but

I could feel their curious glances. I was in someone's way, maybe everyone's way.

Matt moved to the next aisle, and I hurried in the direction he'd turned. Overhead lights reflected off everything blindingly, like lying in a dentist's chair. I found the back of his head again as someone moved behind me, the way they had before. I moved, then they moved. *It's just your imagination.* I wanted to look but my eyes were on Matt, who dropped something—pasta—into his cart, then a jar of olives.

I shuffled ahead, felt the movement behind me again. I saw only ordinary people. My eyes flew over the words on boxes, displays. My chest burned, but I wasn't afraid; I was afraid he would get away. The plastic cart handle had warmed under my hands.

A shadow followed me, I was sure of it. Where was Matt? He'd turned the other way, back toward where he started. Over my shoulder, I watched him walk. Overhead, the store manager announced a special. Something on sale. Something new to try.

I got closer. When he moved away from his cart, I could see no computer bag lying there. No odd items, just things anyone would buy. Nothing different, unusual. I felt crazy. Someone ducked into an aisle. I turned and knocked into a teenage clerk, his expression cautious, apologetic, palms up, like he'd caused what he saw in my eyes.

"It's okay," I told him. "My fault."

I circled back to the front of the store. Footsteps sounded like thunder inside my head. Thunder from a snowstorm. I'd watch him leave, then we'd follow. I'd be patient. I'd wait.

The shadow moved behind me.

When I looked back and tried to place it, it was gone.

My cart collided with Matt's. His lips tightened, his eyes absent any spark of recognition. The package he was holding fell. Fruit—blueberries—scattered across the chalk-colored floor like marbles.

I couldn't look away. I couldn't breathe in. I gripped the cart like I might swing it at him. "You son of a bitch," I said.

He moved his cart ahead, shaking his head, pushing mine aside. I turned, reached for his collar, ready to rip him around.

A hand was on my shoulder. I nearly swung.

A manager in a cheerful green polo. A tidy name tag. "Whoa." He laughed a quiet, halting laugh. Now he looked nervous, too. "Everything okay?"

The clerk I'd run into a minute earlier was beside him. They'd talked about me, I could tell. "Let me help you with this." The clerk was leaning down, scooping the berries into one hand. He looked happy to not be alone with me.

"Are you having some trouble this afternoon? There . . . anything we can do to help out?" He could see the tears forming in my eyes. Rage.

The shadows seemed washed away.

"Can I get you something?" the manager asked. He meant coffee, a place to sit. He wanted to get me out of the store.

Breath flooded me as I braced myself on my cart. I had screwed up . . . again.

I turned toward the door and ran.

TWENTY-ONE

Back to the Volvo. The parking lot was a swarm of headlights.

Cal pushed open the car door.

"There wasn't any laptop bag in his car," I said.

"I know: I looked, too."

"And I just made a scene. I saw him. Ran into him. He saw me." I pounded a fist against my thigh, bit my lip with anger.

"It was worth trying," Cal noted, encouragingly. "If it would have been there, it could have been easy. Just taking it."

"He didn't even have it with him. The whole thing seemed stupid. What was I going to do, just grab it and run? Basically steal it? I've never stolen anything in my life."

"So, where to now?" Cal asked.

"Drive by his place?"

"Roger that."

When we got there, Matt's blinds were drawn the way they had been before, touched by only the occasional flick of a shadow.

"What about a diversion?" I said. "Like faking an emergency, pulling a fire alarm or something so that he'd run out and I could run in."

I knew it sounded crazy. Cal blinked at me patiently, seemingly aware that I hardly meant what I was saying. After an hour, he drove me home to Mom's.

Even trying to control my voice, it echoed off the living room hardwoods. Andy's paws clicked across the floor as he trotted between us. I'd left the TV on in the kitchen as I'd rushed out, and the steady drone of electronic voices carried through the house.

"Silver made it sound—"

"I know," Cal said evenly.

"Should we just assume he carries it with him every other time? Every night except this one? I don't get it."

"If I were him, I'd be getting rid of things, not buying soda or chips or whatever. I'd be covering my tracks. I'm just saying, we don't know much about how this research happens. Would Matt really be working on it at home?"

"I don't know," I admitted. "I know it takes a lot of funding and time—a hell of a lot of time." Andy brushed beside me as the clock in the living room chimed. "I mean, it's not as though the virus is brand-new."

"Paolo told me about your father," Cal said. When I hesitated, he shifted in the chair. "Sorry. He told me after that first night. The first American case of H1-N24, right?"

Right, I thought. It made sense Paolo would have mentioned it.

"Do you remember him?"

Cal's directness made my head swivel.

"Yes." I was quiet for a second, then heard myself continue. "He was tall, with kind eyes," I said, discovering that I didn't mind talking about the memories. "He had a calm voice—it was always comfortable to be around him." My fingers began working the bottom hem of my shirt. "Later, he was away a lot, traveling. Far away. Africa. My mom told me he was doing important work."

"That must have been nice to know."

"I resented it, honestly. After the news came, I used to say I hoped I never did anything important at all. I thought doing something important meant you went away. Of course, then I end up dating a guy doing *important* work."

And then he went away.

"On H1-N24," Cal said.

"Of all things," I said.

Cal gestured in the direction of the kitchen. "Okay if I get some water?"

"Oh, God, of course." I pulled out a glass, started filling it from the refrigerator dispenser. "There's food, I think, if you're hungry."

"Just water's fine," Cal said. "But I could eat if you have something."

I glanced inside the refrigerator at the nearly bare shelves, angling the door so Cal couldn't see their emptiness. All that remained was what Mom had left—two sticks of butter, a carton of now-questionable orange juice, and some chardonnay from who-knew-when. Hypomania turned me into a bachelorette. And not the reality-TV kind. I'd last eaten when? I couldn't quite remember. A banana. I'd definitely eaten a banana earlier that day.

Nutrition, I thought. Something I'd get back to.

"A little short on food at the moment," I said, placing the glass in Cal's hand.

I began to follow him back toward the living room when the TV caught my eye. Nashville's skyline appeared on the screen, then an empty field, then highlighter-yellow police tape. Some of the footage I'd seen before. The burn case. National news now. A description of burning skin, temperatures, speculation about someone's unthinkable possible motives.

I saw Allie's text in my mind. The word *serial*.

My mind still whirring about running into Matt, I turned up the volume, listening. My jaw clenched as I fixated on the screen. The same gravel-voiced anchor who talked about flooding in Asia and wildfires in California was now describing wooded areas around Middle Tennessee, tire marks, a state bureau of investigation. The apocalyptic strangeness of a celebrity news anchor saying the names of nearby streets and neighborhoods, talking about a possible serial killer among us.

"This crazy world," I said, unable to stop looking at the TV screen. "The guy in the woods they found burned—they're talking about it on the cable networks now."

In the living room, Cal was quiet.

"Cal? There's something else I haven't told you. You might think it's crazy. There was an image on Paolo's camera."

No reply.

"An image from Gainer Ridge. Do you know that place? It was where that body was found."

More silence. When I walked into the room, I realized Cal had begun pacing the floor.

"Cal?"

"Sorry, I don't like watching that stuff." His voice sounded shaken, angry even.

The news? That case?

Then I got it.

I found the remote, clicked off the TV, and found Cal standing at the end of the couch. He looked ashen. Around us was the faint buzz of sudden silence. I took his hand. He eyed the door like he was going to run.

"Let's sit down," I suggested.

Cal nodded in agreement, wiping the back of his hand across his forehead. "Sorry," he said, "I'm okay."

Circumstances change, but the triggers, and our responses to them, tend to linger. Same response, different setting; difficult to unlearn. It's what kept the person alive before.

I squeezed his hand, which was now cold. "Afghanistan, right?"

Cal reached for the glass of water. "It just happens sometimes. Even a word here or there. A sound, a smell."

I'd heard before of news programs, specific images, as triggers. We'd been talking about the Marines an hour earlier, I realized, part of me wondering if I should have remembered somehow and been more sensitive to what he'd told me.

Cal reached down and softly touched Andy's head. His solitary job and hobby, his country home, all began to make more sense. No alarms, no surprises.

We sat until he felt calmer.

His voice returned to sounding the way it had earlier in the evening. He sipped at the water, hand shaking slightly as he returned it to the coffee table. "I can't believe I'm saying this to a psychologist. My ex asked me to get help for years."

"I can help you get to the right person," I offered, the tiny vocal fluctuations separating personal and professional lives having dissolved. "I know—believe me, I really know—it's not easy."

"Okay, thanks." He raised his hand to stop me. "Another time. We have to focus."

He was right.

I pointed at his wrist. "What's your watch say?"

"Seven o'clock."

Thirty-six hours, I thought.

Think.

My phone chirped, and he jumped, then sank back into the couch. I turned it over, recognizing the caller immediately.

I squeezed Cal's hand. "I'm sorry. I really should take this."

"Go."

"You're okay for a minute?"

He waved me off.

A second later, I was shivering on the front porch, Allie's voice in my ear. The light bulb had burnt out beside the front door. In its absence, shadows spread around my feet like puddles of ink. The night chill reawakened me. Seeing her number made the other half of life come rushing back—I was under investigation. I pictured Allie wearing her expression from earlier, after I'd pushed too hard, asked too much.

"Emily? Can you talk? Is anyone around right now?" She sounded scared, off balance.

I'd walked outside without my shoes, and now, soles on the rough concrete, my feet were freezing. Through the window, I could see Cal tousling Andy's fur, Andy leaning into his touch.

"At the moment, I'm outside. Sorry about before. I didn't mean to just show up."

"Emily, listen . . ."

I was in deeper trouble, I thought. Detective Mason was coming to arrest me. It was only a matter of time.

"I shouldn't be calling you. But I just have to."

I switched from one foot to the other, my toes curling into the denim on my shin.

"Between us?" she asked. "Okay? Team rules?"

I wasn't sure where her newfound trust was coming from. In

the face of everything, it felt all the deeper and somehow humbling. "Of course, team rules. Just us."

A pause as she hesitated.

"You know the burn case you asked me about? Last week?"

"Yeah, of course. It's on TV. We were just watching . . ."

Something told me to go no further, as if raising the stakes might stop her from saying why she'd called. I guessed she'd seen what we just had. I leaned toward the front windows where I could see the dark screen.

Through the phone, I heard the click of her door closing.

"Emily, there's something new. Definitely unexpected." Her words were hurried, like a tape being played slightly too fast. "An hour ago, a burn victim woke up in ICU. He'd been in a coma for two weeks, so the nurse didn't know what to make of what he was saying. They'd thought it was an accident—a lot of meth cases come through there. Accidents, again and again."

I knew this. Hospital budgets, ethical nightmares.

"Okay . . ." I had no idea where she was headed.

"Well, they thought this guy was the same. Country guy, not the usual homeless type. He wasn't talking, obviously, and had no ID. They assumed it was drugs. Then he woke up. Emily, he told them he'd been drugged. Then set on fire."

My heart pounded. Cars whooshed down the road behind me. My eyes were on the back of Cal's head, his hand on my dog.

"Emily, he said a name—Matt. He said *Matt*, specifically. I mean, it's a very common name, but what are the chances? Where are you now? Are you somewhere safe?" Her voice lowered farther, a whisper now. I pictured her face turned away from the door, elbows propped on her desk like a shield.

Was I somewhere safe?

What's safe? And who's chasing whom?

"I'm home," I said. "I'm fine. Allie, how did you hear—?"

"The hospital liaison called me to report it . . . as a crime. She said she didn't know if he was out of his mind or what to make of any of it. But Emily, the hair on the back of my neck stood up."

"What about Detective Mason? Does he know?"

"Yeah, he'll be there first thing tomorrow morning, if not tonight. That place is going to be jam-packed with cops very soon. Emily, just stay where you are. I want to send a patrol to keep a lookout around your house. Consider this an apology for the way I acted earlier. For acting like you were crazy."

I extended the phone to check the time. Just after nine.

"Where'd you say he was?"

"I didn't." She coughed. Then I could hear the fatigue in her voice. "He started in Vanderbilt's burn unit, then transferred when he got stable. The nurse said he barely survived the twenty minutes in the ambulance."

I traced a half-hour circle around Vanderbilt on a map in my mind. She'd said rural; rural meant north and west. The other sides of town were developed that far out.

I guessed. "Summit Medical?"

I could hear her breathing. Her voice sounded stern. "Emily."

She'd answered for me. "Got it," I said.

"Emily, please, please, don't go anywhere. Whatever is happening, this is psycho. A serial killer."

I looked at the time again.

My old friend. I hoped in my heart that she'd actually meant to tip me off—I'd have done the same for her. My hand found the cold brass doorknob.

"Thank you," I said, before hanging up. "Allie, thank you so much."

"Emily, no . . . really—"

But I hung up.

Of course I was headed there.

TWENTY-TWO

Cal turned as I walked in.

Everything had changed. Now I was the one at the door, the one who suddenly wanted to run.

"What?" he asked. His gaze was steady but his hands were still shaking.

It was almost too crazy to say.

"You're not going to like this," I told him.

He gave me a look.

"Any of it. All of it. What I just heard, and where I'm about to go." I grabbed my coat.

"Tell me."

Summit Medical was about thirty-five minutes out with no traffic and me speeding. No time to be vague. "Well, look . . . thirty-five hours to go, right? I guess I better just tell you."

I relayed what Allie'd said, trying to line the pieces up so it didn't sound completely nutty.

Cal looked at me in a puzzled way that I recognized. It meant my words had come out way too fast. I tensed and released my hands a few times. "Let me say that again," I said.

He squinted. His mind, like mine, surely searching for connections.

"I don't get it. Are you saying what I think you're saying?"

"Look, I don't really know what I'm saying, but I know I need to go there. Like now. I know I need to find out what I can."

It was a nightmare that kept unfolding. I needed to peel back the next piece.

He'll try to stop you. The panic attack was fake.

Allie lied.

Cal stood. "I'll go. I'll drive."

I didn't hear him, not really. "Sorry to kick you out. You're welcome to stay." I was trying for politeness; I could see no real reason he'd want to hang around my mom's house.

He slung his arms into his coat. "What? No, I said I'm coming."

"You'll be okay? I mean, is that a good idea?" The question came out unedited, wrong. Ahead of myself, an imaginary version of me had already blown into the Breathalyzer and started off. My heart raced.

"Let's go," he said.

There was no time to discuss it.

We set off rumbling in the Volvo through back streets to the interstate on-ramp, then onto the steady, nearly trafficless straight-away off I-65 North. Stars above the skyline were tiny pinpricks above the glowing window patterns in white, yellow, and blue—offices closing down as the tourist centers came alive. The city breathing collectively at night.

Cal had pulled down his cap. It looked like a shield around his eyes. Like blinders, focusing him. I tugged at the tips of my hair; I still wasn't used to it being short. I leaned against the window, and the glass felt cool against my forehead. Here I was again, scheming to get into somewhere I didn't belong.

"I have to find a way in . . ."

"Emily." Cal patted the dashboard. "Come back."

I had the feeling of waking up despite already being awake.

"Am I missing something?" he asked.

"I don't know," I admitted. "But I have to talk with the patient. If I'm wrong about there being a connection between him and the murders, it'll only cost us an hour. But I have to see. Okay?"

"And you know he's at Summit?"

"Approximately." I said this with confidence.

Cal nodded. "She told you the patient's name?"

"Of course not."

"So we're going to the hospital where you think this patient is, even though you don't know his name? How do you plan to find him?"

"So many questions, Cal."

He looked back and forth between me and the road.

"I mean, how hard can it be? I'm seventy, eighty percent sure this is the hospital, and I know that patient is in ICU. I just have to get in." I knew my words were running over each other, again—like a wave rushing on top of another wave. "Any ideas?" I asked. "About how I do that? This time of day, it could be strange. I'll . . . find a way. I mean, I have to."

I considered presenting myself as a psychologist, running up to my office for the old department badge in my desk drawer. But I'd sworn to myself I'd keep my professional integrity. Besides, I was already in enough trouble with the board for the DUI. I was already in enough trouble generally. I didn't want to think about what would happen if I was caught trespassing while on probation.

"What about a diversion?" I tried again. "A fire alarm? I might be able to get ten minutes alone with him?"

He laughed a little. It was nice to hear. "Emily, that's what you said about getting into Matt's. Is that from a movie or something?"

"Just ideas."

He shrugged. "It wouldn't work that way in a hospital, anyway. Aside from breaking some serious laws and getting caught on camera, an alarm like that would just throw everything into lockdown. No one in or out."

"I've got an idea: why don't you try to walk in first?"

Says Mr. Just-Grab-the-Laptop.

He's right, though.

Right again.

I patted the dashboard. "Won't this thing go any faster?" I asked.

————

At the hospital, Cal backed into a space at the far end of the lot. When I shoved my door open, he didn't move.

"Wish me luck," I said.

The swoosh of Summit Medical's doors reminded me of an airlock as I limped into the wave of overwarmed air. The interior smelled like guilt—the guilt I had over my accident. A psychiatric hospital smelled different—that was all fear. No, this sterile air smelled like a DUI; like pain, like crawling across blacktop. Like the flash of the face of the boy in the back seat of the car I'd hit—I knew he'd never fully leave my mind.

The cane was long gone—that was from hurrying—so I made my way in the walking boot. Like every hospital, it seemed some-how both sterile and germ filled; I shoved my hands into the front pockets of my jeans.

Behind the desk, a security guard reclined, arms folded over his bulbous midsection. A massive beard that I restrained myself from analyzing flowed down his chest. On a screen, men in green uni-forms silently crashed into men in silver uniforms in blinding white snow. The guard's fist subtly pumped as I approached.

I swallowed, realizing I was sweating under my arms. Music played through the hallway speakers. Rod Stewart, of all people.

Focus.

I was going to say what, again? Right—I was going to improvise.

The security guard rocked forward in his chair, hand resting on a clipboard. "You signed in already today?"

I shook my head.

"Oh! God." His eyes flicked back to the screen, at some athletic ineptitude.

The round, institutional-style clock above him said it was nine forty-one.

"Need to scan your driver's license," he muttered, opening his palm.

Again I had the sense of moving in slow motion.

If Mason looks at hospital records, he'll know you were here.

Thirty-five hours now. Soon, it wouldn't matter.

"Where are you headed tonight?" the guard seemed to remember to ask. Skepticism audible in his tone like a first raindrop from a dark cloud.

A tinsel garland was strung down the hall, even though Thanksgiving was still weeks away. Chrome-colored elevator doors were polished to mirror reflectivity. They showed the other side of the hallway like a screen.

If you go up, they'll keep you here. It's a trap.

It was no trap, but I did have to lie.

"L and D." I smiled. Truth usually leaked out of me, but for the time being Labor and Delivery would have to do.

He nodded. The previously pumping fist extended a thumb, pointing. I thanked him and strode past, wondering if being hobbled in the boot made me look more or less suspicious.

In the elevator, departments were listed. I found ICU on level four and pressed up, lighting the button beneath my finger. I imagined Detective Mason behind me, maybe already driving toward the hospital, already knowing which way he would go. When the door opened, I stepped out onto the floor. Luckily, the department wasn't massive, and the doors were partially glass.

Between the elevator bank and the nurses' station, the hospital smell hit me again—unmistakably medical, and full of fear and memories. Why was that, exactly? For all the advances of medicine, couldn't someone figure out how to improve the scent of recovery? My ankle throbbed. My fingers pressed where the cuts in my palms had recently mended.

I started down the corridor, then I froze. I could see the blonde of a nurse's hair—alone, talking with no one, eyes apparently fixed on her computer screen. There was no excuse in my mind for being where I was. Getting on the elevator was one thing; strolling around, popping into patient rooms would be another.

She sat still as a statue.

Wait.

When you stop, you think. There's almost no way not to. Like air travel, like a straight interstate, like no TV—all your thoughts and doubts surface and demand contemplation.

I waited for what seemed like forever.

Really think about this. It's too crazy.

Be patient.

A bead of the sweat from under my arms ran hotly down my side.

Standing there, I tried to get a sense of how the floor was organized. Newly admitted patients seemed to be in the first few rooms, a special mark outside their door noting an intake. Allie hadn't said the name, but from her description I was looking for a male between thirty and sixty, obviously bandaged over much of his body.

A tone sounded, and the nurse buried her phone in her blonde hair before striding down the hall, away from me. When she disappeared into a room, I followed the hall, looking through the glass pane of each door.

It was late but not late enough that everyone was asleep. TV light coated many of the white blankets with blue flashes. In the first room was an elderly man; in the second, a woman about my age. At the third door, I stopped. White bandages ran up an arm from fingertip to shoulder. The nurses' station still empty, I clicked the door's metal lever and pushed inside.

When I pulled the door closed, the man looked up at the sudden sound. His watery eyes showed confusion at me not being in scrubs or a white coat. The dry-erase board beneath the TV listed the date, the day of the week, and his name in black marker. *James Mandel.* Allie had said he'd been unable to speak for months; I was sure talking with a stranger was going to seem very peculiar. We shared the soundless, softening gaze of two unfamiliar animals approaching each other. A gentle nod, slow movements. I pulled a privacy curtain around the bed and sat down in a wheelchair beside him. I eased closer.

His eyes seemed expectant, slightly scared. Half his face was pink and damp, likely from the moisturizer his nurse had applied—healing to the point where it had begun to look like human skin again. His hairline now began halfway back on his scalp; the gray clumps that remained were as thick as a wig. In the middle of his face was his half-nose, twisted upward, scorched. His breathing was a soft murmur.

"Mr. Mandel?"

He nodded hesitantly.

Machines cast shadows over his bed, humming softly. The windowsill where cards from loved ones normally sat was bare. Right—he was indigent. Who knew how long he would even be able to stay.

The TV was muted, but the images reflected in his eyes—alternating intensities of pale light. He'd been awake for only a day but already seemed to be in the sort of half sleep that warps time in a hospital—where *Judge Judy* blends into *Maury*, into a nurse coming in, into physical therapy. Someone always knocking on your door; someone always with a pill, a question, a form to sign. Now, I was that someone.

The joints of the wheelchair creaked as I leaned forward.

I touched my chest. "I'm Emily Firestone. I'm sorry to come in to see you right now. I know you're trying to rest. I can't imagine what you've been through."

He stared at me blankly. For a moment, I thought he might not reply. Maybe he'd call for a nurse, or close his eyes, finding talking impossible. "Okay," he acknowledged finally, in a deep Tennessee drawl, surprisingly clear-cutting through all the apprehension and damage. "You the cops?"

"No," I admitted. "I'm here because I need your help."

"No, thanks."

I heard the flames in his voice as he spoke.

I leaned behind the curtain, glanced at the door. No movement outside, yet. The windows were only blackness and our reflections. Below, flaxen halos in the lot where Cal waited.

"I just want to ask you a few questions. Is that okay?"

His head cocked, suspicious. His eyes closed contemplatively, then they popped back open like a doll's. "Where're you from?"

Nowhere, I thought. "I'm just me," I offered as a kind of explanation. "I'd wait until you had recovered more, but I don't have much time."

He shrugged.

A shadow moved under the door—the nurse passing by.

I lowered my voice. "I understand you told the case manager about the person who attacked you. Can you tell me what you remember?"

He looked toward the foot of his bed, over the length of his body. "The man who did this? You're looking for him?" His voice cracked as if he was repelled by the memory's general direction.

"I think the person who attacked you also hurt my friends." I wasn't able to say the word *killed*. "I'm trying to stop him from hurting anyone else." It sounded very Scooby-Doo when I put it that way, but it was basically what I was trying to do.

He shook his head, but his eyes stayed on mine. "Don't."

"I'm sorry?"

"Girl, stop." His head rolled to the side. I tried not to stare at the horrifying burn pattern down his neck. He was in too much pain.

Coming had been a mistake.

"Maybe I'll come back another time. I'm sorry, Mr. Mandel." I started to stand.

He reached and grabbed my hand, rough surgical tape scratching at my dry skin. I fought against yanking back. His eyes, black from iris to pupil, seemed to shiver. Vibrate. I sank back into the wheelchair.

"I mean, don't. Don't look for him."

I touched the top of his hand, reassuringly. "I have to, Mr. Mandel. And there's just not much time."

"Honey," he said quietly, "you don't go looking for the devil."

The hair on my neck stood up. I looked around me, behind me, as though someone was coming. The air seemed to siphon out of the room—the space dead still suddenly. The clock's ticking was the only noise. I wanted to not be as afraid as I was; I don't like needing protection.

He squeezed my fingers. "Just don't. You seem like a nice girl. Good life in front of you . . ."

He was trying to help, but I shook my head. "I'm so sorry. Please, Mr. Mandel. What do you remember?"

His voice neared anger. "I'm telling you—"

Warning me.

"—you should stop."

"Mr. Mandel—James. I don't stop. It's actually a problem. If you can tell me about what you remember, I want to try to help. Did he tell you his name?"

"You're not a cop?"

"No."

The side of his mouth tightened with disappointment. "Said his name was Matthew."

I straightened, drawing a shallow breath into the top third of my lungs—as far in as air would go. My cheeks became hot. "You're sure?"

"Said it a few times. Almost made a point of it."

"Did he say his last name?"

His head rolled slightly back and forth.

"How did Matt—Matthew—approach you?"

His eyes went off of me, back toward the ceiling.

"Thought *he* was a cop when I first seen him, real neat. Come to break up our tents on the river. Then I saw the white coat. I was halfway up the bank, near the road, away from the others. It's why he talked to me first. He asked if I'd like to make forty dollars. Fifteen minutes' work.' Emotion flooded his voice—the sadness of not being able to return to that particular moment and make a different choice. "I didn't always live outdoors. Just a lot of things happened all at once. My back. I had a metal job, but couldn't do it no more. I don't do shelters—too many crazies. Rather camp, just be outside. You know?"

I understood.

"This was two weeks ago?"

"Yeah. But hot. Seventies even at night. He wore a coat like doctors wear, asked me if he could give me a vitamin shot. Forty dollars. But I hadn't worked since May; everything was gone."

I swallowed, guilty to be so impossibly privileged. The idea that five months of unemployment could take away everything stung. Suddenly, I missed DHS.

He wiped at a tiny trail of mucus that ran onto his top lip and blended into moisturizer. "The guy said, 'It's just vitamins and being monitored for a little while. To see the effects.' I didn't know. Stupid." He shrugged beneath the blanket.

"White—is all I remember. Seemed strange, I guess. But plenty of strange shit happens living like this. He seemed nice. Didn't want sex. I asked him if it was okay I'd been drinking that day, and he said it was. Didn't talk much, but didn't sound like he was from the South.

"That was it, the first time. Simple. He gave me the shot, just one, here in the arm." He reached across his torso and tapped his left bicep, where the mossy wings of an aged tattoo peaked beneath the sleeve of his gown. "He said he'd be back the next week, that he'd pay eighty dollars then, and told me he only needed one volunteer so keep the arrangement to myself."

I thought I heard a fragment of hope in his voice as he told that part of the story, as though the money promised to him might still appear somehow, despite everything.

He cleared his throat. "Next week, at nightfall, I followed him to the van again. His hand shook so bad the needle almost slipped off my skin. He wouldn't look at me, just at my arm. I remember asking him if everything was all right."

Tears brimmed in his eyes, then. Mine, too. His head thrashed back and forth against his pillow.

"He started asking, like real caring, how I'd been. How was I feeling. Was I okay? Any congestion. He asked me that."

I nodded.

He stopped. He looked reluctant to continue, like he'd come to the entrance of a dark cave.

My hand gripped the grooved plastic handle along the side of his bed.

"I guess I fell asleep. I don't remember that part. Woke up sweating. In the fucking woods somewhere. Sun had gone down, only light was from the dome in the van. Sliding door slamming woke me up. I was in a chair like from a school, my hands behind my back, tight with little zip ties. Against metal. I don't know how he got me upright; I was out of it, dead weight. My arm was bleeding at the elbow, and he wore a medical mask over his face, a gown like they do here. Told me to relax, tied a cloth over my face when I started to yell. I couldn't hear traffic, anything. Guess I passed out. Must've drugged me." James coughed a little, and spit hung from the edge of his lip. "Was fuckin' recording me when I came to again."

"How could you tell?"

"Things he said. He wasn't talking to me; he was talking into the camera. Said the date, time, a few other things I didn't get. Light from the phone or whatever was bright. I could hardly look into it."

"Did you feel sick?"

A look came over his face. The edge of tears. "A little; I don't know. Not really. He wore a mask and glasses, then. Wanted no part of whatever he gave me. I tried to spit on him. Just made the rag on my face wet. Whatever injection he gave me didn't work either or should have worked faster or something. When he turned the recorder off, he went behind me. I could see he wasn't all there. He started mumbling some kind of prayer, then he told me he was sorry for what he was about to do. I said, 'Man, just stop. You don't have to do this.' He said something about the whole world owing me a debt, something crazy like that. I thought I could run and I tried to stand, but he'd zipped my legs to the chair. I felt a hard blow crack the back of my head."

I nodded, like I understood. Like any of it was comprehensible. I guess I'd had some practice at hearing things that were unspeakable. After working with abused kids, very little shocked me anymore, but my hands were still sweaty; my breathing stayed short and sharp.

He jutted his chin toward the foot of the bed, voice cracking. "Then he did it."

I knew what *it* was.

"Sprayed something on me from a distance. Fumes—gas." James looked down at his body. "Guess he thought I was unconscious. Then . . . fire. The wind picked up, or he didn't have enough of the gas. He was wrong about being far enough out that no one could hear, though. They said two duck hunters found me, called an ambulance."

My heart hammered. "What did he look like?" I asked.

Mouth downturned, his eyebrows gathered inward. "It was night. Only light was from the van. Dark hair, thinner guy. Medium everything. I don't know."

He was describing everyone. I stopped myself from frowning. "How old was he?"

"How old?"

I nodded.

The TV program shifted, lights changing from pale blue to white.

His bandaged hand touched his chin. "Can't say."

"You said you thought he might be a doctor. A young doctor?" I pictured Matt's hair flopping over his right eye.

"Maybe forty."

It couldn't be right, I thought. My body seemed heavier. This had to be Matt. *But forty?*

"Did he say he was with a hospital or medical center?"

"No. Don't remember—"

"But you'd recognize his picture?"

"'Course."

Before I could look for my phone, I realized I'd left it—somewhere. In Cal's car? With my cane?

Then, a knock at the door. Two swift raps, then the door opening. The nurse from the station, arms folded.

"Goddammit," I said.

TWENTY-THREE

"Hang on." I yanked the armorlike Volvo door shut. "Hang on, I'm thinking."

"Okay." Cal folded his hands in his lap. He hadn't asked anything yet.

Inside the car was warm. A thin white fog coated the windows, dotted with smudges I assumed were Olivia's fingerprints.

A police car pulled into the lot and parked beside the entrance. Another followed.

Allie had been right—Mr. Mandel was going to have a busy few hours. I'd walked out just in time.

I wasn't sure how much of the story to retell. I figured Cal could do without the details of the fire.

"Everything he said sounds right, but he's confused about Matt's age," I said. "I need a picture of Matt."

"How far off?"

"Ten, fifteen years."

Cal sank back into his seat. "Oh, Emily . . ."

"I know, I know."

I had tunnel vision. I was neglecting the obvious. This had always been a long shot, and a weird one at that. But still. Something was there. It simply could not be a coincidence. Even if they were impossible to articulate, I knew the connections were real. I knew it. And I could live with tunnel vision to see this through.

Thinking, thinking . . .

We started back onto the nearly empty highway, both of us

quiet. I was half exhausted, half wide awake. If you've never been manic, it's impossible to describe.

Cal was muttering something.

"What?" I asked.

"I asked if you're okay."

"I'm fine."

I was not fine. I didn't trust my understanding of time. Even if it wasn't late, so much had happened that the day felt both impossibly long and like it had not yet begun. My hands shook in my pockets.

Cal drove.

At Mom's, I climbed out. Cal followed me.

"Tell me you're going to get some sleep," he said.

I looked up at the window of my old bedroom, dark and vacant. Actual rest seemed an unimaginable triviality. "I'd be lying."

I climbed the porch stairs. He did the same. If my head wasn't spinning, I might have asked what he was thinking. As it was, I pushed open the door.

In the living room, Andy paced vehemently, agitated. His fur seemed to stand on end. Had someone been here? I told myself I was imagining things. Yet nothing would have surprised me by then.

Cal pointed at a space in the middle of the living room beside the couch. "This floor okay for me for a few hours? I need to power down."

"Um, sure. But there's a guest room, Cal. You're more than welcome to it."

He began unlacing his boots, pulling them off. "It's better out here. I'm way off schedule; lying in an actual bed would be weird. Don't ask. What about you? You really should rest."

From the way Cal was talking, I had the feeling that he'd be in full REM sleep within minutes. He took off his coat, rolled it and set it under his head.

"There are pillows, too."

"Fine, really."

I needed to think. "I may make some tea," I said.

He closed his eyes. "You should lay down."

It'd been, what, thirty-six hours? Yet sleep seemed like a place that I could never get to. So inconceivably far away.

"I'm going to take Andy out."

I clicked a leash onto his collar and tapped down the sidewalk as best I could. My ankle throbbed, which was no surprise considering the amount of walking I'd done that day, but it seemed an example of the body's unfair limitations. With each stab, part of me wished I was younger, playing college soccer again—before the aggregate of minor injuries had begun to nag. Before the accident. I longed for a time when I could simply will my body to do things and they would happen. Now my high school friends were pushing babies in strollers, sipping coffee—or even more preciously—chai tea. And married, for God's sake.

I felt old.

More than that I felt alone.

I think I let myself contemplate life for a moment just to suppress the experience of meeting James Mandel. Who had endured pain I couldn't imagine. Part of me felt guilty for even trying. When he'd described the man who'd burned him, I'd pictured Matt's face, but was Cal right to doubt it? Even I had to admit that the connection seemed unbelievable.

I shuddered as I pictured him spitting—or trying to spit—at his attacker through his gag. It reminded me of an article I'd read, maybe a decade earlier, about primitive biological warfare. Tuberculosis patients being forced to spit in the mouths of captured enemy soldiers. What a world, I thought. What a fucking world. I told myself that after Matt was in handcuffs and I slept, I was going to get back to working with kids. Just kids.

Back inside, Andy curled beside Cal. I took off my boot and paced for a while, my socks slipping along the floor. There was the breathy, oceanic sound of cars on the street.

I switched off the light, lay back on the couch. It was like a sleepover, or something, with Cal on the floor beside me. Beams of yellow light lined the floor through the slats of the window shades.

I shut my eyes.

Just for a second, I thought.

———

I see a woman from behind, the sky around her a light, heathered blue, like a baby blanket. High, cotton clouds. She's walking in front of me and I follow her. No smell, no texture, just the hallucinatory, slow pace of her footsteps and the faraway, indifferent chatter of birds. She whispers something I can't hear. I try to follow closer, but in the maddening passivity of dreams, I can't.

She's in the woods, then stepping into water that's a river and a lake at the same time. Wading in—shins, knees. She's up to her waist. Just imagining the cold turns all my skin to gooseflesh. I think for a second when she turns that she's my grandmother, but I know she only looks like my grandmother. She's actually me.

And I understand it's not her whispering; it's a voice from the shore. We both turn to find the voice. There's someone calling my name and we both open our mouths to respond.

I feel a strange sense of acceptance and awe, like a glimpse into the vastness of a galaxy. I feel like a part of something larger.

———

It was dark and I was sweating despite the cold. I looked down to where Cal lay fast asleep, his breathing rolling, automated, unconscious.

I took a shower. Left Cal asleep on the floor. I slid my arms into a jacket and drove toward Matt's apartment. Since I knew he hadn't brought a computer in with him, my basic plan—which was stupid—was to snap a photo of him with my iPhone, then run the image over, or somehow get it to Mr. Mandel to ID. Some part of me expected to do this without Matt's knowledge.

Of course, nothing remotely like that actually happened. Crouching between two bushes, I froze with the knees of my jeans in the dirt until I snapped a few blurry images of a person who was likely Matt but honestly could have been anyone.

I drove home with the fully risen sun in my eyes.

Cal was awake; Andy paced by the front door.

I explained where I'd been.

"Not a great idea."

"Thanks," I said, smiling a little.

He sounded military-calm but incredulous, hair sticking up at an angle created by the curve of his shoulder as he'd slept. "Even if it was, you'd need a legit camera with a lens for distance."

"What did you say?"

"I said forget about getting a picture of Matt with your phone."

"No, about the lens."

"That the zoom on your phone isn't powerful enough. More than a hundred feet, you'd need an external lens—telescoping. We need to think of something else. Public records search . . ."

Cal kept talking, but I stopped hearing him for a moment.

My medication was upstairs. I'd gone three days without it. It would put me to sleep, and I knew it.

There was no time for stability.

"I actually may have just the thing we need," I said. "How fast can you get ready?"

Cal leaned forward and picked up his boots.

TWENTY-FOUR

Cal met me at the office after he stopped at home. His boots creaked heavily on the wood floor. "Your office. I like it; it's . . . soothing."

I glanced over my shoulder as he looked around, my voice fast and muttering. "Thanks . . . I need some patients soon. Otherwise, it's just an expensive place to hang out during the day."

I pulled Paolo's camera down from where I'd set it earlier in the week, then dropped back onto the soft fabric of my patient couch, the camera's pleasant weight resting in my lap. The juxtaposition of the familiar and foreign struck me, like the nearly wrong feeling of enjoying housesitting.

"It's been a while since I've seen that." Cal smiled. "It's kinda nice, actually—almost like he's here with us."

The thought took me aback, but Cal was right. I liked that, too. Like a friendly ghost, like electricity in the room. I wondered what Paolo would think about what we were doing. About Cal and me.

Stop. Focus.

I found the tripod he hiked with and the case that held all his gear and set it down gently, bracing it between my feet. Blood rushed to my face as I leaned over it, an insistent pressure behind my eyes. Inside, the lenses were encased in thick cylinders like artifacts— like I'd discovered something and had only begun to understand its power.

Canisters, glass. I chose the telescopic lens, unlocked the hard plastic casing and felt its weight in my hand, then carefully snapped it onto the front of the camera.

Cal was asking something.

I couldn't hear. I felt like I was waking up.

"Emily?"

I pressed the power button, and unbelievably, the camera's screen illuminated, offering a hundred instructions. In my mind, I could hear Paolo's voice in echo, giving directions.

When I twisted the lens, I could see all the way through Centennial Park. How far had Paolo told me it could see? I backed up, squinted, turned to the windows of a restaurant. Still nothing—the reflection was a blank stare back at me. I opened three more canisters inside the bag before I found what I was looking for.

The filter. The fish filter.

I opened its case, attached it to the front of the lens. It was like a curtain had been pulled back. Across the street, what had been a silver sheet now revealed a bartender wiping out glasses. At the far end of the counter, a man sat alone, teeth like white porcelain as he bit into his breakfast.

I braced my elbows on the top of the couch and scanned the street through the camera's digital display. The image was sharper than my eyesight.

Click.

"Emily?"

Click.

I found a dewy glint of sunlight on the yellow edge of the stoplight. *Click.* I found the crumbled sidewalk, the creaky gate I'd held on to for dear life when Marty showed me the office. I dialed down the light intake, zoomed in on flakes of rust. *Click.*

"Are you there?"

"I'm here." I flicked back over the two shots I'd taken. I wasn't ready for an exhibition, but I was getting the basics down.

Click.

"I have an idea," I said. "Humor me. This won't take long."

He looked at his watch.

I leveled the lens and found the windows of the restaurant across the street. Vague shapes, upright, human, silent. Just the sound of my breathing, then Cal saying, "I'm going to get coffee."

I'd stopped for coffee on the way in, but I wanted more. I didn't turn my head. "Get me one?"

I heard the door close as he left.

I detached the filter and set it back in its case, then put the case over my shoulder I made my way toward the end of the hallway, where the door leading to the roof was rimmed with sunlight. Behind me, my shadow followed me like an apparition. I was in my head now, I knew When you're manic, nothing feels impossible; the world seems expansive but vaguely nightmarish. Sensing my grip on reality slipping, I began hoping Cal wouldn't be away long—to stay grounded, I needed him with me.

On the roof, the hallway's silence gave way to a symphony of city sounds. The ten days that had passed since I'd been up there seemed like a year. That was before meeting with Sandy, before finding her.

I swallowed hard, pushing the image of her face from my mind as I dropped onto the tar paper, the acrid smell of it somehow both registering in my nose and not mattering. I aimed the camera toward the medical center. I focused the lens, altered the light intake. The distance was correct, but the reflection made seeing impossible, like peering at the surface of water in the morning.

I retrieved the filter from the case and attached it to the camera lens. Like before, the glass appeared transparent, revealing the entire lab. I let out a small gasp.

A gust of wind pushed against me and I inched back from the roof's edge.

How many times had I tried to picture the lab? Here it was, not very different from what I'd imagined. There was an empty office that I knew must be Silver's because of its size. It was separated by a wall from two rows of computers. Then there was an open space with some lab equipment, then another wall, then a hallway leading to a darker space which I assumed was where the animals were housed.

I recognized Matt's slumped shoulders right away and wiped

my warm palms down my sleeves. On the lab's far end, Silver was talking with an assistant who wore a white coat. I didn't recognize her at all, but her eyebrows were knitted intently and she nodded slowly as Silver's lips moved.

The camera's plastic warmed in my hands as the battery indicator flashed a red, empty cylinder. I dug through the case until I found a charger, connected the camera.

Beside the charger, I found my phone.

I dialed the number of the florist my family had always used—where fifteen years earlier, I'd picked a dove-white boutonniere for prom. Where I'd ordered the flowers for Paolo's service.

A second later, Becky, the owner, came on the line. Her voice was instantly familiar. Part of me didn't want her to recognize who was calling. I couldn't believe what I was about to ask, and that I was calling again so soon. With a family friend, you feel like you owe explanations even if you don't. I wondered if she'd heard about my accident, if she'd be curt and disapproving.

No. Accustomed to occasions of all kinds, I was sure, she sounded warm but surprised. "Well, hello again. Was that two weeks ago you called? Everything okay with the order?"

Refrigerators hummed in the background. We quickly caught up, her asking about Mom.

"What can I help you with?"

"I need something a little unconventional, Becky."

She laughed. "Emily, if you wanted something conventional, I'd be surprised."

Fair enough, I thought, smiling. "Is Tommy still doing deliveries?"

I pictured her assistant of twenty years. Blue baseball cap, tall, rail-thin. Nose like a hawk's.

"Who else could I count on day in and day out?"

"Great. I need to send something simple to the medical center. But it has to be today."

"Wow, today." She sighed a little. "Oh-kay. What's the address?"

The click of a pen.

I pictured the ID badge around Paolo's neck the year before. I knew the lab address by heart. "They're going to Matt Cianciolo. And the card is a little strange, okay?"

"Yep. Ready when you are." I could hear her shifting the phone from one ear to the other. Nothing was going to faze this woman.

"'Matt, I knew it was you. Paolo, Sandy. They're talking to James Mandel in the hospital now. Forget about Europe.'"

The sound of pen scribbling on paper. "Aaaand . . . got it." Her pen clicked a final time. Probably not even the strangest card she'd handled that morning.

"How busy are you guys? How soon can Tommy make it over there?"

"Hang on, I'll ask him." The sound coming over the line muted as her palm went over the phone. A few muffled exchanges back and forth. "By one thirty," she said. "Will that work?"

I knew getting a delivery done even by then was an immense favor, but even a few hours felt agonizingly long. "Sure. Please tell Tommy the closer he can get to ten on the dot, the better."

I suppressed awareness of my bank account and gave her my credit card number. Then I thanked her profusely, promising to stop in soon.

While I waited—for Cal, for the delivery, for the camera to charge—I heard Cal's boots jog heavily up the stairs. He met me at the door, a white paper cup in each hand. Why did he always smell like Irish Spring soap? It was like we were living in a commercial for it or something. He handed me the coffee, motioned toward my jacket.

"Chilly?" he asked. His voice echoed in the hall. I took him up the second stairwell onto the rooftop deck. Steam rose from the silver metal arches of the medical center, like the building itself was breathing. It looked sinister, white and red lights glowing in what remained of the morning fog.

Cal picked up the tripod, swung it in slow motion like a softball bat. Leaning against my desk, he started slipping his field jacket off his shoulders. "Want to tell me what you're planning now?"

The coffee was hot, delicious.

About twenty-five hours now till Matt left.

Behind Cal, the sky looked like brushstrokes of gray and yellow. Above his beard, his cheeks reddened in the cold as I told him what I'd done.

He bit his lip, squinting slightly as he took in the plan. "So you want to watch as the flowers get delivered to Matt? Can I just ask what you're hoping to actually see?"

"He's going to look guilty," I explained, quickly. "He's going to freak out when he sees it, tear it up, try to get rid of it."

"Emily, anyone might tear it up. You would. I'd throw it away, too, if it came to my office." He sounded apologetic for having to point out something so obvious.

I shoved aside the doubts swirling inside me. I pictured the accusation in Mason's eyes as he'd leaned forward; the watchful gaze of the young cop walking me down the stairs of Sandy's condo; Allie avoiding me. I hated feeling crazy.

I knew it was Matt.

I flashed back to his expression in the supermarket, a carton of blueberries scattering across the floor between us.

The cold made me shiver, but that didn't matter. Up for days, everything I thought made sense. "Maybe I have something to prove, okay? I just have to see for myself," I said. "I need this. I just do. I need to see this right now."

Even beyond what I needed, part of me still hadn't let go of the idea of showing a photo of Matt to Mr. Mandel.

Cal looked at his watch.

"Look, it's already done now," I said, my hand on my hip. "I put the order in and I'm going to see what happens. Aren't you curious?"

Cal shrugged, nodded. He set the tripod onto the tar paper and smiled. "I saw an old movie like this once," he reflected. "Jimmy Stewart, Grace Kelly."

"That sounds like validation," I said.

"It's something, I guess." He shook his head, finished the coffee. A pause.

"Thank you," I said finally.

I checked the time on my phone and wondered where the flowers were right then. I pictured the yellow delivery van bouncing down West End.

Cal unscrewed the tripod legs, angled the mount.

His phone rang. He raised his index finger, turned to shield the phone from the rushing wind. The back of his brown field jacket contrasted the soft sky. The tar paper crunched softly as he paced to the other end of the small roof, the ten or so feet giving some minuscule buffer of privacy.

"Good morning to you, too. Where's your mom?" His voice was steady, even I could tell who'd called without any explanation.

The call was a fissure, a short break, through which I could glimpse exhaustion I couldn't yet feel. I rubbed my eyes, snapped my attention back to the camera.

Did anyone deliver coffee? I wondered, craving even more.

"Day after tomorrow," Cal said into the phone. "Yeah, I'm off today. I'm working on something with Emily . . . Right, that's her . . . No, he's not here, it's too cold. He's at her house."

Cal turned, mouthed to me, *Andy*.

I nodded. I couldn't help but eavesdrop, and smile.

"Because we're at her office. She doesn't bring him to work . . . Yep, same building, we talked about that the other day. Olivia, stop. Where's your mom?" He coughed, rubbed his neck. "Well, you may need to tell her it's time to get up, honey. She'll be all right. It's after nine o'clock. She'll be fine. Promise. Call me back if you need anything."

He ended the call, dropped the phone into his jacket pocket.

"Sorry," he said.

"What for?" Pretending not to listen as much as I was, I'd closed one eye and was watching through the aperture instead of the screen. It made the medical center seem an ocean away.

He shrugged. "I know we're trying to concentrate here. She's just bored I guess. This happens sometimes when she spends the night at her mom's apartment."

"What happens?" I figured I might as well ask. Until the flowers arrived, we were basically watching people watch other screens. Nothing riveting. I rubbed my hands together, warming them.

We went to the stairwell to stay away from the wind, checking the time occasionally.

Cal folded his arms. Answered my question. "Her mom stays up too late, then sleeps in. I'm not judging, really. She's actually a great mom but lives a musician lifestyle. It seems like a lot of staying up late."

"You don't sound judgmental at all. You're being pretty understanding, if you ask me." He hadn't asked me. Which I knew. I was dangerously close to not minding my own business.

"Well, I don't have to worry about most of what she does now. We're not trying to be together, just coparenting. If Olivia's not affected, then her mom's coming and going, late hours—whatever—are fine by me."

Cal and I stood side by side, arms folded, checking the camera every few minutes. The battery indicator showed half full. Plenty.

"Is this recording?" Cal pointed at the unnaturally sharp image on the screen.

"Yeah."

Time creaked ahead. I was biting my lip so hard I could taste blood.

Cal looked at his watch again.

About sixteen hours left.

It was strange to watch Matt working through a compact screen only a few inches wide—it was as if what was happening were a silent movie and Cal and I were the only audience. There was a peculiar loneliness to being at that distance and, at the same time, a shocking, voyeuristic thrill.

I pictured Paolo and Sandy in that office. My eyes drifted over the stations I assumed had been theirs. A wall separated where they worked from the part of the lab that housed the animals. From our angle, only a fraction of a few cages was visible.

"Weird work, right?" Cal whispered. The intimacy of watching gave the illusion that our voices might be heard.

Concentration and squinting pinched my voice. "He believed in it."

"I'm just saying, I think the animals getting sick and all. Ferrets sneezing on each other."

"No, I know what you mean. I guess they have to study that stuff somehow."

"Where's everyone else?"

I shrugged. "Time off because of Sandy? Packing to leave tomorrow for London?"

"Makes sense," he said softly. "So, why's Matt not packing?"

I wondered that, too.

Right at one thirty, it began.

Matt sat closest to the lab entrance. At once, his expression changed, head turned.

"Here we go," I said. "There's the delivery."

Cal glanced over at me, then back to the screen. I wove my fingers through his and his palm squeezed into mine.

Matt stood and walked to the door. He was still for a moment, then he stepped backward with a quizzical expression, a large, clear vase between his hands. Looking around, he settled on placing it atop a filing cabinet. He was squinting, making a face as though it smelled.

"Are those . . . ?"

"Lilies. I had to pick something," I said.

The lab assistant, seated beyond the partition, didn't look up or move. Dr. Silver remained in his office with the door closed.

Slowly, Matt reached for the plastic stake that held the envelope on which his name was written. He glanced over the partition as his thumb slid under the seal. He held the card in front of his face, leaning in like he was reading a foreign language. Then his head jerked back. He ran to the door. He looked out into what was surely by then an empty hallway, closed the door again, and turned the card over. He shook it like a fresh Polaroid, eyes wandering back over the flowers, circling them at a distance.

"Hmm," Cal said.

I realized I was holding my breath. I stopped biting my bottom lip and let myself exhale.

Matt turned the arrangement around, inspecting it. Even held it up and looked at the bottom. He rubbed the back of his neck, then folded his arms like they were a barrier. He paced, picked up his phone, paused, set it back down. I wondered why he didn't simply call the florist and ask who had sent the flowers.

Then my stomach dropped.

Matt dropped the card in the wastebasket beside the vase, rubbed his forehead, and returned to his computer, shaking his head back and forth. Then he leaned forward as if rereading his work.

"Hmm," Cal said again.

My little movie had ended abruptly. Twenty seconds, max.

I let go of Cal's hand, paced the tar paper.

There were shreds of possibility, fragments of maybe. Just threads I had no energy to follow. They were wrong.

This was wrong.

And I knew it.

I didn't know what I'd even hoped would happen. Face in my hands, I felt like screaming. The feeling of falling. Of failure. Of starting again.

I felt stupid, spiraling with confusion.

I thought about Mr. Mandel describing a man in his forties, without a southern accent. It had all made sense before. Now, it looked like I'd forced all of it. We had nothing to go on.

"It's okay. It was a good idea," Cal said. His teeth were chattering.

"I wasted our time. This was nothing."

My mind spun, considering possibilities. It was so strange, I actually felt guilty.

Was Mason going to come arrest me?

Was I guilty?

Cal didn't say anything, and I was glad. Wind gusted so strongly I winced.

But then, who?

"How can he not . . . ?" I started.

"Hey." Cal pointed.

"What?"

"Silver's moving out of his office."

I returned to the screen, which by that time seemed like a movie in its fifth hour. I moved to turn off the camera. The battery was down to about a quarter full.

Cal grabbed my shoulder. "Give this a second."

Matt stood, and both men looked at the flowers. Dr. Silver touched his chin, and Matt motioned toward the door. The assistant on the other side of the partition either couldn't hear or didn't care—her gaze stayed on her screen. Matt plucked up the card, opened it, and handed it to Dr. Silver.

I imagined I could hear them talking. Silver knew exactly who had arranged that delivery. I pictured a sheriff deputy in the stairwell, restraining order in his hand.

I was already on probation.

I thought back to the intake area at the courthouse, recalled the warm, smudged surface where I'd pressed my fingerprints. The vacant stares of people in line, waiting.

I was so exhausted that watching made a part of me almost giddy. It was bad. So bad, I nearly laughed. "I may need some bailing out in a few hours, so let me go ahead and write down my mom's number. Would you mind calling her? She'll know what to do. She's unfortunately familiar with that process."

Cal stayed focused on the screen, his body tense like Andy's when he spotted a squirrel.

"Shhh," he said. "Silver went back in his office and shut the door."

The battery indicator on the camera dropped again. I reached again to turn it off.

"Wait," Cal said. He sounded impatient.

Matt returned to his computer, rubbed his eyes again, typing.

"He took the card," Cal said.

"Who?"

"Silver. He shoved it in his pocket." Cal panned the camera slightly to the left and focused on Dr. Silver, seated behind his desk. "He took it with him. Why would he do that?"

"I don't know, Cal. He's probably about to report me."

The battery indicator began flashing. Only a few minutes left.

"Nah, I don't think so. He might have told Matt he saw us, but why take it further? And it doesn't look to me like he's about to make a call."

Cal was right. Dr. Silver stretched his neck from side to side, as if working out a kink. He leaned back in his desk chair, his expression dazed.

This was different. A man who didn't know he was being watched.

He read the card again.

His face changed. Like he'd just taken off a mask that looked a lot like him.

He stood, then sat again, raking fingers through his hair. He pursed his lips and gently hit his desktop with his fist.

That was fear. Frustration.

The chill hit Cal and me simultaneously.

"Holy shit," Cal said. "He's not calling anybody. He's glad you think it was Matt, but he looks nervous as hell."

Cal was right.

I couldn't talk. Everything had just taken a sharp turn. What I understood was upside down. Hatred bloomed inside me. It pressed against my skin, flushing me like a fever. "Do you think he . . . ? Paolo? Sandy?"

"I don't know," Cal said. He walked quickly, his back to me. His boots sent a slight vibration through the tar paper roof.

I thought back to James Mandel's description of the charming professor in a white lab coat in his early forties. Now my mind inserted a face into the story. I imagined the depth of evil inside Silver as tears of . . . what? Of pain, maybe, stung my eyes. The possibility of Silver having somehow poisoned Paolo was unthinkably horrible. I pictured Paolo's expression as he'd spoken with such admiration about the man. He'd looked up to him like a father and been so naive. We both had. I'd been to a party in his home, for God's sake. I'd been impressed, too. It took my breath. I searched for what Silver's motivation could possibly have been, blankly, emptily— like white paint on a white wall. Then fury burned behind my eyes.

"Silver kept us chasing, suspecting someone else. He was buying himself time," Cal said. "It's not Matt's computer we need." Cal cleared the path between me and the door, but his eyes narrowed like he was estimating something.

Mania pushed me forward. Textbooks describe the feeling as "confidence," but it's more like an inability to grasp the significance of obstacles. "How . . . ?" I couldn't talk, was stumbling over my words. "What do you propose?"

Cal picked up the camera, his other hand holding the tripod tightly. "Tell me everything you remember about what Sandy said she saw, and where. We need to charge this battery. You have to watch for me while I go in there."

TWENTY-FIVE

"You? Why would you go?" I followed Cal into the hallway, our voices echoing. Marty's dark office to my left, mine to my right. Cal's jacket was cold as I grabbed it, the fabric rough under my fingernails.

"Because I can get into the computer and download what we need. What would you do? Grab it and try to run out of the medical center?"

I pictured Vanderbilt Police surrounding me. He had a point.

"It's the only way," he said. His speech accelerated as his southern accent deepened, blurring the hard edges of his words. His eyes had caught fire. "Do you think I want to do this? I don't. I'm scared. It's a fucking bad idea. But it's not the scariest thing I've ever done. And it's the right thing to do if there's a chance to stop him. I don't want to have seen Silver reacting like he did. I want to live in last week, go to sleep at my house, work my job, tinker around in my yard. But I can't—not today." He pointed an index finger north toward the medical center. "I've gotta go; there's no other option. I can't let what we think happened stand."

I understood. I couldn't get Silver's reaction out of my mind either. I shook my head to clear it. So, why was I holding Cal back? He'd chosen to help me, for God's sake. He was about to take the risk for both of us. What accounted for my impulse to stop him?

I pressed against my temples as if holding together the image of what we'd seen. Picturing Silver's expression felt like a near miss by a speeding car—heart racing after jumping back to the curb.

I used the wall for stability, staggering, telling Cal every detail I could remember about Sandy's description of the data and where she'd found it. "But she didn't find it on Silver's computer; she saw it on one Matt used."

"It's a closed network; remember what Silver said? His computer will have access to all the others." Calm and steady.

"How are you going to get in without anyone seeing you?" I asked.

Cal raised the camera. "Just watch his office, just the way we were before. The lab's front door is open—people were walking in and out. You saw how everything's arranged. Matt's back is to the door and his eyes are locked on that screen in front of him. Those assistants are behind the wall on the other side. They won't notice me slip behind him. I only need about thirty seconds. I'll text you when I get close. You text me when Silver walks out."

"We're going to wait until he walks out? He could be there all day."

Then Cal read my mind. "I'm not going to pull the fire alarm, Emily."

Think.

I snapped my fingers. "I'll call him when you get there and say I'm downstairs. Somewhere that's a five-minute walk. He already thinks I'm that crazy, especially after the flowers. He'll come down, and you'll slip in. You just need a minute, right?"

Cal nodded. "Less."

My stomach was tight.

He paused, squinted at the doubt showing in my eyes. "Emily, we need this. Right now, all we have is a reaction."

We'd known evil the second we'd seen it. But Cal was right—a smile was not evidence. There were too many questions, too many possibilities. Lies to unravel. We needed to take the next step.

Then it hit me—Silver really could have been weaponizing the results. The idea that Matt had been doing it seemed far-fetched in hindsight, but Silver was fully capable of navigating a deal like she'd described, of manipulating samples, of faking data.

My mind flashed to Paolo's description of an H1–N24 outbreak. I pounded the wall with my fist to stop myself from shivering.

"We have to stop him now," I said.

"I'm sure I have a few thumb drives in my glove box. I'll grab one on the way there," he said. "I don't even have to get in his email. If he typed it on that computer, there's a trail. Even a hard delete would only take me an extra minute to find. Two minutes if he thinks he really wiped it gone. But honestly, I doubt he did. I got this."

Cal located an electrical socket, plugged in the camera, and turned it on to verify that the battery was indeed charging. His hands shook, the metal buckle on the strap rattling against the plastic case.

"In the time it takes me to get over there, the camera will be charged enough."

Cal was both there and somewhere else. But, in a strange way, his distance made him more present. Even more focused. "It's going to work," he assured me. "Watch. Okay? Keep watching."

"Okay."

Cal straightened his back. He checked the cord once more.

Would this work? I wondered. Another part of me thought, *Why not?*

Something Marty had said in supervision once, years before, came to mind: *Ideas don't have to be complicated to be effective. Sometimes simple strategies work best.* Of course, he was probably talking about something like behavioral interventions for bed-wetting at the time, but still.

"Here," Cal said, extending his hand, nodding at the phone in my front pocket. "I'll put in my address. After I leave the lab, meet me out there."

I handed him the phone and he navigated to a maps app. "We can't look here?" I motioned toward the decade-old laptop resting on my desk.

Cal shook his head. "I'll need the computer in my home office to break anything they've encrypted. Once I have access at home, it'll take ten minutes."

"Then we'll call the police?"

"Right." He dropped the phone back into my palm. "Okay?"

"Okay."

What did he just do to your phone?

Stop. It's just paranoia from lack of sleep.

I let out a breath, nodding quickly.

Cal squeezed my shoulder and tromped down the stairs.

The sound of his Volvo starting.

I was alone.

It was one forty-five, I noticed. About fifteen hours from then, Silver would be in the air, on his way to London—or somewhere away. If he'd been making a weapon like Sandy suspected, who knew where he might be going, ultimately.

When the camera had charged adequately, I went back up on the roof and resumed my position on the tar paper—elbows and knees grinding into the dusty black material, my senses too heightened to wince at the slight petroleum smell coming off of it. I rubbed my eyes as my body tensed, rejecting its return to the cold. My heart, which in my office had slowed to a heavy gallop, was back to jackhammering. My pulse throbbed against my windpipe. The sky was brighter by then, an atmospheric blue so vivid it looked nearly unnatural. I adjusted the light meter on the camera, powered on, and found the lab.

I swallowed, texted Cal: NO ONE'S MOVED.

A second later, his message appeared: I'M HERE, READY.

I glanced at the time. He'd gotten over there fast, I thought.

There was a small piece of guilt to watching Matt; in that moment he looked younger. I couldn't help but see him as a person, like me, who lacked full understanding. The me of thirty minutes before could relate—Matt there working diligently, unaware of what had been going on all around him for—how long? Years? Was he in danger? Were the others in the lab?

My fingertips were cracked, trembling in the cold. A fleck of blood had dried against the nail. GET READY, I typed into my phone.

This had to work.

I dialed Silver's number.

Watched as his head turned. He picked up the receiver.

His voice mirthful, ripe with lies. "Hello?"

"Jay, this is Emily Firestone. I'm standing where we met yesterday, and I have something very important. Something you'll definitely want to see. This is evidence, Jay. Trust me."

Before he could speak, I hung up, held my breath. My eyes focused on the tiny screen. I couldn't blink.

Silver stood and stretched. He leaned and touched his keyboard, took his jacket from the back of his office door. Slipping it on, he leaned toward his reflection on a framed diploma. Smoothed his hair.

You bastard.

His office went dark. He was gone. Off to meet me.

Cal had predicted the sequence. ANTICIPATION? OR DID HE KNOW?

A shadow bobbed in the square hallway windows as Silver strode away.

Cal's message appeared: THAT WAS HIM?

Where had he stood to see but not be seen? The plainness of what he was doing seemed unbelievably gutsy.

I texted: GO.

The lab door opened and Cal slipped in, looking like a movie actor who'd wandered onto the wrong set. He moved quickly through Silver's office door, leaving the light off. Like he'd predicted, Matt, who must have been used to ignoring movement behind him, barely shifted in his seat, the screen a steady glow in his eyes.

The screen lit Cal's face, his exaggerated silhouette huge on the wall behind him, making him appear all the more focused.

I was counting to myself. Thirty seconds. A minute. Another.

Matt glanced over his shoulder, rubbed his neck, and turned back to his screen.

COME ON.

Time passing at its own pace, both stubborn and indifferent.

Another thirty seconds.

Cal stood. He looked at the screen, froze with hesitation, sunk back into Silver's desk chair.

Shadows moved in the hall—amorphous shapes, identities impossible to discern.

CAL, COME ON.

Another minute passed that seemed like an hour.

Finally, Cal stood again, waved the thumb drive up to the window, showing me, and moved quickly back out into the hall.

Matt never flinched.

I stood, turned the camera off, looked up at the sky to thank God. Then I gathered up the camera, tucked the tripod under my arm, and headed up the stairs for my keys. Cal would tell me what he'd found, then we'd call Allie, who would call Andre Mason. This would all be over in a few hours.

My phone lit up—Cal.

"Oh my God, you did it," I said, answering.

His breathing was fast as he walked. "Emily, it's bad. This is bad. It's not just a poison. This is bigger than us. Leave now, meet me at my house. Go."

"Cal? What is it?"

"Emily, *go*. Now. I'm leaving."

I hung up, dropped the phone into the pocket of my coat. Sprinting to the door as best I could with my ankle, I reached for the light switch.

Then a voice came up the stairs.

"Dad?"

TWENTY-SIX

At first, the voice was so faint I couldn't even tell to whom it belonged. But a part of me knew. A pinprick, a grain of sand inside me dropping so fast its wake left pure nausea. The height from the top of the stairs spun my stomach.

I jogged down, the boot like a block of cement around my foot. I dragged my fingertips against the walls to keep from toppling forward.

"Please, no," I said to myself. An auditory hallucination, I wished, birthed from utter fatigue. We'd get the thumb drive into Mason's hands, then I'd submit to the sleep that so desperately wanted to shatter my consciousness.

But I hadn't imagined anything.

"Dad?" No question it was Olivia. Playful, curious. It made sense after the phone call.

She was already in the stairwell when I found her. Bright-yellow raincoat, sandy-brown hair in a tangle. Her eyes and mouth in a delighted, if slightly impish, smile. Her freckled cheeks, reddened by the cold, were the color of some tender flower.

I'd spent enough time with kids to read the expression immediately. Accomplishment. Pride.

"Miss Emily, I walked here by myself," she said enthusiastically, two thumbs to her chest like she'd just won a prize.

Fuck, I thought.

I worked to keep my voice calm. "You walked?"

"I walked from Mom's. It's less than two blocks." She pointed behind her, voice confident using the borrowed phrasing.

I sank onto the stairs and put my hands on her shoulders. The sound of rumpling vinyl as they ran up and down the arms of the raincoat she'd worn for some reason. "Honey, you should not have done that. Where's your mom now?"

Please say *right outside*, I thought. I wanted there to be a running car in the driveway, a harried mom rushing in the door. There was neither.

Cracks showed in Olivia's expression, my concerns seeming to dilute her pride in having found her way. She'd so clearly hoped for enthusiasm in exchange for her big triumph.

"With Billy."

Who the fuck is Billy? I wanted to scream.

"Who?" I asked.

"Mom's writing partner. She's usually gone an hour, but sometimes it's more. But not much more. Really." She could see that all was not right in my eyes and flipped into the mode of defending her mom. "She put on a movie; she'll be back before lunch. There's plenty to eat."

"Honey, it's okay."

It was not okay. Cal's words rang in my memory: *Like having two kids sometimes.* But there was no time for judgment. This had happened. Cal and she would sort it out later.

"Where, um . . . where's my dad?" she asked, looking past my shoulder.

A flock of golden leaves spun like a miniature tornado at the bottom of the stairwell. I brushed a wind-tangled twist of hair off her cheek, regretting already what I was about to tell her. "I'm on my way to meet him. I was on the way out the door." A truth so incomplete it sounded dishonest.

"Oh." She flashed disappointment.

Then just as quickly, she linked her tiny fingers through mine, tugging me the rest of the way up the stairs.

"Dad said this is your office? You work here?"

"I do." I was trying to sound calm, but adrenaline had raised the pitch and volume of my voice. And, aside from that, I was wild-eyed, surely. The space felt unsafe suddenly. I forced in a deep breath to calm down.

We went into my office and I pulled the door until I heard the brass inside clink. My heart thundered in my chest as I dug for my phone, dialed Cal's number.

We'd talked—what? Two minutes earlier.

Pick up, I thought. Please.

No answer.

On a wire outside, black birds—two together, one apart.

He's driving. He's turned the ringer off, or can't hear it over that old engine.

Panic swelled inside me.

Olivia kicked off her boots and reclined on my couch, stretching her fingertips and toes as she tried touching both ends. "It's quiet here," she said.

It was true. The heat was off-cycle for the moment, waves of distant traffic the only sound.

I shook my head to snap my mind back. Three days, three hours' sleep. My chest felt hollow. My mouth was an empty coffee cup.

If ever there was a time to be freaked out, it was right then.

I texted him: OLIVIA SHOWED UP HERE. WE'RE UP IN MY OFFICE. PLEASE ADVISE.

No response.

"Yeah, it's supposed to be quiet. It's supposed to help people relax when they're talking."

"They just talk when they're here? Like, talk and talk and talk?"

"No, not really." I was keyed up, trying not to sound snappy. "Most are kids, like you."

I was thinking, thinking. I couldn't take her back to her mom's. Dropping her off alone in an empty apartment was irresponsible, unthinkable. But would she be safer there than with us?

"What do they talk about?" Olivia continued.

"All sorts of things."

"Like what?"

I just couldn't possibly explain right at that moment. I'd pulled my phone from my pocket and was staring at it, willing it to ring. "Honey, I'll tell you another time. Do you know your mom's number?"

"Nope." Her curls swayed as she shook her head. She was propped up on her elbows, pumping her feet as if working imaginary pedals.

I pictured Detective Mason pulling up just then in a police cruiser. I'd have to explain everything wearing freezing-cold handcuffs. Olivia would be in the company of police—or worse—taken to DHS, for God's sake.

They'll think you kidnapped her.

That wouldn't really happen.

Would it?

Wind rattled the windows as I looked down at the street. Coming from the direction of the park, a car slowly passed down the side street. Was it a police cruiser? Unmarked? It was big enough.

Maybe someone else.

Was I being paranoid?

I pushed off the couch. "Honey, we need to go."

"Why'd my dad leave?" Olivia asked.

"He went to the medical center for a few minutes. Come on, I'm going to run you home."

"Why'd he go to the medical center?"

"I'll tell you on the way. He's taking longer than I thought," I explained, picking her raincoat up from the floor. I opened the door.

In the stairwell, I texted Cal again, as if doing so would make him reply sooner. LEAVING NOW, GOING TO YOUR PLACE.

Something had gone wrong.

I pulled the front door closed behind us. Outside, the sky was the same low gray it had been all morning. Olivia ran her fingers through dust on my truck that'd never washed away. We climbed in. I blew into the Breathalyzer, turned the keys.

"What's that plastic thing? That?" She pointed, her expression curious, wanting clarification. We pulled away. We needed to move.

"Oh, this? It makes sure I'm healthy before I start driving."

Her nose wrinkled. "You're sick?"

"Not anymore. I was, before, but now I'm fine. It's just to make sure I'm safe to drive." I looked at her. "Which I am, obviously; otherwise I wouldn't be driving you." I meant to sound reassuring but was obviously creating the opposite impression.

I caught her glancing down at my boot, her eyes flicking over the scar on my hand.

Kids love the truth.

"I made a bad decision," I admitted, "And . . . drove when it wasn't safe. I wouldn't do it again, but they need to be sure. So I have this gadget for a while."

She nodded. "So why are you crying?"

I wiped at my eyes, not wanting to admit I was terrified. "I'm sorry. I'm just trying to figure something out."

"What?" She blinked.

Where in the hell we're going, I thought.

"How best to get ahold of your mom or dad," I said. "Somehow we obviously got turned around."

Just a little more time. If I got us to a place away from danger, then Cal would pop back up.

No one comes back, remember? Stop hoping.

My heart recovered a memory of a rocking sailboat, of nausea, of being lost. But goddammit, I was going to take this little girl somewhere safe.

Behind us, the same car passed again. A plume of exhaust drifted up as it pulled to a stop.

No, I was imagining that.

Who could I call?

Allie.

Driving, I dialed the phone, wiping away tears and the snot draining from my nose with the rough sleeve of my sweater.

"You shouldn't do that and drive," Olivia informed me.

Least of our problems, I thought.

Allie answered and relief flooded me.

"Hey! Allie, it's me." Finally, a stopgap from the world having fallen completely apart. A path to safety, to Olivia getting away from whatever was happening. "Allie, I'm in trouble. Really, this time, really, listen. I know, I know, but listen—"

Dead air came through the line. Try not to sound maniacal, I thought. Try.

"Hi, how are you?" she began, before a small hesitation. "Great to hear from you."

The calm calculation in her voice stopped me cold.

"Allie, listen."

"I'll be just a moment," she insisted in a clipped, banal tone, like a hurried flight attendant.

Beyond her voice was the sound of movement. Her standing, a door closing.

I wore people out. But this was different. Different from every other emergency I'd bothered friends to untangle. It was life or death.

I pulled the phone away from my face to check the time. Almost half an hour since I'd heard from Cal. Anger pressed inside me, but weakly. Really, it was fear. A terror of falling and never stopping.

Allie was back on the line, her voice completely different—a harsh whisper, exasperated. "Look, they know you were at Summit last night. I'm an idiot for telling you any part of that. For feeling like I owed you an apology. This gets us both. I'm lucky I haven't been arrested. This is you tampering with a witness. This is me colluding."

I was shaking my head. "Stop. Allie. Cal's gone . . . I was wrong about everything. Matt Cianciolo's not involved. It's—"

She cut me off, abruptly. "Where are you right now? Never mind. You know something, Emily? Andre Mason is going to arrest you today."

"What? No, Allie—"

"And honestly, right now, I can't tell if that's a bad thing. At least until everything gets sorted out."

Olivia had tugged open the visor. She was opening and closing the business card–sized mirror to illuminate its light, which—unbelievably—still worked.

I could not get arrested right then. Not that there's ever a great time to get arrested. But me in a cell meant not finding Cal, meant not protecting Olivia, meant me losing what remained of my career. It meant Jay Silver flying away to London—or anywhere he wanted.

Allie sounded as though she'd just straightened her posture. It felt like the phone call was in its final few seconds. Maybe someone had walked in.

Or maybe she's recording you.

"My advice?" she said. "Let him bring you in. Go directly home, call him, and wait. The longer you run, the worse it's going to look."

I'm running?

"Allie," I was shouting. "It's Silver. Jay Silver."

But she didn't hear me.

"I sure as hell hope they're wrong, Emily. I sure as hell hope you had nothing to do with people dying—and that I haven't helped you."

"You need to stop. Listen."

"Call Mason," she said. "But call your lawyer first. That's my advice."

Then she hung up.

Tires hummed over the road, wind gusts shoving wickedly at the windshield. I dropped the phone into a cup holder, trying to keep my eyes ahead.

Stay focused.

"Miss Emily? Are you okay? Where are we going?"

"Your house, honey. Your dad's going to meet us there."

At a stop sign, I wiped at my eyes, picked up the phone and began mapping the address he'd entered. "We'll find your dad super-soon, I know it."

I did not know it. *I'd like to thank the Academy, the Hollywood Foreign Press.*

The map function on my phone moved slowly, the spotty cell service making our position disappear into a gray grid.

"Lean back," I told her. "Just to be safe." I touched the back of her hair, my kidnappee, briefly imagining Detective Mason's owlish eyes as I explained absconding with her.

A bright room. Then a disciplinary board. Then a jail cell.

I stopped myself.

How had I gotten here? Boyfriend dead, suspected as a murderer, alienated from an old friend, and relying on a six-year-old for directions as we drove into the countryside.

TWENTY-SEVEN

Down the road we flew, the agricultural South around us. Fields were speckled with livestock, even that close to the city. Stacked stones; ghosts from the Civil War. The road sensibly straight until it curved to the will of limestone. Overhead, four black birds swept the gray sky in a loose downward spiral.

My phone chimed, an area code I didn't recognize. I reached for it then stopped short, my hand balling up. The near accident I'd had answering the phone while driving Cal flashed through my thoughts as I told myself to focus, to stay present.

Olivia looked at me expectantly.

"I'm sorry, That's not your dad calling. Just a salesperson or someone."

Olivia leaned forward, her forehead nearly meeting the dash, dim yellow sunlight turning her hair the color of caramel. She looked up at the birds, silent.

How long since I'd lost touch with Cal? I checked the time. It was after three now—almost an hour since I'd seen him leave Silver's lab. We drove. Miles. I imagined the truck's heat as steam off the engine, mercifully piping hot through the vents. Cars blew past. Tobacco drooped in the fields, laying still as in submission, afraid to sway in the wind. I looked in the rearview mirror; the road behind us was empty.

"That's it." Olivia pointed, finally. "With the white mailbox."

Dust whirled up behind the truck as I turned into the long ruts of the driveway. We bounced toward the house, only the green roof's peak visible until I topped a small rise. Then the rest of the wide, white porch came into view.

Cal had said it was country. He wasn't kidding—the place looked even more bucolic than I'd imagined. In a neat row along the side, four Volvos rested in various states. A tire swing he'd obviously hung for Olivia swayed like a fish in a too-small bowl, continually encountering glass.

I'd hoped that we'd find his Volvo in the driveway. Its absence prickled the skin on the back of my neck. I tried his cell again. Nothing. My finger hovered over the phone to call the police, stopped. What was I going to tell them? That Cal was missing? I knew this routine. Twenty-four hours at least, then they'd talk to me about his right to privacy and start to search for him.

And who was looking? Me, of course.

The person they suspected in one disappearance, one murder. They'd haul me in, and haul Olivia . . . somewhere? State custody? It seemed like an impossible choice. I was in a game with no rules.

I told myself he would be there any minute.

Tall pines lined the acre clearing, throwing long shadows onto the wind-burnt grass. Olivia produced from her pocket a beaded key chain, dog-shaped. Olivia unlocked the front door and the mix of air rushed in both directions through the open door. Inside was temptingly warm.

The orderliness was intense. Countertops gleamed. Chairs were neatly tucked in behind the kitchen table. Shoes arranged in a row at the foot of the coat closet. Everything in its place.

I scanned the hallway. Empty.

Outside, the tire swing continued its short circle.

I could see Olivia's earlier enthusiasm had begun to wane. Even for someone used to trusting, this had turned into a very strange day.

I found a bathroom in the front hallway and washed my face. The circles under my eyes were so dark they looked painted on, like a ballplayer would do if he were trying to block the sunlight of a day-game. The hand towel I dried with smelled like Dial soap.

When I came back into the living room, Olivia pointed at my boot. "What happens when you break a bone?" she asked.

I tried for some sort of answer, exhausted but full of energy. "You have to wear one of these," I explained. "It's really not so bad. Then your body heals itself."

She considered this idea as I watched the road, my hand resting on the curtain as if I was hiding behind it; I rubbed the textured material between my forefinger and thumb. I didn't want to, but I checked the time again. Cold radiated through the old glass.

This was more than not good. This was very bad.

I flashed back to having my chin tucked over the back of the couch when I was seven, eight, looking out at the street, waiting for my father's car—before I taught myself to stop expecting him. There had been a feeling like excitement, like in a movie: watching him come around a sparkling hood—a hopeful, wistful look in handsome eyes. In daydreams, he looked like a film star from the fifties, someone in black-and-white, wearing a suit jacket. Maybe an apology ready for the miscommunication that separated us for so many years; one that I was fully ready to accept.

It didn't have to be real to make me feel better.

Olivia pointed to a door immediately off the living room, asked hesitantly, "Is it okay if I go to my room?"

"Of course. I'll be right here."

Wait, I thought, this is stupid.

If someone—Silver—had found Cal, could he find us here?

I grabbed the hood of her raincoat. "Hold on a second. Honey, stay on the porch for me, okay? I need to write a note for your dad." My head was a buzz of anxiety, a swarm of crickets in summer.

The rural hush made it seem like somewhere a person was waiting. A monster.

He's coming.

The feeling of being Olivia's age, younger, when getting up from bed, walking through a dark house, could terrify. Something waiting in shadow that would get me, kill me.

There's fear, and then there's real fear.

Be the bigger monster. Stress brings out the manic in you.

I turned over the back of a broad, white envelope. Country light cut in through the kitchen window above the sink. Reaching for a pen from a tall mug beside the phone, I knocked them all over. The pens scattered across the worn tabletop, a few dropping loudly onto the floor.

"Shit," I said.

I had to think about how to do this, the point of the pen pressed against the envelope a bead of sweat on my forehead. I uncapped a ballpoint and wrote in large letters.

Olivia's with me. We're okay. We went to my family's cabin.
-E

I heard his words in my memory. It was the best I had.

He knew where Exactly where. *Where the lightning split the tree.*

"Miss Emily?"

In the light of the front door, Olivia was framed like a painting. Like a girl looking to the road for her father from a long time ago. I tried to catch my breath, tried not to act like someone was behind me. I dropped my hands onto her shoulders, my eyes squinting, adjusting to the light. I'd talked with plenty of upset kids at work, but in those moments, I hadn't been the one who was afraid. I glanced back up at the fence line. Still empty.

"We can't stay here, but we're going somewhere pretty close. Your dad will know where we are. We're going to find him, or he's going to find us." I rubbed my hands up and down on her shoulders, my eyes level with hers, and I leaned one knee onto the porch. "All right?"

Olivia's faith in me was beginning to wear thin. Trust is an earned thing, and it's finite. We were reaching the edge of far too much.

"But when are we going to find him?"

"Soon."

"You're sure?"

God, I wanted to be sure.

Back down the road. Opposite direction, to the safest place I knew.

I wondered if it was obvious we were hiding. I remembered playing hide-and-go-seek as a kid, maybe Olivia's age, maybe younger, peering through the slats of a closet door, or from behind the rough-barked sycamore in the back, my heart pounding so hard my chest shook.

Don't find me. Just a little longer. Don't see me. Fall leaves, speckled with black and brown, crunched under my neighbor's shoes. My cousin. My best friend, Meredith. They took turns hunting me. Strange game for children to play, I'd thought, even at the time. *I'm not afraid of these people; I know them too well.*

It was only four o'clock, but the coming dark seemed like an immovable dome. Bars appeared again on my phone. Beside each outgoing number, my phone listed how many times I'd tried to call. Beside Cal's name was a five. I made it six and pressed the phone to my ear. Voicemail again.

Oh, Cal, where are you?

I knew there was no point in continuing to call—heaven knows he would have been aware by then that I was trying to get his attention. Six missed calls and I'd kidnapped his daughter. *What else do you want?*

Late autumn wind shoved at the truck, whistling through the window gaps. Between us, my phone rang again. Same generic number. I swatted at it like a fly trapped inside the truck; I wanted back the space it occupied in my consciousness.

"We're not far now. It's just another little while," I said. "You okay?"

She made a resigned expression. *Not okay, but okay.*

"Miss Emily, are you going to answer your phone?"

I turned it over, looked up. In the other direction, a car rushed past.

Pay attention, my thoughts screamed.

"It's just a wrong number," I hurried to say, "Or marketing."

Or the police, I thought. Someone who was not Cal.

I cleared the breathy windshield with the back of my sleeve.

"What's marketing?" Olivia asked tentatively, registering my annoyance.

I started to explain when the phone began its condensed melody again, like a door slamming again and again in the wind.

"Is it my dad?" she asked. Her hands were fists in her lap.

"No, baby."

My eyes stayed on the road, but my hand hovered over the phone.

"Can I answer it?" she asked.

"Sure," I said absently.

Her fingertip slid across the screen. With both hands she held the phone to her cheek before a stillness came over her.

A moment passed.

"Okay," she said, passing the phone to me.

I put the phone to my ear.

"Emily," the voice said. "It's me."

TWENTY-EIGHT

In shock, sound disappears. Neurons slow time as a defense mechanism.

For an instant, then, time vanished—no divisions between past and future existed.

No sensible ones, anyway.

———

I was ten again, hair rising along the back of my neck an instant before a knock at the front door. All morning, the house had been so quiet it echoed the hallway clock's ticking. My mother, already so edgy that she'd wept earlier when a glass slipped through her hands and broke, rushed through the foyer, smoothing her hair. She knew already, I'm sure.

Because I knew, too.

Silence was a language—a meaningful lull, a body releasing breath.

Out front, two men squinted in the sun, both with folded hands. One had the courage to look at Mom directly. Neither dared to glance at the eight-year-old girl standing behind her.

"Yes," my mom said, answering their question. "This is the home of Dr. Sydney Firestone."

The men stepped inside; the taller of the two closed his eyes. He explained that medical missions carried tremendous risks. A virus, he said, named H1-N24, was both lethal and contagious, and had the shortest incubation period anyone had ever seen.

My mother dropped the kitchen towel she had been wringing between her hands.

It fell so heavily that I swore, for years, I could see a mark where it landed—a curled, shadowy symbol, dented into the hardwood, signifying the rapidity of change.

Life before, life after.

It marked the ease with which people disappear.

But as it turned out, the opposite happened sometimes, too.

———

I coughed, words failing me. "Who—"

"Emily, It's Paolo. It's me. You have to listen. You're in danger right now."

I knew right then that some part of me had refused to accept his death all along. They never had found him. There was a funeral, but he'd never died.

There's perception, then there's thought, and then, beneath thought, feelings reside. But beneath feelings, deepest of all, is intuition.

And I never should have ignored my intuition.

I was now in a reality where his words continued to be part of this world. The impossibility of his voice narrowed my field of vision. The edge of everything blackened.

"I know, it's a shock. I'm sorry. I had to . . . I got involved in something way beyond . . . I wanted to contact you another way, but you have to listen, now."

Through my chest, the stages of grief began to cycle in reverse. Anger, fury burst through. Then disbelief. "Who is this?" I demanded.

"It's me," he whispered. "Emily, you're not safe."

There is no safe, I thought. Safe is a fake idea. The last six weeks began to rewind in my mind like a film.

The ghost who called himself Paolo continued, "I read about Sandy, Emily. The news said she was found by a local psychologist. I knew that meant you were involved. Please. I want you to come with me. At least for now."

"*With* you?"

Like I was going anywhere with him.

Olivia stared at me. Somehow, I continued to drive.

My mind circled the word it wanted like a cord around a tether pole. "Why?" I murmured.

In his sigh, I heard acknowledgement that some explanation was needed before anything else he said could matter.

"I got pulled in way, way too far. Silver wouldn't let me stop, said we had to keep going. I ended up a part of something . . ."

The dirt road to the cabin approached on our left. The wheels spun through loose dirt as I cut past the rusted mailbox, rumbling over the uneven ground. Dusky shadows spiderwebbed over the bare brush and pine straw. We bumped along toward the cabin. At the road's end, the porch was on one side, the property's lake on the other. The truck skidded to a stop. I cut the engine. The country quiet surrounded us with its tiny harmonies, a hush of gentle calling and answering. My heart pounded.

Olivia looked at the lake, then to me. *Can I look at the water?* she mouthed.

I nodded. "Keep back from the edge, okay? Very steep."

Her eyes smiled exactly like Cal's. She trotted through the breezy grass, parting the faint flow of pale green.

It was already getting dark—the sky dimming by the minute.

"Are you there?"

"Yes." How was I continuing to talk? I had no idea.

"Emily, where are you now?" he asked.

"The cabin," I admitted for no reason I could discern. My sense of what was real turned wavy.

Paolo's surreal explanation continued. "We were close. He started testing the H1-N24 vaccine on people. He wanted me there to record the trial, but it all went wrong. The man died. The vaccine gave him no protection when Silver introduced the virus. Silver had to set a fire to stop a possible contagion."

His accent had deepened in the weeks he'd been away—a

strange paradox. As if, alone, he'd reverted to a truer version of himself. He sounded like one of my teenage patients—that blend of embarrassment, relief, and pride in admitting the procedure of a crime.

"After that, I ran. That was the first week of October."

The picture.

"You were there," I mumbled.

I remembered the weekend after—the leafy shadows flying over us in his Jeep, his indifference to checking messages. His half smile.

We're on our holiday, he'd said.

Here's to freedom, I'd said.

His voice broke. "Then I heard what happened to Sandy. That can't happen to you. I started driving back this morning. I'm almost to Nashville now."

Too much; a flood of reality.

"I . . . have to go," I said, hanging up.

The need to find Cal washed over me in a wave.

I went to Olivia, who stared back at me wide-eyed. I swallowed, crouched down, rubbed her arms. "I'm sorry," I said. "Let's go inside where it's warm."

And I was. I was really, really sorry she was a part of what was happening. A pit of self-hatred flared inside me, reminded me of how I infected everyone's life with madness. I'd make it up to her, I thought. Her and Cal. Somehow. I took her hand. I sorted through my key ring and found the key that unlocked the cabin, gripping it tightly between my forefinger and thumb.

"Are you okay?" Olivia asked. She looked at my shaking hand.

On the front steps, my phone chimed again. I slid the key in the front door.

Reflexively, I brought the phone to my ear.

Paolo's voice again, shouting now. "Go to the police. Please, turn around. He knows, Emily. He knows you know—"

Movement from behind the front door.

I felt a sting in the back of my neck.

As I dropped to my knees, I heard Olivia, her scream liquefied in my ears by whatever I'd just been given—as if we were both deep under water.

"There's a little girl here," I protested, drowsily, "A girl . . ."

TWENTY-NINE

Consciousness never left, not fully. The sedative was like a dip into an indefinite dream; light blinked out, but the sound continued, volume low. Murmurs, Olivia's terrified pleas. Then, silence. I felt the sensation of my body being dragged and the horrifying inability to resist. My skull felt dented, damaged. Pain radiated across my left side.

Then, there were slivers of light, like looking through a dark sheet. Just movement, shadows. The sun was a blot on the tree line, casting a thin, pink gauze over the surface of the lake.

I was in a chair, one from the kitchen. My shoulders bent unnaturally, arms behind my back, hands zip-tied.

Just like the murder victims, before they were burned.

Olivia lay beside me, curled on the rug. Her chest rose and fell, dreamily.

Silver stomped past—a different version of the man I'd met on campus, at the fund-raiser, at his party. The elbows of his ski jacket were torn, his hair carelessly askew. He'd hidden in the dark, I now understood. He was muttering about changing the tires on his car to avoid being tracked, his pacing reverberating through the old floor like gentle thunder.

"It's an animal sedative. She, and you, won't feel a thing." He squinted at me, seeming to read my consciousness as defiance.

Like I could be sedated, I wanted to say. Mania, usually so destructive, simply plowed through whatever he'd given me. The same rush that loomed over my life now propped me up, gripped on to the moment. It wouldn't be denied. My mania took a dozen different sedatives, a professional crisis, and a hospitalization to derail. Silver's sedative was just turbulence.

He began opening the kitchen cabinets, stammering—not full sentences, but phrases, the sparks of some deluded fever dream: ". . . to start this . . . they'll think . . . I'm sorry . . . which of these things . . ." The floorboards creaked lightly in the quiet, country dark. The dim hallway light created an odd sense of vacancy, as though the three of us weren't actually there.

Where was Cal? I glanced at the window, praying for his headlights.

"I'll be in England this time tomorrow," Silver announced, shoes clapping across into the hallway, two rolls of paper towels clutched to his chest. His shadow clover-shaped beneath him, knife-sharp and murderous. I gritted my teeth, picturing him boarding a plane in the morning, leaving all of this—ashes, death—behind.

Cold air penetrated the room, cooling my sticky left cheek. Through the stream of blood running down my face, my vision was a blur. I forced my left eye closed. With the right, I saw that my boot had come off. My left leg hurt so bad I couldn't feel it.

"We're going to be okay," I whispered to Olivia, but she was sleeping.

My heart fluttered at an impossible pace, like hummingbird wings.

I coughed, catching Silver's attention. "How did you find us?" I managed to say. My manic voice was lower, scary-steady. I caught him doing a double take, looking at me as if I were a vicious dog. I knew that if I died, it would be with the satisfaction that he'd looked into my eyes and felt afraid.

"The police suspect you, so you wouldn't go to them. I knew you'd come here—your hiding place. 'Down the dirt road after the Concord exit,'" he recited, absently.

I thought back to the party, Paolo bragging about my family's "land."

"Cal's on his way here," I informed him.

"No, he's been detained." Silver opened another cabinet, peering inside. "He's good at sneaking in, but not so good at sneaking out. Breaking and entering."

"You called the police?" I nearly laughed. "He hacked your computer, downloaded proof of what you've been doing. He's telling them everything, right now. It's over."

Silver kept his gaze straight ahead. He mumbled as if replying to a voice inside his own head. "As if I'm that stupid. Whatever your friend found, I put there to find. We've . . come too far. It takes *years* to get a vaccine approved. Years. Trial upon trial, no money. Oversight but no help. Getting strangled for trying to help the world."

When he turned, I could see that his eyes were missing something. They were flat like a shark's or the fields in west Tennessee. He twitched with the same derangement I'd seen in hospitals— edgy desperation, unable to cloak the rolling boil of his thoughts.

A figure from a nightmare. The devil in my home.

I hated him.

A sane person, I knew, would submit to the obvious hopelessness. I blinked blood out of my eye, strained forward trying to stand. My chair nearly tipped over. The zip tie was intractable, cutting into my wrists.

Silver moved into the interior hallway, arms full. The corner of my eye registered another light switching on.

"Sydney Firestone's daughter," he mused, voice echoing off the bathroom tile. "I always wanted to meet your father," he said.

The bitter toxicity of something like lighter fluid wafted toward me. I strained upward, lurched forward, falling helplessly.

When Silver returned, he rested his hand on the doorknob and glanced at me curiously. "I did it, you know." He stopped and faced me. "It works. Just know that. The fourth subject showed complete immunity. H1-N24 is going to be wiped out—like smallpox. Like Polio. It's over."

My mind couldn't register the words, but somehow I knew I would remember them exactly. Forever.

"I never wanted it to be like this," he said. "For you, of all people."

"Let *her* go." My voice broke as I jerked my head toward where Olivia slept. "She has nothing to do with any of this."

But Silver's face turned trancelike as he went to the door.

And then he was gone, down the back steps, leaving the door creaking behind him.

"What are you doing?" I screamed, but I knew exactly what he intended. I was in a wooden structure with wood paneling and floors. I knew that accelerant was hardly needed. A fire would turn the cabin to ash in no time. The lighter fluid smell was strong enough to burn the inside of my nose.

I tried to inch closer to Olivia, the chair legs squeaking as I scraped them across the floor. "Olivia, you have to wake up."

She hardly stirred, perfectly numbed by whatever he'd given her and me.

As wind ripped through the curtains, I heard the first rush of the fire behind me. Feverish energy reddened my skin, widened my eyes. I worked my wrists against the ties as flames rose in a great whoosh behind my back. The curtains had caught fire.

Olivia's eyes barely cracked open. "Hold on," I said to her.

I heard the quiet rumble of Silver's car starting outside.

Keep on, my heart said. You can't stop.

I tried standing, collapsed, tried again. My cheek rubbed roughly against the dusty boards. But falling knocked the slats away from the bottom of the chair, just slightly. I strained my shoulders up, working the plastic into my skin, slipping my wrists down. I'd learned in soccer how to treat my body like a machine—that it was just a thing that could do incredible *and* destructive things. I'd learned about unnatural ways it wasn't supposed to move, but could. I'd learned how to play hurt. Pain, you just ignore it. I knew I'd break the chair apart, even if it wasn't possible. Invincibility doesn't have to be rational to be real.

A rush of air brushed my hair back as flames shot up the living room wall. In seconds, it was all orange and white light, pulsing and alive. My forearms and neck registered the immense heat, my mouth dry from exertion.

I worked my hands looser. Blood where the zip tie cut into me ran into my palm. I pressed the side of my foot against the floor, testing the leverage. I wiggled my wrists further down the slats, collapsing my stomach, then arching my back until one hand, then the other, popped free. I pushed myself onto my hands, brought my knees under me, stood. A rush of dizziness into the front of my head, the headache where I'd hit the floor nearly overwhelming, threatening to crumple me.

I steadied myself against the mantel, brought Olivia to my chest, still mercifully asleep. Her downy breath calm in my ear.

I staggered to the rear door, then stopped. The ceiling was a bitter cloud that I could taste. Part of me knew my eyes stung, but another part couldn't care. Heat pressed behind us, drawn through the open rear door toward the dark wood as the air swam with confetti-like ash.

Headlight beams sliced the dark. Silver had concealed his car earlier, I could see, and now struggled to get it free. The wheels spun helplessly in the grainy sand at the edge of the wood as his engine howled its tantrum, gray arcs rising from behind his rear tires.

I spotted my keys, resting where they'd landed after flying from my hand when Silver attacked me. I scooped them off the floor.

"Hold on," I said, swiveling. I staggered back through the cabin toward the front door. Flames reflected off my truck's dark hood, and in the rippling lake beyond.

Down the porch steps, I could hear the crush of wet grass, then gravel, beneath my feet. My heartbeat was liquid bass, thumping in my ears, my breath a frantic cloud in thin, persistent waves.

The truck's door creaked as I flung it open. I laid Olivia inside, keys jostling in my hand. My ears rang, lungs searching for air as I reached for the Breathalyzer. Spittle ran down my cheek as I blew desperately. I turned the keys until the engine growled to life. I shifted into gear, eyeing the edge of the lake as I cut toward the driveway leading to the road. But before I could press the accelerator,

I sensed movement in the rearview mirror. The driver's side door opened and suddenly Silver was beside us, his face a mask of twisted fury, strained from sprinting. I reached out to block his advance, but his fist landed against my left side, met my shoulder hard, then my skull.

Hot pressure, pain.

He brought his fist down again, this time grabbing the back of my neck. I blocked his reach as he shoved me aside, jumped in the cab, and grabbed for the column shifter. His hand grasped onto the steering wheel beside mine, pulling, turning us. I stomped the accelerator.

The driver's side door flapped with each bounce. I prayed Silver would lose his grip on the wheel as I accelerated toward the fence line that rushed toward us.

The angle of the fire in the rearview mirror began to turn.

The left tires lost traction on the embankment as the truck surged left, screaming.

We rolled—the world inverting, violently. I reached around Olivia.

The hood plunged into the lake with a sound like a wave against a seawall. The engine sobbed a pleading hiss as it followed. Water like liquid black filled the truck cabin, shockingly cold, as we came to rest on the driver's side of the cab underwater.

Then I was a girl watching my grandmother wade into the river, a girl whose head had been held under water during a swim lesson. I was a teenager sitting nervously on a dock during a class trip. I was a girlfriend who'd agreed to try one night aboard a sailboat.

And I was about to drown with a child in my arms.

———

That couldn't happen. I thrashed my legs as lake water filled my mouth.

The three of us turned sideways over the seats. The passenger side door was close enough to the surface that murky light penetrated the window. My fingers found the gummy steering wheel, then pressed buttons, finally grasping and pulling a lever that released something. A clunking noise up front, a swarm of tiny bubbles rising. The hood must have popped open.

Within seconds, breathing room at the surface-side of the cabin had disappeared. Silver flailed violently below me, grabbing at the back of my shirt, my belt. I kicked him, stepping onto his shoulder as I reached for the door handle on the other side, trying to cradle Olivia and push up, out, fighting the suddenness of being enveloped, surrounded.

The lake, swollen with rain, wanted to swallow everything, it seemed. The truck cabin seemed to push inward as we slid along the bottom. Streaks of light from the flames penetrated the surface like angled bamboo stalks, dwindling into darkness. I fought the bulk of my clothes; cold, loose weights around me.

I pushed and my lungs screamed. I was blacking out.

But fully manic, blacked out doesn't mean stop. There is no stop.

You act when there is no energy to do so.

You do the impossible.

My eyes strained. Shapes were barely visible through the murk. I couldn't see my hands. The flow of water told me that the car continued to slide deeper. Silver's grip around my leg slipped onto my ankle.

My hands searched the doors' edges until I found a handle, then another, my lungs burning hotly. I found a plastic piece, the length I'd expected, then could feel the force of a door opening, whatever remained of the air escaping toward the light. I pushed with one foot against the dashboard.

Above, a shape appeared, and Olivia rose from my hands toward the surface.

Pain disappeared, eclipsed by oxygen's singular absence. My head lightened. There was no more breath in me.

A few seconds passed. Silver's grip released.

Then a hand wrapped around my wrist from above and pulled hard.

My eyes closed as I rose toward moonlight, until I found the world again and drew in a furious gasp.

Air.

Another breath, then another.

I was dragged until I found footing, my shoes pressing first through mud, then onto limestone.

I crawled through the silt to the edge, focused on two silhouettes.

Olivia's feet dangled from a set of arms. Her head hung limp, hair elongated by the water, reaching to the ground like the twisted brown vines of some haunted, horrible tree.

The first red lights of emergency vehicles appeared along the road.

I struggled to stand.

And as I did, Olivia jerked, coughing, blinking in confusion. As if waking from a dream, she looked at the person who had just pulled her from the water.

With a shiver, she asked, "Paolo?"

THIRTY

Where the driveway met the road, a car—compact, American, maybe twenty years old—rested at an odd angle. more stopped abruptly than parked. In the dim light, I could see a haze of oxidation across its hood and that one of the rear doors was sadly dented in. I turned and stared at the water's surface for signs that Silver was following, but there were none—only a steady gurgle as what remained of the air trapped inside the truck escaped.

A rush of red lights appeared at the end of the driveway. In seconds, uniformed EMT workers surrounded Olivia, wrapping her in a navy blanket as she answered their questions.

I was sure the first blue lights would appear soon.

Flames reddened the cabin's roof. Overhead, the clouds were gray wisps, hovering in the distance as if looking on.

I approached the ghost who had pulled Olivia and me from the water. Paolo faced the woods. I knew him, but I didn't. I understood now that I'd never known him, really. He'd been wearing a disguise all along. And yet, my heart lit with love when I looked at him, and I hated that. It was a lesser love, but still. Death and resurrection hadn't cleared my feelings.

A door inside me opened, through which I glimpsed the maddening calculus of it all—how Paolo must've swum to shore, how he'd needed me as a witness to his disappearance to remove suspicion around him.

How long he and Silver had carried on.

How fucking long.

The falsehood, for lack of a better word, multiplied exponentially in my mind the longer I considered it. Silver's inconceivable, limitless capacity to forge ahead. To act. To portray his obliviousness during the investigation into Paolo's death, then into Sandy's. To have the nerve to offer sympathy. To sit at a funeral, for God's sake, knowing what no one else did, dabbing at his eyes with some expensive handkerchief all the while.

I wondered where he had left the rest of himself, or where it had left him.

Paolo wrapped his arms around his shivering chest as I studied the details of his face, how pale he'd become. His shape was the same, a little thinner. He'd grown a wispy beard that didn't suit him. His black hair, longer now, caught the fire's light like a raven's wing. His skin was ashen, and a triangular chip was now missing from his front tooth—something he'd meant to have fixed, I was sure. His gaze narrowed with a sorrowful flintiness, eyebrows scrunched deep—maybe from the way he'd lived the preceding months, maybe from facing me.

In a blink, I saw him as he was on the dock the day he'd disappeared, the collar of his polo shirt popped, his Hollywood sunglasses on. His laughter and his cockiness and his enormous dreams. This man looked years older.

What to even begin to say? Part of me wanted to laugh—him being alive was so absurd.

The love I'd let rest returned to my chest with a stunning surge, like the reflexive insistence to breathe. It wasn't right, was it? I shouldn't have felt that way. But feelings aren't thoughts; you don't think them through. Self-awareness offered no disruption.

I remembered what he'd said on the phone, that he'd heard about Sandy and started back to Nashville that morning. That he couldn't let what happened to her happen to me.

My heart pounded.

"Emily, I can't stay here," he said.

"You're not going anywhere." My jaw trembled. "Where did you go? Where have you been?"

His head bent down. "I was terrified, beside myself with what we'd done. I went from thinking I was breaking rules—like some kind of medical outlaw—to being an accomplice to murder in a matter of seconds. The bottom fell out of everything." His voice cracked with anguish.

"Research is slow, even when the stakes are high. Silver worked at a different speed. The way he talked, rules didn't seem to apply. I felt like I could do anything—no, more than that. I felt like not doing everything I could was squandering time. When he suggested we cut sample sizes in half to double them and run sequence variants we hadn't declared, I agreed. He told me he would take responsibility. It was his lab. His plan was to start human testing *now* and make the success look like a home run on the first swing. He was a believer, like a cult leader, but for his own work." Paolo was nearly breathless. He covered his face with his hands. When they dropped, his dark irises reflected the orange firelight. "If it had worked, it would be like finding a golden ticket. No more fighting for grant funding. He told me money would come our way, too."

"Money?" I felt disbelief. Then I thought of Paolo's tendencies toward nice things. I imagined Silver had noticed that about him, too.

He motioned with his hand. There was more.

"Everything in that lab was regulated to the letter. Silver got me to do things for him. He got me to sign for more and more samples. Then to say I destroyed them in an autoclave, when I didn't. We're talking about breaking FBI regulations."

How much had he done? How much killing? Lying? Hiding? I needed to know, but didn't want to. I shivered from the chill of the air prickling up my spine.

I was shaking. I kept looking over my shoulder toward the lake as if Silver might emerge from it. My mind had hit the limit of how much trauma it could contain. An unreal sense of calm began to take hold amid the insanity.

A hundred feet away, Olivia was sitting up, then standing.

An EMT began toward us, then returned to Olivia when I waved him away.

"Then Gainer Ridge happened." Paolo looked away, bit his bottom lip.

I pictured the image in his camera—the one that had made me suspect a connection in the first place.

"Silver had no doubt the vaccine was going to work. He said it was a shame that just he and I would see history. I set up a tripod in the dirt to record. When the symptoms started, Silver was devastated. He was sobbing when he ended that man's life." Paolo swallowed, wincing as if the memory itself had a terrible taste. "I thought I'd deleted every image from that day."

He continued, "When I panicked, Silver told me he'd documented everything under Matt's login. I checked it myself, logged into the computer Matt used. That's what it took for me to see clearly who Silver was. I was living in a nightmare—only then realizing I'd been crazy to trust Silver."

"Sandy thought Matt was making a weapon," I said.

Paolo rubbed his eyes. "That's reasonable, with the faked records. But no, Silver was obsessed with the opposite. Willing to do anything. He got to where he couldn't see the risks. I think you're supposed to feel something before that happens—disgust with yourself, maybe? But each rule I broke along the way I thought would be the last. Each lie became easier. Then it was too late. I'd taken part in killing someone.

"Then immediately Silver wanted to start again. He told me, 'We can't let that man have died in vain. We can't let his death be for nothing.' For just a second, I considered it. And then I knew I couldn't. So I made a plan to disappear. I bought a car with cash. I thought when I got safely away, I would call the authorities. I wanted to contact you, so bad. The medication—I left it out in the Jeep, on the boat. I wanted it to look like I'd taken yours by accident and drowned. I swam to the other shore, a mile, more, climbed up using rocks, covered my footprints, drove east then south on a full tank of gas. I had no phone, only cash."

He reached for my hand and I pulled it away. Silver's frantic self-justification shouldn't have surprised me—doubling down is what people do when their judgment proves bad. When cognitive dissonance hits, people push forward—like gamblers who know their next hand will win because it has to.

"But how could you leave me that way? A suspect in a murder? Then in *two* murders? He killed Sandy, for God's sake."

"I never, ever imagined that would happen," he said. His voice was barely above a whisper but strained, raspy. "I'm sorry. I wanted to tell you when I got home. I was going to call the police and get in touch with you somehow. I prayed you'd forgive me."

I closed my eyes rather than showing any resonance with those words. Once you'd saved your own skin, I thought.

He looked up at me. "Your new hair . . . it looks nice. Pretty."

I kicked his shoe. "Stop."

Paolo's expression clouded with a child's confusion—lost and desperate and selfish. He hadn't understood the consequences for me when he ran, a part of me believed.

I loved you, I thought, but couldn't say the words.

————

In that objective instant, I imagined how horrible it had been for Paolo, too—free-falling suddenly while his fate cruelly reversed. In minutes, he had gone from taking partial credit in medical history to becoming a murderer. It had been the last thing he'd wanted or even suspected was possible, even while he denied the obvious risks. He'd borne the weight of such treacherous secrecy. It might have driven anyone to run for home, I thought, for safety.

Blue lights appeared at the edge of the driveway. Paolo's eyes shifted between me and the tree line. He rocked forward, wincing at the echo of car doors slamming. His eyes, wet and glassy, pointed upward, reflecting the last of the butter-colored porch light.

"I was afraid," he said. "You don't know what it's like to start in a new country, alone. Everything riding on your work. I worked around the clock, took pills to work longer and longer, harder and harder. Pressure, exhaustion—it made me lie. Running, all the time, a gambler trying to pay debts. Cal noticed. I blamed it on you. I'm sorry—"

In the distance, the squeak of a truck's air brake called, followed then by the distant calls of voices. The faraway sound of men devising solutions for large vehicles and an unmarked dirt driveway.

Bubbles rose on the lake's surface above where the truck rested. Concentric circles rippled outward like rolling wrinkles in the dark. I thought of the shocked, yearning last expression on Silver's face, and the horror of his drowned body. My head was dizzy with how close Olivia and I had come to death. I knew the tragedy of what had happened would extend over the coming weeks in the form of an investigation.

"Silver used to tell this story about Edward Jenner developing the smallpox vaccine. Did you know the first time he tested it, he used his gardener's son? Silver couldn't stop. Everything . . . it was too far."

"Too far," I said, my voice breaking. "I loved you with all my heart." *How's that for too far?*

The blue lights brightened, warbling sirens becoming clearer.

Paolo shook his head, as if rebuking himself, then rubbed at his eyes again. He looked up at me with a boy's gaze. A boy who'd grown up in a shack in Argentina with two brothers and a single mother. Stealing to eat. Later, entranced by America. A scholarship student, like me.

"You and Cal?" he asked.

"Stop," I said. A million thoughts. No time. "I mourned you." I kicked his foot again. "You knew I didn't swim."

A flashlight found us. I shielded my eyes. Beyond it, I saw Cal's form, sprinting toward Olivia.

Paolo had an expression on his face that I'd never seen before. It wasn't sorrow, and it wasn't fear.

"Emily, I have to go," he said.

I'll always wonder what he meant by that. From here at the

cabin, facing arrest? Or from here, in this world, living as the person I thought he was?

Without his help, Olivia and I would have been killed. But then, without his involvement, none of us would have been in that position in the first place.

He'd never set out to be a killer.

Neither had Silver.

But was it possible for him to vanish again? The unfathomable shock of the unexpected visit stole away my words. I called Paolo's name as he moved into darkness, shoes splashing through the edge of the water. An EMT's flashlight followed his form until it became a shadow. Then the shadow dissolved, becoming nothing.

And then he was gone, again.

THIRTY-ONE

Light flooded the night until it no longer seemed like night. Half of everything was red, the other half blue—all of it flashing. The cruiser and ambulance windows reflected it all.

Paolo had told the truth—he'd called the police just after our call ended. Dark uniforms approached with guns drawn. Voices shouted over the rumble of large engines. How many? I had no idea. Toward the road, it looked like an army was invading. Hands on my shoulders, under my arms, two people in uniforms directing me away from the lake.

Across the yard, a flashlight shined in Cal's face as he shielded his eyes. A team led him and Olivia toward the open doors of an ambulance, where white light and sterility waited.

Detective Mason appeared and moved toward me like a guided missile. With an arm around my shoulder, he took me to a police cruiser, deposited me in the back.

"Stay here," he said, slamming the door. Then, momentary silence. I couldn't tell if he meant to protect or detain me. The back of the cruiser smelled the way they all do—half like a locker room, half like chewing gum. I sat still, blinking, stunned. In the rearview mirror, I caught a glimpse of myself. I looked like a meth addict who'd wrestled a bobcat.

Time passed, and Mason came back to the car. A shriek of noise from outside as he climbed in the front, then closed his door.

Silence again.

Here we are, I wanted to say. *My old buddy. Another crime scene.*

Together again. But the part of me that joked had shrunken small, too tired to kid.

No cologne wafted over me from his direction. He must have figured something out, I thought.

He turned, arm draped over the seat. "Are you okay?" He squinted at the gash on the side of my head, though the lake had washed away much of the blood.

"I have no idea how to answer that. Are you arresting me?"

"No." He shook his head. He sounded softer. He'd dropped some of the professional bravado from earlier. He sounded serious, almost sullen. Like he'd missed out on something or he'd lost a game and was trying to figure out what went wrong. "Cal filled me in on what you two were doing. I know you think you're the only one who can figure things out, but we were in the process of getting a warrant to search that lab. You're apparently not very good at—"

"At waiting," I interrupted.

"You need to get checked out medically. There are going to be a lot of questions, but you're not under arrest. Not right now."

Neither of us spoke for a moment.

Mason faced forward, eyes on mine in the rearview. He rubbed his neck, right above the rose tattoo. "This isn't a formal questioning, but I got to ask you something, okay?'

"Okay."

"One of the EMTs said someone—black hair, six foot, someone who fits the description of Mr. Fererra—ran from here. You saw him, too?"

"More than saw. I talked to him. He saved our lives." A part of me hated to say so, but it was true.

Mason chewed his gum silently for long enough that I wondered what he was thinking—about the gray deck shoe caught in the water grate, or the prescription pills, or if I was lying or crazy.

Then he said, "That little girl is lucky. You are, too. You must be in shock." His voice was kind. "Probably not what you expected when you woke up this morning."

"Well, I've been awake for three days now, so technically it wasn't what I expected on any of these mornings. But I see your point."

We both watched in silence as a fire crew began to spray water onto what remained of the cabin. A great burst of steam mixed with the white smoke rising into the sky.

Mason turned his head, pointed. "He ran, right? Into those woods? You try to stop him?"

"Something like that."

Mason snorted. Shook his head. "Don't worry, doc. He'll be found. Promise. It's not gonna take long. Probably he'll come to us."

He won't, though, I thought. You'll never find him. None of us will ever see him again.

———

Mason was exactly right—I went straight to the hospital. Two uniformed cops stood in the emergency room on either side of me.

"You guys my bodyguards?"

They didn't answer.

The old me might have found that uncomfortable. Not anymore. Run of the mill by then.

The slimmer of the two said, "They called your mother. She's on her way back into town."

"Thanks."

I wore a gown. There was a flashlight in my eyes, shots in my arms and scalp. Five stitches over my left eye.

"Sorry if this hurts," the resident said.

"Really," I told her, "don't worry about it."

Then there was waiting, emotionlessness. My dirty feet freezing, brushing back and forth on a hospital floor that was supposed to look like wood.

The resident, who looked younger than me, asked what I needed.

"To talk to Cal," I answered.

Both cops shook their heads.

"In that case, something to eat. My Lamictal. Then five days' sleep."

The resident smirked, hands shoved into the pockets of her white coat. "I think you're going to be okay," she said.

EPILOGUE

"Andy," Olivia said. "Andy." She tossed a tennis ball, and Andy leapt, catching it in the air. The ball had been meant to help Olivia learn softball basics—throwing and hitting. It was softer and more forgiving than a traditional softball but by then was covered in Andy's slobber and, because of that, also leaf fragments and dirt. Andy returned the ball to her, and she ran her fingers through the thick fur along his back.

Cal touched his daughter's curls. "Livvy, put your sweater on and take Andy out to the backyard. I'm sure he'd like to run."

She popped up to grab her shoes, the chimes in the grandfather clock echoing her footfalls. When she turned the glass doorknob, Cal said to her, "Sweater."

Olivia nodded and pulled it from the chair back where she'd tossed it.

We closed the door behind us. "I thought I caught the slightest hint of an eye roll then, when you mentioned her sweater," I said.

"Probably." He laughed. "She can roll her eyes all she wants. It's February."

He turned to look at me then, his eyes steady and peaceful, the way land looks from the window of an airplane.

The afternoon was warm enough that being outside for an hour was not completely intolerable. Half an hour earlier, a brown delivery truck had dropped off an auto part Cal had ordered, then retreated to the highway in a wistful haze.

Cal cradled the package as we walked toward the Volvos. We

laid down, crawled on our backs beneath one. The ground was hard. I could feel the cold through my puffy jacket and the blanket Cal'd laid down. I saw Andy's paws and Olivia's bright-blue cowboy boots pacing around the Volvo's back bumper. My mouth tasted like the strong coffee I'd made to keep warm, but the cold I'd been nursing kept me from smelling anything of the underside of the car—which was maybe for the best.

In a whimsical moment weeks before, wine-inspired on his porch at sunset, I'd asked Cal to teach me about Volvos sometime. I'd meant in the spring, May. Or not really ever. But I'd just finished saying I had no afternoon plans, and now that the opportunity had arrived, I simply couldn't wimp out because it was cold. That would be backing down.

He opened the delivery and handed me what looked like a complicated, electrical Rubik's Cube.

"Starter engine," he clarified.

Wind gusted, a high-pitched whistle blowing through the hubcaps.

Cal's voice was slow and patient. "Turn it right," he said. "Just like that. Now just tighten those bolts, and that's basically it."

I'd never considered that working on cars could be relaxing, but I could see what he'd meant. In the information age, consumed with technology, it felt like a throwback. Something my grandfather might have done on a Sunday afternoon. "This isn't too bad, Cal."

When I finished, we stood against the car.

"If you came with a warning label attached to you," I asked, "what would it read?" The question left a hollowness in me, a slight ache of anticipation. Some part of me wanted to take it back.

Cal cocked his head at me curiously, blinking. Then, looking toward the road, he pulled off his baseball cap and scratched the side of his beard, just below his ear, standing still for a moment. "I'll have to think about that," he said.

He handed me a rag that I wiped over my hands.

"Do you think about him?" Cal asked. His smile was somehow

both lost and centered. Maybe it meant acceptance of what we didn't know and never would.

"Sure. Don't you?"

"I try not to," he said. After a moment, he added, "They might find him." Cal raised an eyebrow, just subtly enough that I couldn't tell whether he wanted them to or not.

"No," I answered, surprised at how sure I sounded. "I don't think so. He's in Argentina, or Europe."

"No disrespect to the Vanderbilt police, but federal agents have a few more resources at their disposal—they won't play around. There are the murder cases, and then there's everything they'll uncover about virus samples. That's national security. I'll bet you a dollar Paolo turns up."

"I'll take that bet," I said. We shook hands, even though I knew Cal was probably right—Paolo disappearing *again* would be nearly impossible, especially considering he'd left on foot. Mason had told me that the car Paolo had driven was towed away and searched. Everything Paolo had told me about the way he'd lived matched the evidence they found. Essentially, he'd been living out of the car for nearly a month. I'd had no hesitation in relaying what he'd told me to the investigators, including how he'd gotten away before. I didn't see how he'd eluded them for a single day, but then again, he'd surprised me before. Within an hour of Paolo running into the woods, the FBI had taken over the investigation. They'd begun combing through Silver's lab the following morning, then turning over every inch of Paolo's and Sandy's apartments. Silver's home was locked down. They'd interviewed me twice, each time over the course of an entire morning, sorting through details I would've never considered.

"You're lucky you didn't get arrested," I said, remembering Silver's tactic. In the blur of that day, I hadn't heard many of the details of Cal's dealings with the Vanderbilt police. "I guess I didn't think completely through the legality of the plan."

"I know you didn't." Cal's eyebrow rose. He didn't smile, exactly, but his eyes brightened. "But neither did I. I knew it was breaking the law, but it was the right thing to do."

Then a realization hit me. "You never told me if they cuffed you."

"They locked the door at the substation. No cuffs, though. I told them the truth—that I broke in because it was an emergency. I must have talked a blue streak about what we thought Silver was doing. I couldn't stop thinking about where you were."

"Not to mention Olivia," I said. Across the yard, she climbed the porch steps.

"If I'd known she was there, I don't know what I would have done," he said quietly. "It was only when the campus police got to my phone, saw how many times you called, that they started to believe me—enough to let me call the Metro Police."

As long as we were getting real, I decided to take the conversation a step further.

"You know, my worst fear," I confessed, "is losing my mind. When I think about him, it all gets so twisted. What was real? If some of it was fake, was all of it? I don't know. I think about the impossibility of him showing up just as the truck turned over the embankment."

"I know," Cal whispered.

My eyes found Olivia again.

"You knew him," Cal continued, after a pause. "I did, too. That person existed. We knew that person. And that was real."

The idea was soothing, comforting.

"We're the lucky ones because we both saw the same things. Knew the same person. He's alone, wherever he is. Asking himself who he really is."

It was true.

Witnesses to an experience make it real. We shared that.

Up toward the house, Olivia had devised some sort of game—two sticks and a passage between two of the Volvos. She wanted Andy to play, to figure it out. To chase.

"You know, Silver's vaccine worked," I said. "That night, he told me it did and I believed him. Even while the cabin was burning around us. He was going to present a paper on it in London. Do you think . . ."

"Do I think it was worth it? That the number of people who'll be saved justifies the killing?"

My eyes felt hot. I nodded.

Three people dead, including Sandy. James Mandel left with lifelong scars.

"No," Cal answered quickly. "Murder is wrong. Always. Even a breakthrough discovery can't happen that way."

I knew it was wrong, too, even as a small part of me imagined a girl, somewhere, who would never hear a knock on her front door, or watch her mother's dish towel fall to the floor from shock and grief.

Earlier that week, when a federal agent told me that the CDC had already taken the vaccine and started analysis of its sequencing, I sat up straight.

I thanked God.

"I do feel bad about Matt," I said. "No, more than that. I feel bad *for* Matt, too. He was getting framed for everything going on around him. Everything horrible happening. He must've felt like he was going crazy. Everything pointed to him. The flowers I sent, wow."

Cal squinted, considering this. "Just a regular guy, after all, as manipulated by Silver as everyone else."

"Yeah."

I combed my hands through my hair.

He leaned against me, and I sniffed, shaking off a strange idea.

"What?" Cal asked.

"I had a thought, but it's terrible. I can't . . ."

He shrugged; a pause, a slight smile. "Suit yourself."

"I was just thinking about Matt interviewing for his next job. When he gets asked about conflict with supervisors and dealing with unforeseen complications, he'll have a hell of a story."

"Oh my God, Emily." Cal shook his head.

"I told you it was terrible."

I handed him the rag, only then realizing it was an old T-shirt. He took my hand in his and continued cleaning a spot I'd missed.

"This can be hard to get off," he said.

When he finished, he reached for my other hand, cleaning it.
I looked at him.

He sighed. "So what would yours say?" he asked, eventually. "Your label."

I was great at asking questions. Better at asking than answering. They say being a therapist is the best way to hide.

"'Warning,'" I said, "'Occasionally doesn't sleep. Has unusual thoughts from time to time. Sometimes hears a voice. Difficult to turn off.'"

Cal considered it. "That sounds about right," he said. He draped the rag on the shoulder of his old jacket.

"You didn't answer," I pointed out.

He squinted. "I was thinking," he said. "I guess mine would say, 'Caution: Doesn't care for loud noises. Avoids crowds. Slow to warm up.'"

"It wouldn't say anything about avoiding crazy women, or being judgmental, or being stubborn?"

"Yeah, you're right," he admitted with a laugh. "It would say that about crazy women. I try to steer clear."

I shook my head and smiled. "You're not trying very hard."

We were quiet after that for a long time.

"I'm no good at this," Cal said finally.

"You're not kidding," I said. "But neither am I."

"I guess I'm warned. The label and all." From his pocket, he produced a key with a black plastic rectangle, handed it to me. "Let's see if it starts."

We climbed in, shut the doors.

Not having to blow into a Breathalyzer was nice. Six more months and that would be over.

"It's yours," Cal said.

"What?" I was shocked. "You can't just give me a car."

"Why not? I have three others."

I glanced up. There they were in a line.

I felt like I was on *The Price Is Right* or something

"I'm not sure, Cal."

"Think about it," he said. "You never liked that truck much. And it's not going anywhere now. Besides, now that this one's fixed up, I need to clear some space for the one I'm looking at."

Me in a Volvo. Cal and me together.

My face turned up toward the sky. A feeling of weightlessness.

Who would have guessed?

————

On the first warm day of spring, I returned to the lake where Paolo had disappeared. I rolled down the window on the country road, and my hair, which had grown in slightly, was whipping against my sunglasses. It was midafternoon, and the sky was clear and bright, the world seemingly all solid colors. The kind of light that makes everything seem to radiate from within. At the marina, I stopped in the gravel, same lot as before, and took a deep breath. Sun flooded through the windshield, warming the skin of my bare arms, my neck, my face.

Aside from a pair of the marina's work trucks, the space was empty. Faint birdcall from the nearly bare trees. I slipped off my shoes, slung a backpack over my shoulder. The ground was soft after the previous night's thunderstorm, cool, gray mud pushing between my toes as I followed a trail toward the water's edge. Having no cast around my ankle, no boot or cane, felt freeing, as if the wind at my back was nudging me upward toward the swaying pine branches. My chest rose, my steps were light.

Along the edges of the path, the branches were sticklike and barren, like flashes of lightning coming up from the earth. Aching to be reborn. But here and there, where the sunlight had reached in, dots of green had appeared. Buds emerging. The first signs of life, rising impossibly from tangled brambles.

Winter was ending.

Driving, I'd wondered if I'd be overcome, but calm washed through me as I stepped from the woods into the clearing. The open space accelerated the wind, which was pushing at my chest. A gust raised gooseflesh on the backs of my arms, and I leaned in, pushing again toward what I couldn't reach. The whooshing quiet of vast openness. Space itself, breathing.

The lake's surface was a million ripples marching.

I dropped onto the seawall and rolled my jeans to midcalf before continuing along the edge of the low tide.

I wanted.

I wanted to find just the right place.

I'd told Cal my plans that morning. It was still dark when we woke up, his silhouette framed by the window in the burgeoning dawn. Down the hall, Olivia was surely asleep. Cal sat up slowly, the bed gently creaking. He smoothed his beard.

"I'll go with you," he'd offered.

His arm was warm where I touched it, the bedroom air around us still night-cooled.

"This I want to do on my own," I'd said.

I needed to see the place Paolo and I'd anchored, where the boat with the family had pulled beside us and Paolo had dived in, returning with their keys. I needed to be where these things had happened, where I'd awoken so alone. So frightened.

I stood on the shore, the silty lake gently lapping, freezing my bare feet.

The cold stung in a way I liked.

I remembered Paolo on that day, wind nudging strands of hair on his forehead. The way he shielded his beautiful, uncorrected smile beneath those Wayfarer sunglasses.

This was a visitation. He hadn't died, but he had. He was still on this earth, somewhere. But the person I knew was gone.

I backed into the grass, set down the backpack, unzipped it. I pulled out the tripod Cal and I had planted on my office roof, attached Paolo's camera. The tripod feet dug into the wet ground. I unattached the filter, aimed the lens at the horizon and found the correct zoom. The image was perfectly in focus.

The sun blurred the horizon. The water and the sky blended.

I remembered the look on Silver's face when he'd told me he'd wanted to meet my father. I'd seen the sliver-thin division between insanity and greatness in that instant—a place I'd approached closely enough to understand. I'd felt the sun scorch my wings, flying so high.

I leaned forward, closed my right eye.

My finger rested on the warm plastic.

Breath left my lungs. Now, I thought.

Click.

I pulled back to examine the image.

I made a slight adjustment.

Click. I checked.

Perfect.

Now, I'd go home.

Footsteps behind me. A reluctant voice.

I visored my eyes as I turned.

A teenage boy. I recognized him. He'd been on the dock before, white headphone cord running into his pocket and a hose in his hand. He'd gotten taller since then, stood straighter. He wore a collared shirt, the marina's logo emblazoned on his chest.

"Um, Miss? We're not actually open right now. Can I help you with something?"

I must've looked odd, standing there alone. Yet, his expression was kind. In the distance, trees swayed behind him. A white bird paced curiously along the dock.

"Thanks," I answered. "But I actually just finished up. Now I'm all done."

Acknowledgments

I would first like to thank my family—Rebecca, Henry, and Harper—for being so patient and supportive of my writing. Without your help, this book would never have been possible.

Thank you to my fantastic agent, Rachel Ekstrom Courage at Folio Literary Management, for your tremendous guidance and advice.

Many thanks to Chelsey Emmelhanz at Crooked Lane Books—I can't express enough gratitude for your diligence and insights. Thank you for everything you've done in helping to create this book. You are the very best.

Thank you also to Jaden Terrell and Steven Womack for your kindness and encouragement along the way.